I0779688

JESSICA ANN DISCIACCA

WITCHES *of* TRIORA
the VESSEL

DARK FLAME
PUBLISHING

WITCHES OF TRIORA: THE VESSEL

This is a work of fiction. All of the characters, names, and incidents, organizations, and dialogue in this novel are either the product of the author's imagination or are used fictitiously.

DARK FLAME PUBLISHING

Dark Flame Publishing books may be ordered through booksellers or by contacting Dark Flame Publishing online: JessicaAnnDisciacca.com

The views expressed in this work are solely those of the author and do not necessarily reflect that views of the publisher. Any people depicted in such imagery provided by Adobe Stock or Getty Images are models, and such images are being used for illustrative purposes only. Certain stock images. © Getty Images and. © Adobe Stock.

ISBNs: (Paperback) **979-8-9910142-1-2**, (Hardcover) **979-8-99-10142-3-6**

To those who are searching for their inner powers. Whether you were born with it or acquired it... when you find that ember, ignite it. Feed it. And then conquer it.

CHAPTER ONE

*"O*ur *Father, who art in heaven, hallowed be thy name. Thy kingdom come, thy will be done, on earth, as it is in heaven. Give us this day our daily bread and forgive us our trespasses, as we forgive those who trespass against us; and lead us not into temptation but deliver us from evil."* The entire church made the sign of the cross as we all kneeled.

The wooden pews creaked as the congregation stood from the kneelers and returned to their seats. My bones and muscles groaned as I pushed my weight against my forearm crutches in order to stand. Today, the pain was bearable. There was no fever, and I was able to get out of bed this morning. The Lord had truly blessed me with another day so that I could be able to go out and share his good news with others.

The Montecassino Abbey would soon be swarming with tourists who had traveled near and far to stand in the grace and glory of our beautiful home. Nestled in the mountains of Lazio, overlooking Cassino, our abbey was breathtaking. A true reflection of God's artistry. When Saint Benedict established our church in the year 529, I truly believe God smiled upon the saint. Since its time of creation, no matter how many wars or centuries had passed, these walls remained strong.

I settled back into the bench, placing my crutches on either side of my legs. I took my rosery in between my fingers, sliding the small beads against my palm. Inhaling deeply, I forced the burning sensation in my legs to cease. Sister Francis gave me a small, weary grin that didn't reach her eyes. I nodded, signaling to her that I was okay.

Polio was a unique and cruel sickness. I wouldn't wish it upon anyone, yet who was I to judge God's great plan. I had caught the life changing disease when I was a small child in the orphanage at St. Bernard's. Unable to give me the proper care and treatment that was required, the sisters here at Montecassino took me in and raised me as one of their own. I see God's plan. Without the disease, I would have never been blessed to find my true calling which led me to my family... my brethren in Christ.

Here, I received an education, and nightly treatments that helped ease my pain. I had a roof over my head and food for each meal. I learned my greatest lesson that I repeated to myself daily. What the devil means for evil, God can turn it around for good. Genesis 50:20. I was the living embodiment of this scripture.

After Mass was over, the sisters quietly shuffled from the aisles into the nave as they proceeded to attend to their daily duties throughout the abbey. I waited patiently for them to get a head start before I slid the forearm crutches on, pushing myself to a standing position. Every step was an effort, but I was still able to walk, even if it was with assistance.

My feet shuffled under my long black tunic. Now that I was almost 21 years of age, I was a novitiate. I would live the life of a nun for a year or two before entering into service. It was an honor to dedicate my life to this calling, regardless of how short that life might be. Even though I tried not to ponder upon it, I was aware of the statistics of someone who had my condition. Any day, my muscles around my lungs could become paralyzed and I would die of suffocation. There was no cure for what I had, but I wasn't scared. I had made peace with my impending death a long time ago.

I focused on the time I did have and the good I could do for God's people. My specific talents lay in the kitchen. I loved to feed the people who came to worship. Breads, pastas, sauces, fish. I even sometimes dabbled in baking. Though the sisters didn't indulge in the desires of the flesh, sugar was a weakness of mine I couldn't seem to escape.

I made my way into the kitchen, nodding at the nuns that were already slaving away over the stove tops. I gathered the necessary ingredients, placing them at a small table in the corner before lowering myself into a chair. Eggs, flour, ricotta cheese, potatoes, salt, and pepper. Homemade gnocchi.

I would pair the dense dumpling with a fresh basil pesto sauce. I had harvested a fresh batch of the herb yesterday morning for this very meal. I inhaled the fresh aromas as I smiled to myself. My hands deep in dough, surrounded by the beautiful mountain landscape outside the window of the kitchen... I was blessed.

As I mixed the dough between my fingers and palms, a sharp pain shot up my right forearm into my shoulder. I recoiled quickly, gasping as I sent one of the glass containers to the ground, shattering the jar. I held my shoulder, rocking myself slowly, praying the pain would go away. Sister Odette came to my aid, placing a comforting hand on my back.

"Get the tea," she ordered to another nun, kneeling in front of me. "Breath slowly, child. This too will pass, as does all fleshly discomforts." I nodded, taking in small breaths fighting the tears that threatened to escape.

Tea was placed in front of me as Sister Odette reached into her apron pocket, taking a small vile of black herbs and mixed it into the liquid. She brought the ceramic cup to my lips. "Here child, to ease the pain," she said as I sipped slowly. The warm liquid slid down my throat, instant relief coated my muscles, sending me into a relaxed, euphoric state.

"Thank you," I whispered.

Sister Odette brushed my sweaty forehead with her fingers. "All is well," she whispered, cleaning the broken glass from the floor. "Sister Agnes, Sister Angela, help Sister Seren up to her room. She needs rest."

"I can finish," I insisted, not wanting to leave the warmth of the kitchen.

"That is all for today. You need rest," Sister Odette said shortly as the other two came to my sides, helping me out of my chair. "I will be up shortly with your medicine."

I braced myself on my crutches while the sisters followed closely behind. I was feeling better, but my arms now felt weak and lethargic. My muscle spasms and episodes had been coming more frequently the past month. The doctors couldn't figure out why and though the herbs and medicine helped with the pain, it forced me to sleep. Sister Odette assured me rest was what my body needed to heal, but I hated it. I was tired of sleeping. That's all I did was sleep.

How was I ever going to fulfill my duties as a nun if I was confined to my bed majority of days? I would continue to pray. God had been with my thus far, He would not abandon me now. Not in my time of need.

As we got to my quarters, I opened the door to my simple room. A small twin sized bed, a nightstand, and one dresser. A crucifix hung above my bed. No windows or artwork adorned the walls. My room was simplistic, but it was mine.

The sisters left me alone as I took my veil from my head. I pulled the pins and clips from my hair that confined my long, wavey, dark mahogany locks. I couldn't remember the last time I had cut my hair. As a result, it fell well past my waist and was extremely dense and heavy. I ran my fingers across my scalp, allowing the loose strands to relax.

The door opened a few moments later while I struggled to take off my shoes. Sister Odette approached me with her small leather case of my medicine. I hated needles, but I couldn't deny the relief the serum provided. She knelt, taking my feet in her hands as she slid off my shoes, placing them neatly under my bed.

"Lay back, sister," she said, before preparing the needle. I had known Sister Odette for most of my life. She was the closest thing I had to a mother. She had taken me under her wing when the abbey had given me refuge. She was my teacher, my caregiver, and my spiritual guide.

When my condition took a turn for the worse when I was nine years old, Sister Odette didn't leave my side. I figured it had something to do with my body going through the change into womanhood. That was when the daily shots had begun. It was the only relief the doctors could provide for me. Between the serum and the teas, I was in a constant state of drowsiness.

Sister Odette made the sign of the cross, saying a small prayer as she always did before administering my medicine. She pulled the shoulder of my robe down, wiping my skin with a cleaning agent before pressing the tip of the needle through my flesh. I didn't flinch or recoil. Even though I hated needles, I had become accustomed to the discomfort.

She stood from my bedside, taking her small black pouch with her. "Sleep well, my child," she said, before taking her leave. The small oil lamp on my nightstand was the only source of light in my room. I watched the walls as shadows and figures danced over the terracotta surfaces; they were my only source of company in these moments.

I felt the drug begin to work itself through my system. My body warmed as my limbs began to feel heavy. The pain was subsiding. Tears fell uncontrollably down my cheeks as I closed my eyes and tilted my head to the side.

God, what is your plan for my life? Why must I live in this constant state of pain? What lesson do you want me to gleam from my circumstances? Please, father, speak to me. Tell me of your plans.

I waited for a few moments for an answer, but none came. I was alone in my pain... in my fear. I tried to be strong, but with each passing day, I could feel the weight of my condition begin to take a toll on me.

My brain began to fog as a zinging sensation zapped through my body. I would soon be asleep, too drugged to even dream. I opened my eyes as my vision blurred before clearing. In the corner, sat a dark shadowed figure. His red eyes glowed as if they were small balls of fire, shifting in shade and hues. The figure's head morphed from a bull to a ram, and then to a man.

I locked my eyes on the figure, willing myself to stay awake. The shadowed monster sat still, staring back at me without a single blink. My breathing was calm and steady. A sense of peace and comforted washed over me as if I somehow knew the shadowed figure. As if it was a part of me. Something I had always been missing. I strained to see the being more clearly, but my eyelids began to feel heavy. I blinked once. Twice. Finally falling into my sedated sleep of darkness.

Chapter Two

I woke early the next morning from a heavy sleep. The sun still slept as I dressed and crept down to the kitchen. The room was empty as I began to sift flour into a large wooden bowl. My body was tired, but my mind was awake. As the bread began to rise, I left the kitchen to attend my morning prayers. The isolation and silence were a welcome change.

I headed back down the hallway towards the kitchen, each step more painful than the last. Halfway there, I felt my legs weaken as I leaned against one of the doorways. I took a few deep breaths, willing the pain to dissipate. On the other side of the cracked door, I heard the rattling of jars along with two voices I recognized; Sister Francis and Sister Odette.

"We need to find another solution," said Sister Francis. "The shots are no longer working, and the signs are beginning to manifest more frequently. This condition is too unpredictable, and we are putting everyone under this roof at risk."

"You don't think I know this," snapped Sister Odette. "I am working on finding a long-term solution, but until then, we stick with the plan and the injections."

"You and I both know what needs to be done, sister," said Sister Francis. "It should have been done the moment that wretched woman set foot on our doorsteps with it."

Bam. Something hard, like hands, slammed into the desk followed by a moment of silence. "God has a plan for this," explained Sister Odette. "He always has a plan. It is not by chance the child was brought here, placed under our care and our guard. We will find another way to rid her of these demons. We must."

"You are blinded by your affection for it," said Sister Francis in an unfeeling tone. "You have allowed yourself to become attached. Remember what it is sister. Remember what it is capable of."

I heard footsteps heading towards the door. I stumbled backwards, hiding myself in an enclave behind a statue as I watched Sister Francis leave the office. Were they talking about me? Was my condition progressing to the point of no return?

I pulled myself from my hiding place, knocking softly on the door to Sister Odette's office. She turned to see me in the threshold and offered a small smile gesturing for me to enter. "Good morning, Sister Seren. How are you feeling today?"

"Good morning, sister. Much better," I lied. My pain was worse than yesterday, but I didn't want to worry her. I was obviously causing her stress.

"I am glad to hear that, child. Today should be a busy one. We have a large pilgrimage group scheduled to visit the abbey. We must prepare."

"Of course, sister. I will be of assistance in any way I can," I nodded, turning to take my leave back to the kitchen. My body groaned with each movement as my arms felt heavy with that all too familiar zinging sensation. I winced quietly. In a moment, Sister Odette was there, examining me from head to toe.

"Sister Seren, is it the illness? Do you need a cup of tea?" she asked.

"No sister," I said, plastering a smile on my face. "I am feeling much better today. Honestly." I would have to repent for my lie today after mass, but I hoped God would understand and forgive me for the small exaggeration. "I will be in the kitchen making bread if you need me."

She nodded, allowing me to pass by her as I fought the heaviness beginning to spread down my legs. Once I reached the kitchen, I sat at my normal table by the window overlooking the mountains of Italy. I mixed the ingredients needed to make fresh pasta, making sure not to overdo it. Today, I would not experience an episode. Today, I would fight to be normal.

The bells had rung, indicating that it was time for mass. The pilgrimage of visitors had arrived. Lunch was prepared and ready for them once father had concluded his sermon. I walked into the nave, surrounded by dozens of new faces. They each smiled at me, taking in my forearm crutches. I smiled and nodded back, trying to ignore their looks of pity.

My arms were shaking with each step causing small beads of sweat to from along my forehead and neck. My jaw clenched at the pain. I tried to remain unphased. People walked past me as I struggled to stay upright. With each step, I was losing control of my body. *Not today. Please God, not today*, I prayed silently to myself.

I stumbled as one of my crutches hit the side of the pool of holy water. My vision became blurry, and I fought to stay upright. Sister Francis appeared in front of me, taking my arm in one of her hands as she took in my state.

"Sister Seren, are you alright," she asked, worry spread across her face. I was unable to speak, focusing on my hazy vision. "Sister," she said to a nun behind me, "fetch Sister Odette immediately, and tell her to bring Sister Seren's medicine."

It was too late. My body couldn't take anymore. My vision tunneled. I lost control of my crutches. The zinging sensation amplified. The feeling starting from my spine, spreading throughout every nerve ending in my body. A massive pressure built inside of me, fighting to be released.

Time around me seemed to slow as I became conscious of every singular beat of my heart. One beat. Two beats. Three. Then, without warning, the fourth beat of my heart slammed so hard inside my chest that the wind was knocked out of me. I gasped for air, but none came. I let go of my crutches. My body became paralyzed. This was it. Polio had won. I was about to die.

I could faintly hear screaming in the background as I tumbled ever so slowly to the ground. The faces of my sisters appeared blurred as I fought to remain conscious. Heat inside of me welled. The pressure was too much as it zinged and zapped down my extremities. I willed it to let go of me. To release.

As if it could listen, the pressure found its way to my fingertips, building within my palms. *Boom!* A loud zap crackled through the air. My skull made contact with the marble floor, releasing the pressure from my body. Screaming continued. Darkness flooded my vision. Stars and constellations appeared in front of my eyes. I must have been hallucinating. I focused on the beautiful designs the balls of light created. If this was the way I would meet my maker, I was ready.

Sister Odette's voice jolted me out of my daze. Her blurry face appeared in front of me, blocking the images of the beautiful night sky. *Sting.* I felt a small prick in my arm as my breathing became ragged and uneven. My heart began to slow as a cool breeze tickled throughout my veins.

Sting. A second syringe pricked my arm. Then a third, until my body began to shake from the overdose of medicine. Footsteps continued to pound against the floor as the congregation ran for the exits. I continued to focus on the shooting stars that stretched across the black fog above me.

My body continued to jerk from the drug coursing through my system. My eyes became heavy. I could taste bile rising from my esophagus into my mouth. Foam reached my lips, falling down the side of my face as my body seized. The darkness above me began to dissipate. My heart slowed. Everything around me fell away into the darkness.

"Keep her drugged," I heard a familiar voice demand.

"It's been twenty-four hours. She'll be fine," said another voice. My head spun. I felt like I was going to be sick. I attempted to pry my eyes open, but my temples throbbed. I let out a small moan.

"She's coming to," said the first voice. "Inject her or I will." *Sting.* I felt the insertion of the needle into my arm. My eyes fluttered back as the spinning began. "We will wait until Father Lucas arrives. He will decide what to do with her then."

I awoke in a pile of my own sweat. My hair was matted to my face and neck, and my extremities felt as if they weighed a ton. I took a deep breath in, triggering a cough that rattled my lungs.

"Shh, shh," came a voice next to me. A cool damp cloth pressed against my brow and my cheeks. My vision was blurry, but I could make out the face of Sister Odette hunched over me, cleaning my exposed skin.

"What—" I tried to speak, but my voice was hoarse.

"Shh, my child. Don't speak," she said, looking back at the door in panic. "There is so much you need to know. So much I should have told you as soon as all of this began."

"What do you mean, sister?" I rasped.

"All you need to know is that Father Lucas is on his way to the abbey. You must remain strong. Do you hear me? Do not waiver."

"But Father Lucas deals specifically with demonic abnormalities. Why would he be coming here? And what does he want with me?"

Sister Odette opened her mouth and shook her head fighting to find words. A tear rolled down her cheek as she dropped to her knees at my bedside and began to pray. I reached for her, taking one of her small hands in my own.

"Sister," I whispered. "What happened to me in the service?"

Her eyes snapped to mine. "You remember?" she asked, her voice trembling.

"Not really. I remember feeling the pain from my sickness. I thought it was my time to meet our maker, but then, as I fell, all I saw was darkness and... stars. I must have been hallucinating."

She gasped as she ripped her hand from mine. I could hear her rattling with something on my nightstand before she brought the syringe up to my arm.

"No, please," I begged, but it was no use.

"Sleep child. All will be well soon," she whispered in my ear as I fell, once again, into an endless slumber.

CHAPTER THREE

*B*am! The sound of my bedroom door woke me from my drugged dream. I forced my eyes open to see Sister Odette placing a chair underneath the doorknob before rushing toward me. The candlelight flickered around the room, making it hard for me to see much else. I could hear screaming in the hallway outside, and growling, as if there were animals in the abbey.

I inhaled as the smell of smoke and burning wood filled my lungs. Sister Odette rushed for me, ripping my sheets back, pulling my body towards the edge of the bed. The drug still coursed through my bloodstream, making it impossible to utilize my limbs.

Sister Odette pulled me to the floor, looking back at the door in panic every few seconds. She cradled my head in the nook of her arm as she pushed me underneath the bed. The coolness of the floor felt like heaven on my feverish skin. Banging erupted from the wooden door. I could have sworn the whole room shook as sounds of claws and snarling followed.

Sister Odette gave a final push as she jammed me underneath the four-post bed. "Do not say a word," she demanded. "Not a word."

Bam. Bam. She looked back at the door; her whole body shaking in fear. Her eyes returned to mine. "No matter what, remember who you are Seren. Remember that the Lord loves you and that what the devil meant for evil, God can turn it around for good."

Panic rose in me as tears began to stream down my face. "What is happening," I was able to say. I reached for her, but she shoved my hand back underneath the bed just before the door smashed open with force. In an instant, Sister Odette was on her stomach. Growling and snarling filled the room as two black shadowed monsters resembling wolves sank their teeth into each of her legs. Their ruby red eyes glowed as they pulled her effortlessly out of the room.

I could hear her screaming. My eyes were locked on the doorway, unable to look away as the demonic beasts tore her to shreds. I looked down at the streak of blood that started at the edge of my bed and led to her now dismembered body.

My breathing was rapid and uncontrollable. I fought to hold in my tears even though terror saturated every inch of my body. I willed my legs and arms to move, but they still felt like they were glued to the ground. I clenched my fists open and shut over and over trying to get the rest of my body to wake up.

I heard the hounds go silent as their black, shadowy paws appeared in my door frame once more. They placed their noses to the floor and began to sniff. One jumped onto my bed causing the springs under the mattress to press against my face and chest.

It jumped from my bed to the floor, sniffing in a circle until it stopped; slowly extending its muzzle under the wooden frame of the bed.

I closed my eyes, wishing this was all just a dream. This was it. I was going to die. Not because of old age or because of polio. I was going to die at the hands of Satan's hounds. I began to say my final prayers, praying I had done enough to prove myself worthy of God's love and grace. Then, everything went silent.

I opened my eyes slowly, only to find a pair of swirling red eyes staring back at me: the hound's canine teeth bared towards me as a low growl came from its chest. Drool and a stench worse than anything I had ever smelt came from its mouth. I opened my mouth to scream just before the demon snapped its teeth around my shoulder.

I screamed. My entire nervous system woke in that moment. I reached my free arm out, trying to grasp anything to hold myself back from the hound pulling me into the opening. As my head cleared the wooden bedframe I reached my hand to my chest, gripping my rosary. With all the strength I could muster, I brought my hand up through the air and slammed the end of the cross down into one of its ruby red eyes. The thing whined and whimpered, freeing my shoulder from its teeth. It shook its head drawing its one eye back to me.

Right before it was about to pounce, a figure appeared in the doorway. The hound stopped, turning back to see who had interrupted its meal. The tall figure stood silently, looking at me for what seemed to be an eternity. I forced myself up onto shaky arms as tears streamed from my cheeks. I looked at the stranger and with everything I had left in me I whispered, "please," in between a whimpering cry. "Please help me."

The hound looked back to me and growled. Just before the creature could attack, the male figure brought a gun up in front of him and sent two bullets spiraling into the demon. The hound dropped to the floor. His skin liquified into a dark tar-like substance, steaming and bubbling.

I exhaled in relief, collapsing on top of my weak arms. I fought to push myself upright but struggled. The male figure lowered his gun and walked hesitantly towards me until he towered above. In the low light, it was hard to make out many details about the strange savior. He was tall, with a thin and powerful build. He wore dark black jeans and suede boots. His dark button up shirt was rolled at the arms to his elbow. His hair was well kept. Short on the sides and a little longer at the top. His eyes were like daggers as they peered down at me behind a thick line of dark black lashes.

"Thank you," I willed myself to say before collapsing back to the ground. He reached for me, just in time to catch my head preventing it from slamming into the floor. With my body still shaking from fear and the drugs, he turned my face slowly, so I was forced to look up at him.

His eyes were hazel. He had a strong jaw and was cleanly shaven.

His nose was long and shapely. Everything about him was inviting and alluring, but I still didn't know if he was friend or foe.

I watched his gaze scan the length of my body as if examining my condition. "Can you walk?" he asked in a soft yet demanding voice.

I shook my head.

"Why not? What happened to you?" he asked shortly.

I pointed my finger to the edge of my bed where my crutches leaned up against the wooden posted. "I have… I have polio," I confessed.

He looked at the crutches and then back at my face. He exhaled. With one fell swoop he scooped me up into his arms. My head lay firmly against his chest as he carried me from my room and into the hallway. Screams continued to fill the air as I saw the hounds pounce on anyone who came too close to them. Limbs and blood littered the marble floor. I closed my eyes, wanting this nightmare to end.

A fresh breeze met my sticky, drenched skin once we had exited the abbey. A black car sat in front of the driveway. He placed me gently into a seat and buckled me, leaning my head against the cold glass of the window. I peered outside, back to my haven. Back to my home. Half of the abbey was on fire and already up in smoke. No one else exited the church. They were trapped inside with those demons.

The strange man sat in the driver's seat and started the car engine. "Wait," I said, before he pulled away.

He paused, looking at me through the rear-view mirror. "Yes?"

"The others," I gasped, coughing in between each word. "Save the others," I pleaded.

He exhaled before turning around to face me. "I can't, they're already dead. Nothing I do will save them." He turned back around, putting the car into drive. "You're lucky I got to you when I did. God only knows how you would have survived. You know," he said, looking back at me in the mirror again, "with you having polio and all." He winked, before turning his attention back to the road.

Firetrucks and policia rushed up the road towards the abbey, not even attempting to stop the one and only car that was currently fleeing the scene of the crime. I sent up a silent prayer, praying to the angels they would be able to save some of my sisters, praying they would not get torn to shreds like the others.

The feeling in my arms began to trickle alive as I watched my warm breath fog the glass of the window. I wiggled my toes as the pain from my muscles began to scream alive with vengeance. I squeezed my thigh with my fingertips, holding in my groan.

"What are you—," I started to say. "What are you going to do with me?"

I heard a faint chuckle as he turned onto a highway. I was familiar with the surrounding city of Montecassino, but I had never been anywhere else. "I saved your life," he replied, "isn't that enough?"

"Why? Why save me and not another?"

"Let's just say I had a good feeling about you."

"You saved me based on a feeling?" I asked.

"A good feeling," he clarified, sarcastically.

"What were you doing at the abbey this late anyways?"

He allowed a few minutes to pass before answering. "I hunt those things," he said as if he was unsure of his own words.

"Are you Father Lucas?" I asked.

He began laughing. I could see his brilliant white teeth flash in the rear-view mirror. "Do I look like a father to you?"

I felt a little foolish for even considering that to be a feasible option. "No. I am just trying to figure all of this out," I said softly. "Can I at least know your name?"

He looked back at me in the mirror as a passing car lit the inside of our vehicle. "Antonio. But you can call me Tony for short," he said. "And what shall I call you?"

"Seren," I replied.

"Do you have a last name, *Sur -ren,*" he elongated my name, enunciating every sound and syllable of the word.

"No," I said shortly. "I was raised in the nunnery. There is no need for a last name."

"Interesting," he replied plainly.

"Shouldn't we be telling the policia what happened?"

"And what would we tell them? That large hounds made of shadows attacked the abbey and killed all those precious, innocent nuns? No, Seren. We don't involve the policia in our affairs."

"Our?" I asked, unsure of how I was now involved in his affairs.

"Full of questions, aren't we?"

"If you just got your home shredded to pieces, wouldn't you have a few questions?"

"That's a fair point," he said, taking the exit that was labeled airport. I was able to sit myself up now. I moved my neck back and forth, stretching the neglected muscles.

"Where are we going?"

"The airport. We're headed to Triora," he replied casually.

"What's in Triora?"

"All the answers your heart could desire."

Tears began to fall from my eyes silently. I wiped them away, trying to focus on the outside world. I wrapped my arms around my body, forcing myself to keep it together. I was scared, traumatized, in pain, and confused. I was in a car with a stranger who had just saved me from some demonic power I didn't understand. I had lost my home, my family... everything I had ever known; and now, I was about to fly halfway across the country. Nothing made sense. All I knew was that I was at his mercy. If he chose to dispose of me or leave me, with my condition I would be as good as dead.

Chapter Four

I spent the remainder of the drive saying my prayers and praying for all the souls that were lost this evening. It was four in the morning by the time Antonio pulled into the airport; driving to a private entrance and then onto the tarmac stopping in front of a large black plane that had its engines running, preparing to take off.

Antonio opened my door, reaching inside to pull me up into his arms as he headed for the aircraft. There were two stewardesses waiting for us on a black carpet leading to the stairs of the plane. In beautifully scripted golden letters on the side of the plane it read, 'Luna'. *Moon.*

He nodded to each of them as we ascended the stairs into a lavish cabin with leather seats and gold finishings. He placed me into a chair, buckling me before he headed to the cockpit. I looked around, taking in the grandeur of it all. The stewardesses entered the plane, closing the door behind them as the engines roared.

Antonio returned with a glass of water, placing it on the table. "Figured you'd be thirsty after everything," he said, sitting across from me.

"Thank you," I said, trying to reach for the glass. Just as my shaky fingers wrapped around the cylinder, my arm gave out, sending the water tumbling over. Embarrassment flashed across my face as my cheeks blushed. I looked up at Antonio as he wiped the water with a napkin. "I am so sorry," I gasped. "The medicine is still working its way out of my system."

"Medicine?" he asked, wiping the last bit of water from the surface.

"Yes. I take medicine to help with the pain my condition inflicts." A stewardess set another drink on the table, taking the damp napkins and empty glass from Antonio.

"I see. And how was this medicine administered?"

"A daily shot. Sister Odette—" I froze, feeling the weight of her lost deep in my chest. "She would also give me teas when things got uncomfortable."

Antonio didn't say a word. He took the glass in his hand and leaned forward, placing the rim to my lips. I took small sips, allowing the cool and refreshing liquid to coat my insides. I didn't know how long I had been out thanks to my latest episode. The water stung a little as it scraped against my esophagus.

"Thank you," I said, as he set the glass down, buckling himself into the chair. "How long until we reach our destination?"

"Only about an hour," he said, turning his attention to the window. I noted his jaw tense as he held his chin in between his fingers. "I am sorry," he said watching the plane pull onto the runway.

"What fo—" I started to say, but before I could finish, I felt the familiar feeling of drowsiness replace my consciousness. I looked at the glass and then at Antonio. "Why?"

"Things will make since soon enough, I promise. Now lay back and sleep," he said as the plane took flight. I watched the clouds appear outside of my window just as my own darkness took hold, sending me into a dreamless sleep.

A burning sensation erupted from the inside of my skin crawling up every nerve ending in my body. I jolted forward, more alert than I had been in months. I screamed out in pain as a blinding light above me filled the room. My head slammed back onto the table as I worked to free my arms and legs from the restraints that held me to the surface.

"Make sure she doesn't get free," said a woman's voice. A stranger's face appeared above me. She placed a strap over my forehead, preventing me from lifting my head. My eyes strained as I looked down at my body. I was in a medical gown with three strangers surrounding me.

"Where am I?" I asked in a panic.

"It will all be over soon," said the woman above me as she gave me a small smile. She looked to the other two women on either side of me and nodded. They placed their hands over my body and began to chant: moving their hands slowly through the air above me. My skin lit in agonizing pain. I screamed, feeling as if I was going to be sick. Sweat beaded along my forehead, neck, and chest. I grit my teeth, trying to hold onto consciousness.

I looked down at my body noting small wisps of black smoke rising from my skin. It transferred from me and into the two strange women while they continued to chant and move their fingers above me. My legs felt like they were on pins and needles. My muscles seized and spasmed from whatever they were doing to me. I pulled at the restraints again, trying to set myself free.

"Please!" I yelled, feeling my teeth rattle together. "Please stop!"

"Gina, put her under," said one of the women. The nurse above me nodded, placing a syringe into my IV. Within a matter of seconds, I could feel my heart slow as my body went numb.

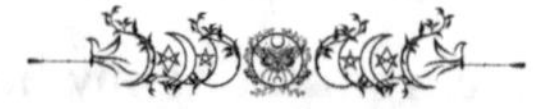

I opened my eyes slowly, greeted by the beeping of a heart monitor. I took a deep breath in as my vision cleared. I was in what appeared to be some type of hospital room. There was an IV in my hand and a nasal cannula attached to my face. My body felt exhausted and weak, but there was no pain.

I removed the tube from my face, forcing myself to sit up. In the corner sat Antonio, reading a book. His eyes met mine slowly. He placed the book down and made his way over to my bedside. I looked up at him, trying to contain my rage.

"How are we feeling?" he asked smugly.

I grit my teeth together. "What did you do to me?" I demanded.

"Any pain? Any signs of Polio?" he asked sarcastically. I paused, turning my focus to my muscles. They were sore, but there was no pain. Not like the pain I had lived with for more than half my life. I looked back at him in shock.

"How?"

He chuckled. "You never had polio, Seren."

"What? Yes, I did. I was diagnosed before I was ten. I've had to be on medication the last decade of my life. What do you mean I never had polio?"

The door to the room opened. A beautiful brunette appeared. Her eyes were chocolate brown, her skin was sun kissed with little freckles that adorned the bridge of her nose, just like my own. Her hair was curly and extended past her shoulders. She appeared to be in her mid to late 40's.

She was curvaceous but small in stature. She was dressed well, in a white satin blouse and a pair of jeans that hugged her frame. She brought her hands up to her mouth as she smiled and laughed. I looked at Antonio and then back at the woman.

"I'll let your family explain the rest," he said, winking at me. He placed his hands behind his back and strolled to the door. He nodded at the woman. "Thora," he said before exiting.

The woman, Thora, walked over slowly, looking me over. I noticed the silver pentagram that hung from her neck. Rings and bracelets adorned her fingers and arms.

"May I sit," she said, gesturing to the side of the bed. I nodded, watching her ever so closely. There was something almost familiar about her, but I couldn't put my finger on it.

"Who are you," I whispered.

Tears filled her eyes as I watched her expression soften. "Oh, sweetheart. I'm your Aunt Thora. Your mother was my sister," she said softly. The wind felt like it had been ripped from my lungs. She laughed again, taking my hand in hers. "I can't tell you how happy I am that you are here. That you survived."

"What? What do you mean?' I asked as a million questions flew through my mind.

She took a deep breath, sitting up straight, placing her free hand on my face. She looked deeply into my eyes and smiled. "You have our eyes," she said, laughing softly.

"Please," I said, pulling away from her. "What are you talking about?"

She nodded, wiping her face. "I am sorry. You must be so overwhelmed. Where do I begin?" She paused, moving to the seat next to my bed. "Your mother, Annalise, was my sister. My twin in fact."

My whole world went spiraling.

"Was?"

Her smile fell. "Yes. She was killed about twenty years ago in a car accident. We thought... we thought you had died with her, yet here you are... a miracle." My legs began to tingle with pain. I winced, grabbing for them. My condition was returning.

"I need medicine," I said, feeling the burning sensation travel up my legs to my hips.

"For what, sweetheart?"

"My condition. I have polio."

She smiled at me tenderly, taking my hand back in hers. "No, you don't, Seren. You never did."

"Yes, I do. I feel it. I am feeling it right now."

"That's what the nuns made you believe, but in reality, you were completely healthy."

"What? I don't understand."

She took her hand back; her face turning more serious as she focused her eyes upon mine. "Those shots and teas they were pumping you with all those years; that wasn't medicine. It was poison. They were trying to prevent you from coming into your own. For coming into your powers."

I laughed at her, shaking my head in disbelief. "What are you talking about?"

"You are a descendant from a very powerful and revered line of witches, Seren. Magic courses through your veins," she said plainly.

I looked at her in disbelief and then started laughing hysterically. I had been through enough the past few days; I must be having a nervous breakdown. That had to be it.

"I know this is all a lot," she said, moving to the edge of her chair, "but I can answer any questions you have about your mother, about your powers, about who we are. And in time, you will have full mobility again. No more pain. We got most of the poison out of your system, but there will be some residual side effects since you had been on it for so long."

"Stop," I demanded, turning to face her. "You're crazy. I am not a witch. I can't be. I am training to be a nun."

"Another lie," she said with confidence. "You are powerful, sweetheart. The nuns were doing everything they could to diminish what is inside of you. What has always been inside of you."

"No!" I yelled, scooting away from her. "I detest all things satanic. I am a child of God. Not this foul creation you claim me to be." Without another thought, I started reciting the Lord's prayer. I watched to see if Thora would start acting out of character, but she just sat there, unphased, looking a bit annoyed. She crossed one leg over the other. As I finished the last line, she locked her eyes on mine, arching one eyebrow.

"Are we done with the theatrics, sweet Seren?"

"I... I don't understand," I said, more frightened now than before.

"First and foremost, I, nor any of us in the coven, are satanic worshipers."

"Coven?" I gasped.

"Yes, coven. Secondly, I personally believe in Jesus, God, and all that bright and shiny stuff. Just because I am a witch, doesn't mean I do not respect other religions or origins about creation. Thirdly, reciting the Lord's prayer does nothing to us or demons for that matter. They know the Bible better than any of your Catholic priests or nuns. They were around when the damn thing was written for Aradia's sake. Why would reciting some retelling of events they were present for harm them?"

I stopped, thinking about her logic. She had a point. I swallowed, trying to relax my nerves. "Then, if not for Satan, where does your power come from?" I asked.

"Our power comes from inside of us. You're born to this, it isn't chosen. The craft is passed down from generation to generation. We use things around us in nature to amplify our gifts."

I giggled uncomfortably. "So, you don't have real magic then. Like the kind that could kill someone or light a building on fire."

She looked at me, appearing annoyed as her foot stopped bouncing and her eyebrow arched once again. She raised her hand slowly focusing her attention on my throat, squeezing her hand in the air in front of me. My lungs felt like they were collapsing in on themselves. I reached for my throat, trying to remove the invisible hand around my neck. I began to choke and gasped for air.

She released her hand, untangling her legs and leaning forward towards me. I coughed, forcing my lungs to expand.

"Yes, niece. I have power. Real power, and so do you."

I scrambled as far away from her as I could until my back was flush with the headboard. She laughed, shaking her head, and leaning back in the chair. She pulled something from her pocket, placing it on the bed next to me. It was a photograph. She nodded towards it.

"Go ahead, take it. I won't bite."

I picked up the photo, never taking my eyes off her. I brought it closer, recognizing Thora and another woman who looked identical to her. They were standing stomach to stomach, both pregnant. They smiled with joy as if they were in the middle of laughing about something in the moment. My mother.

"You... you have a child?" I asked her, fixated on the picture.

"A daughter. Same age as you. Francesca. We call her Frankie for short. You also have a grandmother, your nonna, who is still very much alive. She is away right now but is scheduled to return in a week."

"And... my father?" I met her eyes.

She shook her head, dropping her gaze to the floor. "Your mother never told me who he was. What I do know is that she loved you very much. She was so excited to meet you. To hold you." Thora paused, laughing to herself. "She used to call you little bean. We would talk about what it would be like to raise you girls together. Frankie's father died when I was pregnant with her, so it was going to be just the four of us." I saw Thora's face fall.

"I'm sorry for your loss... all of them," I said.

"Yes, well the universe has a funny way of ripping everything from you only to provide you with the greatest gift of all."

I looked at her with confusion.

She laughed. "My daughter, Frankie. She is the embodiment of the moon goddess, Aradia. A blessing that only appears in our covens once every three centuries."

"Moon goddess?" I asked, trying to follow.

"There is much you will need to learn. Right now, however, we need to get your strength back. Once the poison is out of your system, we can begin honing those powers of yours."

I paused, looking at my legs and then back at her. "So... I am not sick?"

She stood, reaching her hand out to my face. I didn't flinch or pull away this time. Not when her face looked so much like my own. "No, sweetheart, you were never sick. In fact, you are quite healthy. We need to build your muscle density but that will all come in time. You're going to be strong, Seren. Mentally, physically, and magically. You are destined for greatness. It's in your blood." She leaned down and kissed me on top of my head. "Keep the photo. She would want you to have it."

"Thank you," I said, feeling a whirlwind of emotions.

"Of course. I'll check in with you tomorrow. The healers will be in sometime this evening to extract more of the toxin to speed up the healing."

"Was that what they were doing when I first woke? The black fog?"

"Yes. It's their magical gift. They can pull sickness or poisons from another living thing. They take it into their own bodies and their magic kills it before it can make them sick." I didn't say a word, even though I was secretly fascinated. This was all a sin. A horrific sin. I had to stay focused, and not lose sight of who I was.

"Will it be as painful as before?"

"Shouldn't be. The initial extraction was painful because they were taking in so much. Now that there are only residual bits left, it should just be uncomfortable."

"Glad to hear that. Thank you for checking on me," I said, scooting down underneath the covers.

"Of course. Get some rest."

Once the door was shut, I pulled the photo out from under the covers and stared at my mother and aunt. They were happy. Full of joy and hope. My mother. The woman who I had wondered about my entire life. Even with the abbey and the sisters, I still couldn't help but wonder where I came from. Now that I knew, I was unsure if I wanted to know more. This had to be some kind of joke. Was God testing me? And if he was, how was I supposed to stand up to individuals who possessed actual magic?

I felt the contents of my stomach turn and rise. I leaned over into the waste basin just in time to purge black bile from my mouth.

Once I was finished, I looked at the substance. This was the poison my sisters – my family had been pumping me with my entire life. They were trying to kill me. Sister Odette. The woman I loved like a mother injected me with this every day of my life; allowing me to believe I was dying from polio. I shoved the basket away, resting my head on the pillow.

I didn't know what to believe anymore. In the span of a day, I had learned where I came from. That the people I loved were trying to murder me. That I was a witch. And I had seen real demons. How was I supposed to come back from this? What was I supposed to do now? Where did I go from here?

CHAPTER FIVE

"Deep breath in," said the healer, standing over me. This time, there were no restraints or injections. I was hopefully done with those for good. I did as she instructed, readying myself for the discomfort. "Ready?"

I nodded, clenching my fists together. The healer scanned her hands over my body and began to chant in a language I didn't recognize. I watched her eyes closely. It was as if a small drop of black paint was being dropped into the center of her irises. The black inky substance saturated the rest of her eyes, changing them into the deepest shade of black.

The burning sensation began to prick across my skin. It felt like strings were attached to parts of my muscles, and she was pulling them out one by one. I clenched my teeth together, watching the black swirls of fog rise out of my body like steam. Her hands drew the substance to them as they evaporated into her skin.

After ten minutes of working, she began to sway on her feet. A young woman came up behind her, placing her hands on each of her arms. The healer's eyes fluttered as she leaned against her assistant. The black ink magic drained from her eyes, revealing a soft shade of green. She stood upright, looking like she was going to be sick.

"A few more sessions and you should be good as new," she said with a sweet smile. She went to take a step but stumbled as her companion held onto her. I swung my legs around, reaching for her.

"I'm so sorry," I said, touching her arm.

"No need to be sorry, honey. I am sorry you've had to endure this for the past eleven years of your life. This is some strong poison, but not the worst I've encountered," replied the healer.

"How long will it take you to heal?" I asked.

"A few hours of rest should get rid of it for good. Then I can take on a little more tomorrow."

"Thank you," I said, smiling up at her. She was a very tall woman with hair the color of straw that swirled in curls, framing her face. She wore a loose black dress.

"It is my pleasure to help a sister in need," she said, before she was escorted out of the room.

The word 'sister' now had a different meaning. Once, it was my dream to be a sister for the house of God. Now, I was a sister to a witch coven. I went to get back into bed when my door opened and in came my aunt.

"Good morning, sweetheart. How are you feeling?" she asked with a smile on her face. Her hair was pulled back away from her face today, allowing me to see her pierced ears.

"Stronger and more rested," I replied, still hesitant about her.

"Glad to hear that," she replied, reaching for a robe. She held it out in front me, inviting me to put it on. I did as she silently commanded, not wanting to be choked again.

"Are we going somewhere?"

"Your room," she said, smiling at me. "We can't have you staying in the medical wing. I've set up your mother's old room for you. I thought it only fitting." I smiled back at her, not knowing the right words to say.

She handed me a pair of forearm crutches, helping get me comfortable. "Hopefully you won't be needing these soon, but just until you regain your strength and balance back," Thora said.

She placed her hand on my back and ushered me out of the room. I walked through the halls in my slippers and robe as other people glanced our way. I got a few nods and some halfhearted smiles. We ascended a stone staircase that opened to a vaulted ceiling hallway with large floor to ceiling arched windows cut out of one side. A cool crisp breeze fluttered through the openings, meeting my damp skin.

I stopped, taking in the grandeur and beauty of it all. I walked over to one of the openings and peered out onto Triora. A luscious mountain landscape of rolling hills stretched for miles. Not a town or house could be seen from where we were. Only the beautiful treetops and a few rocky cliffs. The clouds touched the tops of the mountains, reflecting the vibrant green shades of the forest. It was breathtaking.

My aunt made her way next to me, smiling at my reaction. "Our coven is built deep into one of the largest mountain systems in Triora. We have a castle on top of the settlement. Some of us stay topside, while others prefer underneath. This part of our home is camouflaged with magic. From the outside, it looks like nothing more than trees and rocks. If someone tries to step on our land, they instantly think twice about it, and choose a different path. It has kept our people safe for a few hundred years now."

"This is magnificent," I said without thinking. Magic was alluring. I was being tempted by my flesh. I pulled my focus away from the beautiful scenery.

"Come," Thora said, placing my hand on her arm as she continued our ascension.

We entered the top portion of the large estate. The walls were made from raw stone, and beautiful wooden mahogany floors stretched throughout the entire castle. Oil paintings of men, women, families, and what appeared to be extravagant balls hung from the tall walls in each hallway.

I followed my aunt up a winding stone staircase until she stopped at a black wooden door. It had a large S carved into it, accompanied by beautiful carvings that were etched around the outer edges of the door.

"An S," I said, "for Seren?"

"No, sweetheart. An S for Salvo. De Salvo to be exact. Our last name."

"I have a last name?" I asked, realizing how stupid I sounded right after the words left my mouth.

Thora laughed. "Of course, you do. A very respected name, in fact." She turned the doorknob, standing back for me to enter. A large, canopied bed sat on the farthest wall. A beautiful nature design adorned the wallpaper on the wall the bed was against as an accent to the room's décor. A sparkling gold crystal chandelier was fastened to the ceiling in the center of the room. Two arched glass doors that led to a terrace were on the exterior wall. A few dressers, a makeup vanity, and a couch that was placed in front of the fireplace completed the room. The walls were a soft calming tone of lavender.

Thora walked in behind me, looking around in silence. "I haven't been in this room in over twenty years," she said softly. "For some reason, even after she died, I couldn't bring myself to clean it out. Something inside of me told me to hold on to hope." She turned her face towards me and smiled softly. "And now I know why. I was preserving a piece of her for you."

I smiled, unsure of how to respond. "It's a beautiful room. Are you sure it's okay if I stay here?"

"Of course, it is," she said, wrapping an arm around my shoulder, pulling me to her side for a hug. "Everything we have, everything I have, is now yours. You are no longer an orphan, Seren. You have a family. A real family who is proud to welcome you into the fold."

I took another look around the room, still feeling overwhelmed and confused about my current and unexpected predicament. My aunt seemed nice, but she was a witch, and according to her so was I. How would I get out of this? Would God forgive me? Had I already been sentenced to Hell the moment I was born?

My aunt stepped in front of me, placing a hand on my shoulders. "What's wrong, sweetheart? What is troubling you?"

I opened my mouth, but I felt foolish for even saying it out loud. So far, they had saved me from an illness I thought was going to kill me. They've provided me with a home and all the material things one could ask for. I even had a real family.

"I— my entire life, I've been taught about the evils of this world. I've been taught that unless you act, pray, and believe a certain way, you are doomed to hell. Now I discover witches are real. Demons are real. And not only are all these things real, but come to find out I'm one of those things as well."

She smiled softly. "I can't pretend to understand what you're going through. Once you learn our ways and see how we honor the land, life, and everything around us, I am confident you will change your opinion about the meaning of the word witch. I can't promise you that all you will learn and see is good. Our craft is about balance. Give and take. That includes life. But overall, we honor the gifts we are given and give back to the lives around us."

I paused, looking to the floor as the question I so desperately wanted an answer to pressed against my lips. "Since..." I started, "since we are 'witches', does that mean we go to Hell after we die?"

She touched my face gently, brushing a piece of hair back from my cheek. "We are not evil, Seren. Some witches are, just like normal people can be evil, even some Catholics. I believe we are judged by what is in our hearts and what good we do here on earth. As I have said, I believe in God, and in his son Jesus. But there is much more I believe as well. In time, based on your own experiences, you will find your way and be able to answer your own questions. That is how it should be."

"Thank you for being so understanding," I said.

"Anything you need, I am here. Now, onto the more fun parts of your room." Thora walked over to the double doors along the wall and pulled them apart, revealing a large room that was my very own personal closet. I had never seen so many shoes, purses, and clothing items before in my life. On the back wall, in the center of the room, sat a large wall of jewelry.

At the abbey, I had three robes, perfectly identical to one another. We were taught that things like clothing, jewels, and materialistic items were a sin of the flesh. Just another thing I would now have to get used to, I supposed.

"All new items were stocked for you once you arrived," explained Thora. "Everything you should need, including undergarments," she paused, pointing to drawers along one of the walls, "purses, and accessories can be found here. If you need anything else, don't hesitate to ask."

She picked up a manila envelope on one of the tables and handed it to me. "And this, is your identity. Your true identity," she said. "We looked through the abbey's records after the policia got through putting out the fire. There is no mention of an adoption or of a Seren. We checked with the local courts as well. Not to insult your former care givers, but it seems to me that they didn't want anyone to know you were there, let alone alive."

"So... I don't exist. I never did?" I asked.

"Not at the Montecassino Abbey, but you do here, Seren." I opened the envelope, taking out each individual document. My picture was on all of them, but I had no clue what they were. I looked at Thora as I held the cards in my hand.

"What are these?" I asked.

"Your passport," she said, pointing to a document with the name Seren Lucia De Salvo labeled across it. "This allows you to travel anywhere you wish in the world. A codice fiscale card for taxes. This just keeps the law from looking into us too hard. We have to appear normal. And a birth certificate to prove you exist."

"And these?" I asked, holding up a few plastic cards with numbers on them.

"Credit cards. You have access to the family coffers now."

"Is there work I can do to pay for my keep?"

She laughed. "No, sweet girl. We are very wealthy. No need to trouble yourself with work or financial responsibility. Once you get settled and you decide what you want to do with your life, we can discuss career options. Until then, enjoy life. Explore the city. Get to know yourself and others around you."

I looked at my license, reading my name silently to myself. "Lucia?" I asked, reading over my middle name.

Her smile stretched across her face softly. "Your grandmother's name. She is the head of this coven. Your mother was next in line, born only a few minutes before me. Since her passing, I have assumed the second seat next to mother. Once I am gone, it will fall to Frankie."

I shook my head, placing all the items back into the envelope. "Thank you, Aunt Thora, truly."

"Anything you need," she said, kissing me softly. "I mean that. Now, why don't you take a shower, get some fresh clothes on, and relax. I have placed some books on the table in front of the couch that should answer some of your questions about your gifts and lineage. They are Frankie's, so once you are done, you can return them to her room which is two doors down to your left."

"When will I get to meet her?"

"This evening, I hope. She is on an errand right now, but she assured me she should be home this evening before dinner. She is very excited to meet you."

"I look forward to it," I said, moving to peek into the very large and extravagant bathroom.

"If you need anything," said Thora, moving towards the door, "we are all here to help. Oh, and your cellphone is plugged in on your nightstand. Your number is written on the pad next to it. I went ahead and programed some numbers in it to get you started."

"I— I don't know how to use a cellphone," I admitted, wrapping my arms around myself.

"I see. Well, I am sure Frankie will be eager to teach you when she comes home. Relax niece, you're home," she said softly, before shutting the doors behind her.

Chapter Six

After I took a much-needed bath, I found the most modest thing in the closet, a black pair of jeans, a short sleeved black crew neck shirt, and a pair of black boots. I sat on the couch in my mother's old room and just stared. I wondered who she was and what kind of mother she would have been. If she was anything like her sister, I believed I would have had a good life.

She grew up in this room. It was designed and decorated for her. She slept in the bed I would now sleep in and sat on the couch I now sat upon. It was as if I had stepped into her life, taking her place in some way. I stood with my crutches, going to the dresser that contained old photos of her. There was one when she was a teenager. She was standing by a black horse, smiling from ear to ear. Another with her and Thora on what I assumed was their birthday. They were laughing as their faces were smeared with cake. I couldn't help but chuckle.

Photo after photo of my mother, Annalise, appearing, beautiful and beloved by those who were around her. She looked normal and happy. I wondered how she died and I survived. What happened to me? How did I end up at the abbey?

All my memories of the sisters and Montecassino were now tainted. These women had raised me with the intent of what? Killing me? They were all dead now, so I would never know. My entire life had been a lie. The sisters that I thought had loved me, detested me. My faith was shaken, and I now questioned everything.

Then, there was Sister Odette. The woman who I thought of as a mother. The woman who raised me in her image. Tears fell from my eyes. She was dead. No matter the anger I felt that was directed towards her, she was dead, and she was never coming back.

I let myself mourn. I cried for the nuns that I had trusted. The home that had sheltered me. The peace that I had once thought of to be divine. The women I looked to for guidance and comfort. The life I had desired my entire existence.

Everything had changed now. Everything was different. Nothing made sense anymore. I fell to my knees, lacing my fingers together as I prayed to God for guidance. He still existed. He wasn't a lie. He couldn't be.

I sat back on the couch, hesitantly grabbing the first book on top of the pile Thora had left for me. It didn't have a title. I opened it to see an outline of seven groupings. Luna, Étoile, Terre, Eau, Sole, Fuoco, and Vento. After flipping through the pages, I quickly discovered that they were the original seven covens.

Under each coven, the book outlined the history of each. The leaders, the bloodlines, who married who, and what powers and unique gifts came from the merging of different witches. The seven covens had spread out amongst the seven continents over the centuries, but they all began here in Italy.

A knock came at my door. I placed the book down and hesitantly made my way over to answer it. I cracked the door slightly to see Antonio standing with his hands behind his back on the other side. His smile flashed as I balanced myself on my crutches.

"See," he said smugly, "didn't I tell you all your questions would be answered?"

"Oh, don't worry. I now have a million more," I replied, relaxing a little.

"I have no doubt you do. Why don't we grab something to eat, and I'll help fill in some of those blanks for you. What do you say?"

I looked out in the hallway. "Am I allowed to leave?" I asked, unsure.

He laughed, taking a step closer. "You are not a prisoner here, Seren. This is to be your home, not a cage. You are a grown woman. You get to come and go as you please. See who you wish, and do as you wish, whenever, wherever, however. That also means you have the right to decline my invitation for an early lunch."

Everything inside of me told me to stay in my room, but I no longer trusted that little voice. I wanted answers. I needed them. "I'll go. I can't remember the last time I ate," I said, grabbing the wallet of personal belongings I had put together.

"Excellent," he said, pulling the door closed behind us. I followed him through the halls. He walked slowly, making sure not to go too fast. I felt so embarrassed about my condition. "Don't worry," he whispered down to me. "We will start working on your rehabilitation tomorrow."

I stopped, looking at him in shock. "Can you... can you read minds?"

He laughed, ushering me along to continue walking forward. "No, rest assure I cannot read your mind. But I did read your face. I can tell you're uncomfortable. You were also looking around at other people as if you're embarrassed. I put two and two together. I'm very good at reading people. I can sense a liar a mile away."

"That's unnerving," I whispered.

"Some think so. I quite like the little party trick." He led me through the front entrance of the castle, out to a courtyard. He opened the door to his black sports car which looked very expensive. I slid into the passenger seat as he took my crutches and placed them in the back.

Once we pulled off, he took me through a beautiful, scenic route into the main city of Triora. The buildings were old, but well preserved. Life seemed simple and stress free here. Farmers markets were on every corner. Clothing hung from windows above. Children played in the streets as mothers cleaned and socialized.

"Do you know how to drive," Antonio asked.

"What," I said, snapping my focus back to him.

"Have you ever driven a car?"

"No. I rarely left the abbey let alone got driving lessons," I admitted. "Honestly, I didn't think I'd be alive long enough to benefit from learning."

"Well, we'll have to remedy that as well. Then you can pick whatever car you'd like."

My eyes widened. "You mean... you are going to buy me a car?" I asked in shock. "Oh, no. That's okay. I don't need anything else. This is all too much."

He laughed as he pulled into a parking spot along the curb. "Didn't your aunt explain how this all works?" He tapped on the wallet I had on my lap. "We are all grossly wealthy. It doesn't matter how much you spend; the money will be there."

"Is it some type of magic?"

"A little. Our seers foresaw how to set each of our covens up for financial wealth and stability. With the right investments and business ventures, we will never have to worry about financial hardship."

"So, each of the seven covens have their own bank accounts?"

"I see you've been reading. Yes, each of the seven have their own investments and sources of income." He got out of the car and helped me onto the curb. We were in front of an adorable little bistro. He helped me into a chair on the patio before sitting across from me.

A beautiful young girl greeted us as she made eyes at Antonio. I wasn't really rehearsed in flirting, thanks to my upbringing, but she was absurdly obvious. He ordered espresso for the both of us, and then a pasta dish. As she left, he winked at her. I thought she was going to fall over onto the sidewalk. He laughed, taking a sip of his water.

"Is... is that your girlfriend?" I asked, curiosity getting the best of me.

"No. I don't have one of those. I just know her family from frequenting their restaurant over the years." He leaned forward in a secretive manner. "Why? You think she has a crush on me?"

I pulled away, uncomfortable by the proximity. He laughed. "I'm sorry for being so nosy. This is my first time in a new town and around... normal people, I guess you could say."

"Don't worry. We'll get you adjusted to our sinful little playground in no time."

I shot him a glare. He laughed, reaching into his pocket. He brough his fist out towards me and placed the item on the table just as the espresso arrived. I looked down at my rosary, cleaned and sparkling as if it was brand new.

"Thought you might want that," he said, taking a sip.

"How did you? When did you get this?" I asked, hesitant to touch the thing.

"After I killed the beast and scooped you up, I figured you'd want it. To bring you comfort or whatever you use it for."

"Thank you," I said, running the smooth and familiar beads in between my fingers. I didn't know if it symbolized anything to me anymore, but I would keep it, just in case.

"You're welcome," he said, watching the people pass. They nodded and smiled as us as he returned the gesture.

"Do they know what you are?" I asked.

He turned towards me and cocked his head to the side. "And… what exactly am I, sweet Seren?"

"Well… a witch," I said plainly. I was done being polite and timid. I wanted answers and I wanted them now.

"Actually, I am a warlock. Males are warlocks. And yes, some of them have an idea, others have no clue. Some fear us, most love us. We have been good to this town and in return, they are good to us."

"But you're from the Luna Coven, correct? You don't live here."

"A quick and observant study you are. I am going to have to watch out for that brain of yours. Yes, I am from the Luna Coven. You are from the Étoile Coven. My family resides in Sicily most of the time. When our generation was young, the coven leaders knew that our age bracket would contain the two prophecy vessels, the moon goddess, and the horn god. If you were born within a specific set decade, the elders decided to contain us all to one location in order to watch and observe our powers to find who the gods were. I was born and raised in your new home. So, regardless of where my family may live most of the year, Triora is my home."

"I know my cousin Francesca is the moon goddess, so does that make you the horn god?" I asked.

He smirked. "No, that honor was not given to me. Our horned god has chosen another, Orion Camerino from the Soleil Coven. He is currently 26. When he was around 15 his strength manifested. His powers and innate gifts resembled our horned god. Your cousin will be 21 in September. She started showing her gifts when she was around 13. A quick developer that one. When Frankie turned 20, the coven leaders announced them as the reincarnation of the gods, and they are now engaged."

"How old are you?" I asked.

"I am 25. And you?'

"20. I'll be 21 in October." He nodded his head without another word.

Our pasta dishes arrived. The aroma nearly sent me hurdling face first into the dish. I folded my hands and bowed my head to say a prayer to thank the Lord for the food I was about to consume, but stopped, unsure of the ritualistic custom. I slowly unfolded my hands, not daring to look at Antonio.

Remembering my manners, I used the fork and twirled a small helping onto a spoon before placing the buttery and lemon concoction into my mouth. My eyes shut as I slowly chewed the perfectly cooked pasta. I never wanted this moment to end. I let out a small moan of satisfaction as I allowed the contents of the dish to slide down into my stomach. I opened my eyes to find Antonio looking at me as if I were the most interesting thing in the world. I placed the fork down, moving the napkin to dab my lips.

"That good?" he asked, finally digging into his own dish.

"It's wonderful," I replied, feeling a bit embarrassed.

He laughed at me, chewing his food as his gaze met mine. The sunlight hit his multicolored hazel eyes. I watched as they reflected the colors of the plants, the stone, even my hair. They were entrancing. I leaned forward, trapped inside the prisms of color.

"Find something else you like?" he interrupted me, placing another fork full of pasta into his mouth.

I shook my head, turning my focus back to my food. "I am so sorry; I don't know what's wrong with me. That was rude."

"No need to be sorry. I've trapped plenty of damsels with these bad boys," he said, tapping a finger to the side of his eye.

"Well sorry to break it to you, but there will be no trapping of this damsel." I took another bite.

"Confident, are we?" he laughed, swallowing his food. "You just might be a Salvo after all."

"And what is that supposed to mean?"

"Let's just say that the women in your family are known for their... talents. Not just with magic but with... extracurricular activities." I paused for a second, trying to follow his meaning. He must have seen the confusion on my face because he leaned forward as he whispered, "They're known for their beauty and their talents in the bedroom."

I pulled back, appalled by the information. "Oh," I gasped, not sure of what to say. "I— I— I'm a nun. We don't—"

"Come now, Seren. You weren't a nun yet. And now that you know who you are, you are free to explore that side of yourself."

"Can we please change the subject," I said, trying to shove my mouth full of food to shut it up.

"Of course. I am sorry if I made you uncomfortable. Not something we should talk about on our first date."

I choked on my food. "Date?" I gasped.

He laughed, taking a drink of water. "One-on-one meal, beautiful scenario, I plan to pay. It's a date."

I shook my head. "I am sorry if you got that impression, but I don'—"

"Stop, stop," he interrupted, reaching across the table, and gently placing his hand on my forearm. "I am just teasing. I am sorry. I will stop. It's my sense of humor. I tend to push people's buttons. Sometimes I go too far. Now, in lieu of changing the subject, what do you wish to know about our little magical family?"

"The legends, about this town and witches. Is it all true?"

"Some, but not all of course. There were witches here during those horrific two years. 1587-1589. During that time, this region experienced poverty, famine, and plagues. It was all due to a poor harvest season. Our three main exports were and still are: wheat, wine, and chestnuts.

"The church needed someone to blame so they looked to a poorer section of the city, La Cabotina, and found a group of women who were widowed. These women were also known for being healers. The town accused them of causing the poor harvest and all the terrors that followed. They even said these women were cannibals. In reality, they were only trying to help their townsfolk. Thirteen were arrested and sent to prison along with six more that following year. One died during a torture session. One threw herself into the void, and another five died in prison over the next year."

"So, they were just normal people?" I asked.

"Not all of them. Two of your ancestors and one witch from the Soleil Coven were involved with the efforts to try and save their home. They escaped. All records of them have been erased. They returned to Castle Salvo where they lived out their lives in silence."

"And witches aren't cannibals?"

"We prefer our pastas over human flesh, but... there are groups of witches who have strayed from the old ways. Who prefer to use darker methods to gain power."

"What do you mean?"

"Groups of witches have left the original seven over the centuries forming their own dark coven. They use human sacrifice, blood rituals, and dark magic to commune with demons and things beyond our world. Where our magic is derived from the earth and natural elements inside of us, the dark coven gains their power through blood magic. The process of taking life in exchange for unnatural power. We are not those people, nor do we have any contact with them. They are why witches have been given a bad rep."

"I see. And who is the moon goddess and horned god? Do you praise them?"

"In a way, yes. The moon goddess, also known as Aradia, is the three phased goddess. The maiden, mother, and crone. Our religion is called Stregheria. It is one of the oldest religions known to date. The goddess has power over the moon, stars, and sea. She can mask reality, pierce illusions, awaken intuition, and spark vision. She is the very embodiment of enlightenment.

"The horned god is Aradia's male consort Cyrus. He is the embodiment of the male power. God of nature, the hunt, wilderness, sexuality, and the life cycle. Together they power our world and create a balance among all life."

"And every third century, Aradia and the horned god are reincarnated in two witches so their power can be replenished back into the earth?"

"Exactly."

"Do they have to marry for the ritual to work?"

"Our records don't say specifically but, every time they have been reborn, their souls seek the each other out. They are mated. Meant to be together and find one another over and over again. We have documented that even when the two are married, they still seek out others sexually, but they are dedicated to one another, and their power together brings in the golden era for the covens every century they appear.

"Our businesses thrive, more witches and warlocks are born. Love flourishes. Along with our powers and natural gifts. We have been blessed to have been born during such a time."

"And do the witches and warlocks believe in marriage? In monogamy?"

"I would say most do. Just like some humans couples, ours like to mix things up from time to time, but overall, when you are tied to another, that is a life commitment we do not take lightly. Divorce happens just like it does all over the world, but not as frequently among our kind."

"When is my cousin's wedding?"

"I believe after the new year."

"And how is she? My cousin. I assume you know her well since you were raised together."

He sat back, taking his espresso with him as he sipped casually. His dark blue button up shirt was cleanly pressed, and his dark washed jeans fit his legs well. "She is persistent. Loved by her people. Powerful and very beautiful. Everything needed to make a good leader."

"And her fiancé?"

Antonio exhaled. "He, on the other hand, needs some work. He has an immense amount of power. He is well trained, deadly in fact, but lacks the mind for politics. He is quick to act and does so without thinking through his actions sometimes. There are specific expectations he does not seem to care about."

"And do they love each other? Or is this more of an arranged marriage? I figured they would love each other because of the whole soulmate, destiny thing."

"I'm not going to presume to know their feelings, but from what I can tell they are not afraid to explore each other and the possibility of a relationship if you get my meaning. The moon and horned god's mating bond does not take place until after the ritual is conducted. Only then are the memories of the gods transferred into their hosts. Then, the mating bond usually clicks into place."

"And all the covens are in support of this?"

"They all mutually benefit from the return of the gods. In the past, there has been tension between the covens on political platforms. Each coven conducts themselves differently and chooses to focus their magic and skill sets."

"What do you mean?" I asked, finishing off my pasta.

"Your coven, for example, are highly skilled in politics and focus on astrology. The Étoile Coven has many people positioned in different government structures around the world. Their powers are more focused on mental and physical control. My coven, Luna, care more about financial gain. We have a plethora of businesses and are involved in the stock markets in the United States and other financially beneficial investments.

"Terre and Eau focus on the earth and the green movement. They are more of the hippie mindset. They are known for their naturalistic ways and use a lot of elements to strengthen their magical abilities. Vento Coven lean more towards scientific development. There was a time when they would experiment on live humans. Fuoco and Soleil are more military and tactical based. Both are very wealthy due to their inventions."

"So, they each have infiltrated some larger worldwide organization to have a foothold if needed to support the witches' endeavors?"

"You could say that. They all have a different outlook on how their lives should play out. Individualism you might say. Some covens are freer with themselves, whether it be with money, sex, or drugs. Others are more of the rule following kind. They like order and do not take any risks."

"Will there be anything else?" asked the young server as she peered down at Antonio.

"No, darling. Please put it on my tab," he said, flashing his bright white teeth in her direction.

"Of course, Mr. Simonelli."

"Now," he said, leaning towards me, elbows on the table, "what would you like to do next?"

"I really have no clue," I laughed uncomfortably. "My daily schedule has been set for me since I can remember. I've never been able to choose what I do with my time."

"How about this... I take the top down off the Jag and we go for a little scenic drive. Fresh air will do you good and you'll get to see the beauty of your new home."

"Really? Are you sure? You don't have anything else better to do?"

"Not for another three days," he winked, standing as he extended his hand out to me. I took it, pulling myself up before reaching for my crutches. "Ah," he said, stopping me from putting them on. "My one condition is that you walk back to the car only using my hands for support."

"Antonio, I can't," I replied.

"You can. You can do anything you set your mind to. Now, eyes on me. One step at a time." He held out his other hand and I took it, balancing myself as my legs began to groan.

The first step was the hardest, but then the second step found its courage, and then the third. I was sweating and my heart was racing by the time I settled into the seat of his car, but I had made it without collapsing on the sidewalk. In only a few days of being here with the witches, I was already healing.

He loaded my crutches in the back seat. He slid into the driver's seat, pressing a button that collapsed the soft fabric of the roof and looked over and smiled. "See, I told you, you were capable. I'll have you walking in no time."

"Did you forget to tell me you were a physical therapist?" I said with a small laugh.

"Kind of... I'm working towards my PhD in medicine," he said, matter of fact as he pulled from the curb.

"I thought the Vento Coven was more of the medical mind?"

"They are, but I've always had an interest in medicine. My investments are in medicine and medical equipment, as was my fathers, and grandfathers. I felt that in order to understand my business better I would benefit from being in the field."

"Wow," I replied, not knowing what else to say.

"You're impressed, aren't you?" He winked, with a devilish grin.

"A little," I admitted. He laughed, zooming us up into the mountains. For being so young, he had accomplished so much. My life paled in comparison. Now that the church was no longer an option, I was struggling to even begin to fathom a life for myself. But in this life, I would be able to walk, to run, to possibly have a relationship and a family, but most importantly... I would be able to live. To grow old and have a life of my own. To learn and explore the world beyond the church.

My hair fluttered in the wind as we swerved up and down the back roads of Triora. The trees and vegetation were magnificent and tranquil. The air smelled crisp and the nature around us seemed to open its arms as we sped down each path. I felt the warmth of the sun on my cheeks and allowed myself to smile. I would no longer let fear determine where my life led me. I would be my own maestro in my symphony. I would find my path. My calling. My purpose.

Chapter Seven

"Come on," demanded Antonio, "two more steps and you're to your door. Then, I will let you relax." My legs were aching from the pain. He hadn't allowed me to use my crutches the entire way back to my room from the driveway. My sweaty fingers held onto his hands for dear life as my body shook.

"I thought you said we were starting therapy tomorrow?" I said, between hefty breaths of exhaustion.

"I saw how well you did at the restaurant and changed my mind. You will walk again, Seren. I will make sure of it."

We got to my door as I braced myself against the frame. "Antonio, I am very grateful for all your help, but... why do you care? What is in this for you?"

The smile from his eyes fell as he made sure to keep one hand firmly planted on my lower back. "I had a younger sister. Giana. She was in a car accident back in Sicily when she was eighteen a few years back. They said she would never be able to walk again, but I worked with her every day until we made progress. She died about two years ago from other complications. Helping people somehow makes me feel close to her again. Like her death wasn't

"

for nothing."

I reached out, touching my hand to his arm. My heart swelled with pain for him. "I am so sorry for your loss. Truly. Magic couldn't have saved her?"

"The car accident wasn't what killed her. After she began to recover and was on the mend, we found out she had a hereditary condition that was going to kill her regardless of what our healers did. We tried everything, but sometimes nature must take its course."

"If it's worth anything, you sound like an amazing big brother. She was lucky to have you," I said, smiling softly at him.

"Thank you. It does mean something. Now, let's get you inside so you can get some rest," he said, taking me by the arm as he pushed the door open.

Inside, sat my aunt and a girl around my age. They both stood as I entered, with smiles on their faces. The girl had long black, straight hair. Her eyes were a brilliant shade of green, her skin was tan with the same set of freckles that my aunt and I shared. She was at least five inches taller than me with legs that most women would die for.

"Hello," I said hesitantly. The girl's smile exploded across her cheeks as she took off towards me. She wrapped her arms around my body and squeezed.

"I am so excited to meet you," she said, pulling back to look at me. I wobbled a bit as Antonio positioned his hands around my waist to steady me. "Oh, right. I am so sorry. I didn't mean to take you out," she laughed. "I am Francesca, but please, call me Frankie."

"Nice to meet you, Frankie. Your mother has told me wonderful things about you," I replied.

She looked back at her mom and smiled. "She's told me wonderful things about you as well," she continued. "I can't wait to get to know you. I've always wanted a sister and, well... with our mom's being twins and all, I figure we basically are sisters. And I hear we were born exactly a month apart. How crazy is that?"

I laughed, feeling a sense of joy I had never experienced before. "Fate," I whispered, smiling up at my beautiful cousin.

"I agree," she said, taking me by the arm and helping me to the couch.

"How was today?" Aunt Thora asked, looking between me and Antonio.

"I would say it went well," he answered. "Would you agree, Salvo?"

"Besides you almost killing me with all the walking we just did, yes, I would have to agree. I learned a lot," I replied.

"Good," said my aunt with a smile. "Thank you so much Antonio. We will see you at dinner this evening."

"Of course, Elder Thora," replied Antonio. "Nice to see you as always, Frankie," he nodded at my cousin. "Seren," he said with a wink as he took his leave.

Frankie rolled her eyes. "That one is a flirt," she said, still holding onto my hand as we sat on the couch together. "You'll have to watch out for him. Seems to me he found something he likes."

"Now, now," said my aunt as she sat in a chair across from us. "Antonio Simonelli would make an excellent match for any young woman. Plus, we haven't had a wedding between our two covens in decades. This could be a very good thing."

I looked at them both, unsure of what to say. "He's... uh... nice," I replied. They both started laughing hysterically.

"Don't worry, niece," said Thora, "we aren't in the business of arranged marriages around here."

"Unless you're the moon goddess," added Frankie under her breath.

"Last time we spoke on the matter," replied Thora, "you were quite happy with the arrangement. Don't act like you haven't had your eye on Orion since you were young. I know you better than you know yourself, darling."

She shrugged her shoulders. "I mean... he is hot," she said, plainly.

Thora scoffed. "Oh, Frankie, have some class, for Aradia's sake."

"What? He is. Don't act like you haven't noticed mother. I don't care what age you are. If you're alive with a pulse you notice when that man enters the room." They both started laughing again. A small giggle rose from inside of me. Their laughter was contagious. "You'll see, Seren, just wait. God or not, that man is a work of art."

"That is your future husband you are talking about," added Thora.

"As you so often like to remind me," Frankie said, leaning back into the chair. "Now, enough about me, tell me about you. What do you like to do?"

"Well," I said, "I was raised in an abbey so there wasn't a lot of choices to choose from. Over the years, I did find joy in cooking. It was really the only thing I looked forward to most days."

"Cooking?" said my aunt. "That's something we can work with."

"Aradia," said Frankie, "I couldn't imagine growing up in a nunnery. I feel for you, cousin, really, I do."

"Francesca!" gasped my aunt.

"No, it's okay," I said. "Really. I've only spent a day in this beautiful town but, I've already begun to see how narrow my views of life have been. I am open to learning and experiencing... life."

Frankie sprang forward, taking my hands in hers once more. "Oh, I am so glad to hear you say that," she said in an excited tone. "I thought we were going to have to spend months converting you, and talking about religion, blah, blah, blah."

"Francesca! That is enough," said Thora.

"Now, once we get you up and walking," continued Frankie, "I am going to take you to all my favorite haunts. We are going to get completely hammered and dance the night away, just us girls."

Thora rested her forehead on her hand. "Aradia, please help me,"

Thora pleaded.

"Oh, mamma," Frankie said, tossing a pillow at her. "Just because I will soon have the goddess inside of me doesn't mean I don't get to live. And it sure as hell doesn't mean I don't get to build a relationship with my long-lost cousin."

"I'd like that very much," I said to Frankie.

She looked back at her mother. "I love her already. Oh," she gasped, turning her attention back to me. "Did mamma tell you about the ball that we are hosting in July?"

"Ball?" I asked with confusion.

"I figured finding out she was a witch was enough for one setting," answered Thora.

"Yes," continued Frankie, "coven members from all seven are coming here in July to welcome in the summer season. It is one of my favorite events. And this year, we're hosting!"

"Sounds... wonderful," I said.

"It is," Frankie said, before gasping. "You don't have a dress, do you?"

"Oh, I have a million in that closet," I replied.

"No, no, none of those will do. We will have to go shopping... tomorrow. Just in case it needs altering. This is your first witchy ball. The first time everyone will get to meet the daughter of Annalise De Salvo. It must be perfect."

I felt the heat rush to my cheeks. An uncomfortable feeling settled inside of me as I tried to remain unreadable.

"What is it, sweetheart?" asked my aunt. They both stared at me for an answer.

"I... I don't really like being the center of attention. I'm more of a behind the scenes person," I admitted.

Frankie began laughing. Her mother hid her smile, but it didn't go unnoticed.

"Oh, Seren. You have so much to learn," said Frankie.

"What my daughter meant to say," interrupted Thora, "is that when you come into your powers, we are confident those feelings of uncertainty you are feeling will change."

"Plainly," added Frankie, "you will need to get used to being the center of attention. You are a Salvo. We are one of the most powerful and oldest families in any coven. We are gifted, talented, successful, and beautiful. People will envy you because of your last name alone. And when you come into your power, they will envy that as well."

"Our family lived a long time hiding our true gifts," explained Thora. "My grandmother, Francesca, finally decided enough was enough. She allowed her gifts to flow and took pride in our strengths and didn't hide her power because it might make others feel inferior. She passed that down to her daughter and then to us. We embrace who we are and are proud of the gifts we've been trusted with. We bow to no one and to nothing."

I smiled, not knowing what to say yet again. "I see. Well, I am eager to continue to learn about our family history," I replied, glancing at the books on the coffee table.

"Any questions you have," said Thora, standing from her chair, "we are here to answer. Come Frankie, time to let your cousin rest."

Frankie leaned over, kissing me on the cheek tenderly. "I'm so glad you're here, Seren. We're going to get into so much mischief together. I can't wait." She pulled away smiling from ear to ear.

My aunt brought over another pair of crutches to the couch before bending to kiss me on the head. "Your cousin means well. She's a free spirit, that one," she said.

I laughed. "Really, I didn't notice," I replied.

"Get some rest, niece."

CHAPTER EIGHT

"That's it, that's it," encouraged Antonio. "Almost there. You've got this. Just a little bit further." My hands and arms shook on the bars as I forced my legs to work. I did as he instructed, not relying on my upper body strength.

I got to the end of the row of bars and all but collapsed. Antonio caught me before I could hit the ground. I was drenched in sweat. This was my 20th time walking back and forth on my own and it wasn't even nine in the morning.

"Excellent," he said, all but carrying me to the bench. He knelt in front of me, rubbing my calves and moving towards my thighs. His eyes looked up at mine. "Is this, okay?" My body moaned with delight as he worked the stress from my muscles.

"God, yes," I said, allowing my aching muscles to enjoy the massage.

"You're making great progress," he said, moving to the next leg. "I know it's painful now, but the more work you put in, the faster you'll be able to walk on your own." He stood up, taking a seat next to me and handing me a towel.

"You're really good at this," I noted, wiping my brow.

"Thank you. One of my many talents, I assure you," he said with a wink, passing me a bottle of water. I laughed, downing the entire bottle in a few gulps. I looked around me as witches practiced fighting maneuvers. I felt like I had stepped into a boot camp.

"Will I learn how to do that?" I asked.

"Eventually, yes. There are people and things out there in the world that want to kill us for our powers. Better to have a full arsenal of skills at your disposal, just to be on the safe side."

"What wants to kill me?" I asked, surprised by the new bout of information.

He laughed. "One thing at a time Salvo. For now, let's just focus on getting you healthy so you can run for your life... just in case something decides to chase you."

My eyes widened in fear. What was out there? What was he talking about?

He laughed again. "Sorry. My pesky sense of humor again." He turned his focus to two men fighting in front of us in the center of a circle.

I watched them closely, studying each calculated swing, dodge, and punch. How was I ever going to catch up? I needed to master magic, knowledge pertaining to each coven, fighting, shooting, and walking. All while learning how to be a normal citizen out in the real world. And let's not forget... somehow, my prude self also needed to live up to my seductive and powerful family's reputation. I was royally screwed.

I felt an elbow hit me in the arm, snapping me out of my self-doubt and pity. "What's that mind of yours worrying about now?" Antonio asked, turning his body to face me on the bench.

I huffed, not wanting anyone to see my insecurities. "It's nothing," I said, wishing he would stop being so observant at times.

"Seren, you can talk to me. I'm not going to judge you. I am here to help," he said softly, placing a hand on my arm.

"I... I have so much to catch up on. How am I ever going to be one of you? You all were trained for this life since birth. I just... I don't see how I am ever going to fit in here. Between the rehabilitation, mastering whatever power I might have, all the studying, and let's not forget living up to my *family's legacy*. God, has my cousin always been that beautiful? No wonder the goddess chose her to be the vessel. She's damn near perfect."

He began laughing, which caught me off guard. I looked at him, not knowing what I said that he found so funny. "Frankie is easy on the eyes, but she's not the only one in the family that got blessed with looks," he said, pinching my chin between his fingers. "Stop being so hard on yourself. You need to be your biggest cheerleader. It won't matter if I believe in you, or your aunt, or even the moon goddess herself. Unless you believe in yourself and put in the work, all this will be for nothing. You're the only one who can determine what you are capable of."

"It's... it's just a lot," I said, with a huff.

"I get that, but you're here. A few weeks ago, you believed you wouldn't live to thirty, yet now you have a whole life in front of you waiting to be written. You couldn't walk a few days ago, yet today, you just did 20 laps all on your own. You are powerful Seren De Salvo. I see it, your aunt sees it. Now, it's time for you to see it."

I looked at him, feeling a warmth in my heart I had never felt before. I had never had anyone believe in me or compliment me in the way he had just done. The nuns lived a very isolated life. I wasn't used to having someone to confide in.

"Thank you, Antonio. For everything," I said.

"Anytime, beautiful," he said, standing. I felt my cheeks blush. "Come on, let's get you a shower and then some breakfast."

The next few days, I pushed myself harder than I thought possible. Even when Antonio wasn't around, I was up, forcing my legs to remember how to walk. I graduated from my crutches to a cane. After a few more sessions with the healers, I no longer felt as much pain. Twinges here and there continued, but nothing compared to the constant state of discomfort I had lived with the past eleven years.

At night, I continued to pray and study the Bible searching

for my truth. Every story I read, I cross referenced, looking for the inconsistencies or things that couldn't be explained. Most of the stories that I researched had historical backing to their timelines. Characters and events could be found and were documented in other languages from different regions of the world. Artifacts mentioned in the Bible had even been found and where now on display in museums for all to see. Everything I had been taught wasn't a farse. So where did that leave me?

At the end of the week Antonio left on a business trip he avoided telling me much about. I was curious, but I didn't push the subject. I went to the library after my therapy and buried myself in our history. I learned all I could about witches, the covens, our origin, and the gods and goddess. It amazed me how similar different parts of each religion were to Christianity.

It was nearing midnight. I was curled up in the library underneath a blanket nose deep in book about Aradia, the queen of witches, better known as the moon goddess. She was the daughter of Diana the moon goddess and Lucifer, not the Christian Lucifer, but the god of the sun. She was the liberator of our people who had been oppressed. She empowered the witches, warlocks, and their descendants. When she found her mate, their power united, giving their people physical power and protection.

I heard the door to the library open behind me. My head popped up as my eyes strained in the dim light. A female figure stood in the doorway; eyes deadlocked onto me. I placed the book down, standing to my feet, unsure of who was before me.

"Hello, can I help you?" I asked, trying to make out the figure. An older woman stood by the door. Her white hair was braided away from her face and pinned up in a bun. Her frame was thin. A black suit hung on her body in the most elegant of fashions.

She took a few steps towards me, bringing her face into the light. She had thin lips with dark eyebrows. Her eyes were small, but still bright as if there was a fire behind them. Wrinkles adorned her face, showing her age, yet familiar freckles scattered the bridge of her nose.

Before I knew it, she stood before me. I watched a single tear escape her eye as her mouth began to quiver. "Bambina," she whispered. She reached out her hand, combing my hair in the most intimate way.

"Nonna?" I asked, confident I knew who stood before me. She smiled, nodding her head as tears fell from her face. She wrapped me in an embrace against her as she cried. A part of my heart filled in that moment. I felt like I belonged. Right here, in her arms.

She pulled back, touching my face softly as she examined every inch of me. She laughed and smiled, tears continuing to fall down her cheeks. She looked down at the cane that I used to support myself. Her eyes turned furious.

"The nuns did this to you," she said in an assertive tone.

"Yes, but they're all dead now," I said, still feeling the pain of that reality.

"Good, come and sit," she said, ushering us back to the couch. "Studying about the moon goddess, are we?" she asked, placing the book on the table in front of us.

"Just trying to catch up on our history. On where I come from," I said, feeling an instant sense of peace and comfort around this stranger I had only just met.

Her eyes softened as we sat in silence. "You look so much like my Annalise," she said, reaching out to pinch my cheek. "It is uncanny. All these years, I believed every trace of her was erased. My heart ached without closure or answers about what happened to her. About what happened to you. Yet here you are. More beautiful than I ever could have imagined."

I smiled, feeling a sense of pride. "I've dreamt of this moment. Of a family of my own for so long. I feel very blessed," I replied.

"We are blessed child. You are exactly where you are meant to be. With your family. With me," she said, pulling me back into her chest. I sat there for a moment, relishing the motherly affection I had never experienced, yet dreamt of. Everything made sense. Everything felt right.

"Now," she said, settling in on the couch beside me. "I want to know everything. Every detail about your life. No matter how big or small."

I smiled, pulling the covers over my legs. That night, I shared my life with my nonna. We laughed, cried, and listened as we both shared the stories of our lives with one another. In the early hours of the morning, while the sun rose over the horizon, the stranger that I had met a few hours ago had become my greatest confidant. My greatest strength. My most valued friend.

Once Antonio returned, I worked harder and longer until I no longer needed the cane. I was far from running a marathon, but I could walk on my own. He was right. It was painful at first, but I got stronger every day.

My nonna began to teach me all she knew about magic. Different spells, different branches of elemental magic and how they all tied back into one source of power. I took page after page of notes, documenting every word that came out of her mouth. I wanted to make her proud and I wanted to live up to our name.

Antonio continued to work with my physically. Now that my legs were functional, we needed to work on my stamina. He was kind and patient. After only a month, I felt like I had known him for years. I trusted him. He had saved me and helped restore my body. I would have been lying to myself if I didn't notice how attractive he was. But I wasn't the only one. No matter where we went, girls flocked to him. All he had to do was smile and they would all but lift their skirts for him.

"Two more laps," Tony demanded.

"How about you take the day off from being my drill sergeant and revert back to just Tony, my friend," I said, feeling the burning sensation in my limbs. Thankfully, the water in the pool was crisp and refreshing, but I had been swimming for an hour now and was beginning to feel fatigued.

"The more you complain, the more laps I am going to add," he said, sitting on the edge of the pool, fully dressed. His black dress pants were rolled up to his knees as he dangled his feet in the water. His shirt sleeves were rolled up to his elbows per usual. I resisted from staring to long, but recently, I couldn't help myself. Especially when he smiled at me, which seemed to be often.

"Alright, that's two more," I gasped, treading water. "What's my reward today?" I gripped the edge of the pool wall next to him as he smiled, leaning in close to my ear.

"The way you've been staring at me all morning tells me exactly what you want, beautiful," he whispered. The brush of his lips to my ear sent my entire body into a warm frenzy. Feeling embarrassed and unsure of these new sensations and desires, I did the only thing I could. I reached up, wrapping my arms around his neck and pulled him, fully dressed, into the water. I swam back, laughing as he came up from air.

"And now I know what you look like wet," I said, smiling at him as he looked back at me with shock and surprise.

"Oh, you are going to regret that," he said, pushing off the wall towards me. I screamed; swimming as fast as I could for the opposite side of the pool. I barely reached it before he slammed against me, pinning my hands to my sides. I had been this close to him before, with all the therapeutic exercises we had done, but this was a different type of closeness.

"You can't out swim me, beautiful," he said, looking down at me as he caught his breath.

"I can't out swim you *yet*. Maybe in a month. Look at all the progress I am making," I said, smiling up at him.

"Mm, believe me, I am watching," he said, bending his head down towards mine. The smell of him, a rich mixture of cologne and something natural like rosewood made my body tense. He was warm as I became very aware of every part of our bodies that were touching.

His chest rose and fell against mine, as I remained still, not daring to move. Not wanting this moment to end. I had never wanted a man before. Never desired another. The feeling of him was more than I could bare. I secretly hoped he would kiss me. *No*, I thought, shaking the desire from my head. This wasn't right. This wasn't the Christian thing to want or think but... I wanted him to... to touch me and allow me to feel him.

His eyes filled with desire and want as his breath remained ragged. I tilted my head up to him as he trailed his fingers against the length of my jaw. His other hand braced itself firmly against my back, pulling me against him completely. I reached up, moving my fingers to his jet-black hair. He closed his eyes at the contact. A yearning deep inside of me awoke. My entire body electrified at his touch.

"Seren, we—" he started to say, but before he could finish, I placed a finger over his mouth, gently brushing his soft, supple lips. He moaned.

"If you want to stop, I understand," I whispered, continuing to take him in.

"I—," he started to say, but paused as his eyes buried themselves into my own. He began to lean slowly into me. Everything inside of me blazed alive. In this moment, nothing matter. Not religion. Not the oath I had once made to myself. Not the dangerous line we were now approaching. All that matter was this feeling that had come alive inside of me.

I closed my eyes, anticipating the feeling of his lips. The taste of him. But I was left wanting. "Seren," he whispered a moment later.

I opened my eyes to see darkness all around us. Small droplets of water were frozen in the air. There had to be thousands of them. The pool of water was lit with an entrancing and illuminous white light that was coming from... me. I reached out and gently touched one of the droplets. It fell from the air back to the pool.

"What is this?" I asked, as we both looked at each other with smiles of amazement on our faces.

"It must be your power. It sure as hell isn't coming from me," he said, taking in the magnificent moment.

"My power? You mean, I actually have power?" I said with excitement.

He began to laugh. "Yes, Seren. See, told you, you were a witch."

I screamed, wrapping my arms around him as I laughed. We pulled away from each other, locking eyes once more. That fire immediately relit inside of me. I touched his face softly, as his eyes blazed with desire once more. I wanted him. I wanted this. I slowly leaned into his lips, anticipating the ta—

"Seren," I heard my nonna's voice boom with authority from the other side of the pool. It snapped any tether of passion I had as I pushed away from Tony with such force that I ended up submerging him underneath the water. He resurfaced, just as the suspended rain droplets came crashing down to the surface. My white light faded away and the darkness that had surrounded us dissipated like fog.

My nonna looked at both of us and then at the pool and the wet droplets that surround the edge. "Good," she said without feeling. "Your power has finally surfaced. Now the work begins. Get dressed and meet me in my rooms. Now," she demanded, without another word.

I looked back at Tony and blushed. He laughed pushing me in the arm as we swam to the ladder in the pool. We dried off, not saying a word. I didn't know what to say after what almost happened. All I knew was that whatever just happened between us, I enjoyed it. I wanted it. But... my religion. My vow. I was torn between the religion I had always known and this new path full of so many inexplainable possibilities.

"Have I ever told you your nonna scares the hell out of me," Tony said, finally breaking the silence.

"My little nonna? I don't see why," I said, smiling back at him from under the towel.

"Oh, you haven't seen her magic yet. Just wait. Word of advice, don't piss her off."

"But she loves me. I'm her little bambina," I said in a teasing manner. He snapped me with the towel as I jumped back. "Hey, not fair!"

"Just checking those reflexes of yours. Not bad."

"Well, I better go get changed and do as she requested. I guess fun time is over."

"For now," he said, winking at me. I laughed, making my way back to my bedroom.

CHAPTER NINE

"Focus child," nonna snapped, as I peered down at the bowl of water. "Clear your head and control the element. You are made of water. You command the water. Your power is like an ember inside of you. Now light the flame and make it your bitch."

I looked at my nonna in shock as I tried to smother my laughter but failed miserably. I covered my mouth with my hands as the small squeals of amusement slipped between my fingers. She giggled, sitting on the edge of the table next to me.

"What? An old lady like me can't cuss? Is it not the proper thing to do?" She allowed herself to laugh, bopping me on the head. "Now focus. Imagine what you want to happen in your mind. The brain is the most powerful weapon you can possess. Visualize a single droplet rising from the center of a ripple. Form it in your brain just like you form the dough underneath your hands when you bake. Make your vision a reality."

I did as she commanded, pushing every thought, every feeling out of my head. Every distraction. Smell. Sound. The only thing I could see was the water in the brown wooden bowl in front of me. I focused on the water so intensely that I began to have tunnel vision, but I didn't stop. I took a deep breath in, feeling the vibration inside of me awaken as a deep pressure built. I exhaled, controlling the force as my body lit with gooseflesh.

I focused on that feeling, controlling it until I saw a ripple begin to appear in the water. Small o's formed over and over again. Starting from the edge of the bowl, pooling towards the center until small particles of water rose, building into a single droplet. I pushed my power outside of me, raising the water high above the bowl. I held it there for a moment before allowing the droplet to fall back into the bowl.

"I did it," I whispered, proud of myself.

"Yes, bambina, you did it. Don't get too cocky. You can't do much with a single droplet. Onto bigger spells."

Antonio was sent away on another 'work trip'. I was beginning to get very suspicious with the lack of willing information I received when I asked about his business away from the castle. He would be away two weeks this time. Though I had no room to voice my opinion, I was disappointed. We never got to finish what we had started in the pool, and I now decided I wanted to explore that option, if the opportunity presented itself again.

Just because I wanted to pursue a potential relationship, didn't mean I didn't believe in God. As my power grew and my knowledge along with it, I was making peace with the reality that I would never become a nun. The more I learned, the more I craved. Knowledge was power. Power was strength. And now, more than ever, I wanted to be strong.

With Tony gone, Frankie did not hesitate to step in. She became a welcome distraction and source of entertainment. My cousin, our future elder, had a wild side to her. She dragged me to every under-ground party, rave, and intimate get together the city had. As July approached, so did Triora's annual wheat festival. The city embraced any opportunity to throw a party.

At night, with my cousin by my side, I felt alive... invincible. I was introduced to the very thing I that had been forbidden to me my entire life. Dancing, music, alcohol, and so much more. I now understood the allure of this life. Everything in moderation, I told myself.

I got to know Frankie's friends, Isabella and Gabriella, along the way. Every night we hit the town. We found ourselves drunk off the local wine and dancing in the middle of a huddle of strangers we barely knew. I came alive. For the first time in my life, I felt free, and I was never going back. I was never giving this up.

In the mornings, I would train. I began running with Gabriella, Gabby, for short. She was an enthusiast about physical fitness. We would sweat the wine out of our system early in the morning as we trailed up and down the hills of Triora. In the afternoons, I would study and work with nonna on my magic. I even started baking and cooking in the kitchen. I had never known this type of happiness.

As the ball approached and members of the other six covens began to arrive, I sat in on political meetings with Frankie. We watched as nonna and Aunt Thora conducted themselves and navigated the political matters that were presented. They would discuss trivial topics such as world politics and possible wars and how it would affect the financial standings of their businesses.

Then, halfway through, Frankie and I would be asked to leave. The doors would close behind us without any explanation. I tried to discuss it with my cousin, but she didn't seem very interested in the secrets that were being kept.

"The ball is in two days," stated nonna. "Are you excited to attend your first event?"

"Nervous is more like it," I replied, cleaning up the books we had studied from that afternoon.

"What is there to be nervous about?"

"Our family name is a lot to live up to. I just don't want to make you or Aunt Thora embarrassed is all."

Nonna, snatched my arm before I could walk to the bookshelf. "You listen to me, bambina," she said, with vigor. "You are not an embarrassment. You are a blessing from the triple goddess herself. I couldn't be prouder of you even if I raised you myself. No matter what you are feeling, in two days' time, you will hold your head high and wear your name proudly for all those assholes to see. Your family is proud of you, I am proud of you, and we love you."

I set the books down and embraced my nonna. For being such as badass, she always knew exactly what to say to make me feel better. "Any advice?" I asked, pulling away.

"Don't trust a single one of them. They are jealous and power hungry."

I laughed, shaking my head. "Always the optimist, aren't you?"

"No room for that shit. When you've lived as long as I have, you see people and their true colors for what they are."

We continued to put away the books and supplies. I was becoming more curious about the secrets the council was keeping from Frankie and I. My cousin may have not cared, but I did. I needed to know what was going on and what I would someday be a part of.

"Nonna, can I ask you something?" I said, before my nerves got the best of me.

"Of course, bambina."

"I know I am new to all of this, and I know you and Aunt Thora are still trying to protect me from things I may not understand, but I can assure you, I am stronger than I appear, physically, and mentally."

"That, I have never doubted, sweetheart," she said, patting her hand against my cheek.

"With that being said, I want to know what all the secrecy is about? Why is Antonio really sent away? Why are we learning how to fight and kill? What threat is out there that you don't want everyone to know about?"

She paused, taking a seat in the small wooden chair across from me. She looked out the window of her balcony as she rubbed her mouth with her hand.

"Sit, bambina," she said softly, tapping the spot across from her. "After all these years, do you know your cousin has not once asked me about the parts of the meetings she is excluded from? Not once. Yet after sitting in on a few, you are brave enough to ask." She chuckled, shaking her head. "You are so much like your mother, and you never even met her."

"I don't mean to be nosey or compromise anything—"

"No, you have a right to know. This will involve you someday. It will involve everyone soon enough." She exhaled as I saw the stress of the situation fall heavily on her shoulders.

"What is it, nonna? If I can help..."

Her heavy brown eyes looked at me as she smiled. "We are at war child. For the better part of a decade, we have been at war," she said softly, watching my expression. I straightened in my chair, not showing an ounce of fear.

"Tell me," I said simply.

"There is a dark coven. They go by the name of Obsidian. They are made up of defective witches from all seven covens. The coven has always been. No one knows how or when they formed, but every generation has fought against them. But these past ten decades... it has been different. They've grown stronger. At first, we didn't see them as a threat. Their numbers were small, and their magic was experimental at best. They dabbled in the demonic realm, which is a risk all its own with little reward."

"What is dark magic?" I asked.

"Magic that is derived not of nature but from satanic means. Blood, human, animal sacrifices. Deals are brokered between witches and demons. Power is transferred or given in return for your souls or the use of your body so the demons may walk on this earth once again as they did in the early years after they fell. Recently, the Obsidian Coven have discovered a way to steal our magic with a spell. This action kills the intended target as the dark member absorbs their strength and gifts."

"How is it done? I haven't read anything about this," I asked astonished.

"We're not sure. They have been working on new spells and speaking with demons for centuries. At first, the demons only saw them as meat suits. Our records indicate that the demons would possess them anytime the coven opened their doors to them. They would send the members into madness, using them as a free ride out of Hell until their bodies eventually gave out. Now, we believe that their new leader has somehow brokered a deal with them and are working side by side, gaining new powers and spells that make all this possible."

"So, what happens when our members are sent out on 'work trips'?" I asked, fearing for Tony.

"They are our cleanup crews. When we get a report of demonic activity or the Obsidian Coven's presence being sensed, we send out our members to eradicate and clean up any mess they may have created. We put the demons and dark witches down, Seren. No matter who they are," she said very clearly, with a heavy tone.

"This is why everyone is trained to fight?"

"Yes. We have always trained in this manner, but we have increased the required lessons for each coven to prepare. Speaking of... you should probably begin training now that you are strong enough. There is an excellent teacher arriving tomorrow that I will be speaking with about this matter. Only the best for my bambina," she said, reaching to take my hand.

"How can I help? I want to help and protect our family."

"That responsibility will fall to you soon enough. For now, the best thing you can do is to continue doing exactly what you are doing. Get stronger. Train. Learn. And watch. Always be watching, Seren. Nothing is ever as it seems here." She stood, kissing me on my head.

"Thank you for trusting me nonna." I said, smiling up at her.

"You are my heart, little one. You have repaired a part of me I thought would always be broken. I trust you completely. Now, get some sleep. Tomorrow, the festivities begin."

Chapter Ten

Come on, come on, swirl you stupid blob of water, I thought, holding a large amount of water suspended in the air in front of me. Focusing on the blob of cool crisp spring water, my tunnel vision honed as I ever so slowly bent the water to my will. The water cylinder began to swerve and swirl in a snake-like motion as I gently moved my fingers around the figure.

The door to my room opened, breaking my concentration, send the large water bubble splashing on top of my desk. "Dammit," I said, looking at the soggy stack of papers I would eventually have to clean.

"Oops, sorry," said Frankie, covering her laugh with her hand.

"Ha, ha, laugh it up. I finally got the damn thing to spin, and you go and make a mess of things. As usual," I said, laughing along with her.

"My bad. I just thought you might want to know that a certain tall, dark, and handsome warlock has returned home. But don't mind me. Ya know, since I make such a mess of everything."

"Antonio is back?" I said, feeling an uncontrollable smile stretch across my face as anticipation grew inside of me.

"Hmm, name sounds about right," she said in a mocking tone. "Where is he?"

"Last thing I heard, he was heading towards his room. How convenient for the two of you," she said, making a kissy face at me.

I laughed, shoving her into the door frame as I passed by. "Thanks, cuz, I owe you."

"I'll remember that," she yelled after me as I picked up the pace down the hall.

My heart was beating so fast, I could have sworn others could hear it. I couldn't stop smiling as I rushed towards his room. I stopped in the hallway, checking my appearance. Not the best, but not my worst. I wore I form fitting black spaghetti strap dress that came to my midthigh and a pair of boots. My hair was loose and wavy as it trailed down my back. Frankie had been teaching me how to use makeup which I just happened to apply to my face this morning.

God how I had changed in two months. Yet somehow, I never felt more like myself then I did now. I had determined that I believed in God and the stories of the Bible, but I also now believed there were other things out there. That God had given us nature and the earth around us to manifest our magic and grow it. Why would we have these gifts if we weren't meant to use them.

I continued down the hall, rounding the corner to see him speaking with two other men I didn't recognize in front of his door. I didn't care who they were. I had waited long enough for him to return, and I was done waiting. He turned and locked eyes with me instantly. That devilish smile appeared across his face as my pace picked up. Without thinking, I sprang myself into his arms, needing to feel him.

He began laughing. God, how I missed that sound. "Well, hello to you too, beautiful," he said, pulling me in closely.

I pulled back, as he peered down at me with those beautiful hazel eyes. "I have so much to tell you," I said, forgetting we weren't alone. One of the guys cleared his throat behind me. I turned towards the two men.

"Seren," said Tony, "this is Georgie Vernada and Joseph Dialgo. They're from my coven. Boys, this is Seren De Salvo."

"Oh, hello," I said bashfully. "Sorry for interrupting."

"Seems like we're the ones interrupting," George said, waving a finger between Tony and I. Tony chuckled, dropping his eyes from them.

"It's a pleasure to meet you," Joseph said, taking my hand and kissing the top of it.

"You as well," I replied.

"We'll let you two catch up," Georgie added, pushing Joseph along as he winked at Tony. I felt my cheeks heat with embarrassment.

"I'm so sorry, that was rude," I said, turning back to Tony.

"Don't you ever apologize for greeting me like that. Best damn thing that's happened to me in two weeks," he said, winking before pulling me inside his room. "Now, what did you want to tell me?"

Without waiting for him to turn back around I hit him as hard as I could manage in the back of the shoulder. "Owe," he yelped. "What was that for? You are sending quite a few mixed signals right now."

"That's for not telling me you were going on a suicide mission all those times you got called away for a 'work trip'," I said, with air quotes. "What if you would have gotten yourself killed?"

"You know?" he asked with surprise.

"Yes. Nonna told me. I've been worried sick."

"Awe, I'm touched," he said, moving closer towards me flashing his brilliant white teeth.

"Don't do that," I said, crossing my arms over my chest.

"Do what?" he whispered, running his hands down my arms.

"Flirting. It's not going to cool how pissed I am at you right now. Why didn't you tell me?"

"I am sure your nonna explained our situation to you. It was not my information to share. I was only following orders."

"No more secrets. Please Tony."

"No more secrets, I promise," he said, taking a moment to gaze down at me. I couldn't help but smile. He chuckled, lifting my chin up so our eyes met. "I've got a present for you."

"For me? What for?"

"Ah, I saw it and thought of you, figured it was about time you had your own. Now that you're a real witch and all."

I smacked him in the shoulder. "Oh, now I'm a real witch. Not before?"

"You know what I mean. Now that your powers have manifested." He reached into his bag and pulled out a black box and handed it to me. I opened it to find the most beautiful and intricate golden pentagram necklace. In the middle was a black stone with small white flakes scattered throughout. I smiled, looking at the unique piece of jewelry.

"It's beautiful. I can't take this," I said, handing the box back to his him.

"You can, and you will. No give backs. Now, turn around so I can put it on you."

I smiled, moving my hair out of the way as he gently clasped the chain around my neck. I grazed my fingers over the symbol, turning back to face him.

"Beautiful," he said, "just like you."

"Thank you again," I replied, looking down at the pendent. A mix of emotions fluttered through me.

"What is it?"

"It's just... All my life, I was taught this was the sign of evil. Now, it's a symbol of who I am. What I possess. I guess I am still adjusting to my new role."

"Your past is a part of you, Seren. All of it. The good and the bad. It's perfectly normal for you to ask questions and be curious about what you are learning. As long as you are true to yourself, you will find your way."

"I suppose you're right," I replied, smiling up at him.

"Now," he said, leaning back against a dresser along the wall. "What else did you want to tell me?"

"Well, not so much tell you, but show you."

"Oh, really. Is that my present?" he said in a deep and seductive tone.

"You are unbearable at times. Do you know that?"

He shrugged. "You haven't seemed to mind."

"Okay, stop distracting me and watch." I dropped my eyes from him and held out my hand, palm up. I focused, concentrating on what I wanted to manifest. My power was developing just like nonna said it would. Each time I casted, it seemed to get easier and easier. It was like a muscle, growing stronger each day.

Precipitation in the air gathered into one Mass over my hand until it was the size of my head. I held it there, allowing it to steady before demanding the form to spin and twirl as if it were made of hundreds of snakes.

Tony pushed of the dresser; mouth opened in amazement as he walked closer to me. He smiled with as pride flashed across his face. "You are amazing, I'll give you that," he said, turning his eyes to me. He reached out to touch my face.

Without hesitating I pushed the water formation forward, slamming it directly in his face. He stumbled back in surprise and shock standing completely soaked. I smirked, walking backwards towards the door.

"Oh, I forgot. I need to return some books to Frankie," I said, holding back my laughter.

"Oh, you just now remembered?' he asked, wiping the water from his face.

"You looked like you needed a cold shower. You're welcome. And let that be a warning about ever lying to me again."

"Lesson learned," he said, running his hands through his sexy wet hair. I turned around, reaching for the doorknob. "Oh, and beautiful." I paused, not daring to turn around. "Game on."

I peeked back over my shoulder and gave him a small smile. "Tony, I'm a Salvo. What makes you think you even stand a chance?"

"Call it a hunch," he said, winking at me.

I pulled the door open and left before my instincts took over and I jumped him right then and there. At this point, I was the one that needed a cold shower. I rushed back to my room; remembering I did indeed have books I needed to return to Frankie.

I found her walking arm in arm with Bella in one of the halls. "Hey lady," said Bella. "Where are you off too?"

"I thought you'd be occupied for the rest of the afternoon," added Frankie, nudging me in the shoulder.

Bella's mouth gaped open. "Oh, that's right. Mr. Simonelli is back under the same roof."

"You both need to stop right now," I demanded, pushing my

smile down.

"Making him grovel for it?" said Frankie. "That's our girl."

"Ha, ha," I said, holding the books out towards her. "Actually, I was just returning these books I borrowed from you."

"Ever the book worm," she said, moving past me. "We're headed to meet some of the other coven gentlemen. You can just leave them in my room. Thanks, cuz."

I rolled my eyes. "Sure, no problem," I replied, moving towards her room.

Frankie's quarters were a lot like my own, though she had more of a sensual flair when it came to the decor. I pushed open the door to find a dark room. The curtains were drawn along her balcony window and her bed was unmade.

I closed the door behind me, holding the books close to my chest as I smiled remembering the sight of a very wet and surprised Tony. I chuckled to myself. 'Game on'. That's what he had said. What did that entail, I wondered. I wouldn't mind a repeat of the pool that was for sure.

I shook my head, snapping my mind out of my daydream. I walked over to her bookshelf, gently trying to shove the books back onto her very cramped and messy shelf. As I slammed the last book into a small opening, the bookcase rattled, sending a figuring of Hecate to the floor.

"Awe fudge nuggets," I whispered, bending to the floor, trying to find the small statue in the dark. I heard a low and sensual chuckle come from behind me. I froze... I wasn't alone. I tilted my head up, not daring to move as I strained my eyes to see who was there.

A massive male stepped forward into the small stream of light. He had to be at least 6'4" made purely of muscle. His waist was trim as his back and shoulders veered into a well-built V. He stood in front of me in only a pair of form fitting jeans that I happened to notice were not buttoned.

He was built like a god. Muscles I didn't know existed bulged from every inch of his bare skin. His dark, curly brown hair was a little longer, stopping at his mid neck. His body was wet and glistening as if he had just stepped out of the shower. His skin was sun kissed which complimented his deep brown eyes.

He smiled at me, reveling two long dimples that formed along-side his wide thin lips. A set of white teeth flashed. His face seemed to be formed by Michelangelo himself.

"What is a fudge nugget?" he asked, in a deep a masculine tone.

"What?" I said, unable to form words or a clear thought.

"You said, 'awe fudge nuggets'. What is it?"

I stood, feeling like a child in his presence. I fumbled with the small figuring in my hand, until I reached back to clumsily place it on the wooden shelf behind me. "It's ah... it's just a word I made up. I don't like to cuss, so I make up words instead to replace the more... filthy ones."

He leaned forward slowly, placing his hands on either side of me against the bookshelf dresser. I was forced to bend back, mirroring his angle. His head came dangerously close to mine as he examined every inch of my face.

"You must be the little dove everyone is talking about," he said, focusing on the bridge of my nose. "You look more like your aunt than Frankie does."

"Orion," I whispered, pulling my face as far away from his as possible.

He smiled, pulling away as he extended his hand. "Nice to meet you, Seren." I took his hand, shaking it hesitantly. "Were you that eager to meet me or did you come here with a purpose?"

"I... I was returning some books I borrowed from Frankie. I didn't know you were in here or I wouldn't have—"

"Barged in as I just finished with my shower?" he said, tilting his head to the side with an ornery smile. "This makes a much more interesting story of how we first met; don't you think?"

"Uh, no. No, I am sorry, really," I said frantically. "I didn't mean to—"

"Stop flailing, little dove. It was an accident. No need to get bent out of shape about it," he said, standing tall in front of me.

"I should—" I said, fighting to find words. I couldn't take my eyes off him. "I should go—" I said, stepping to move around him as my foot caught the side of the dresser, sending me plummeting to the floor. Before I made contact, two strong arms wrapped themselves around my waist, pulling me against his hard and firm torso.

I froze, unable to move, think, or make a sound. His deep and dangerous eyes looked at me with something like recognition. In that moment, my heart stopped. Time stopped. Everything inside of me felt complete. My magic responded to him in a way I had never experienced before.

He took one of his hands and placed it softly and hesitantly on my cheek as his thumb brushed gently against my bottom lip. His eyes flickered between mine as if they were searching. For what, I didn't know. The pressure inside of me I now recognized as my magic screamed to be released.

I stood, entranced in this stranger's eyes, allowing myself to give way to my power. I felt a boom of release, just like I had that day at the nunnery when I collapsed. Darkness and fog blasted from within as stars and constellations formed around us. I didn't care. I didn't look. All I could see was him.

His eyes left mine for a brief moment to take in the planetarium that was now floating in midair. He smiled, looking back down at me in awe. I was frozen in his arms, not sure what I was feeling. He leaned his face down, brushing his nose against mine.

"There you are," he whispered, right before I found the strength to push myself out of his grip putting as much space between him and I as possible. I took a deep breath in, feeling as if I had been under water. The stars and the darkness fell away as I panted for breath.

Orion straightened himself, running a hand through his hair. He grabbed a shirt from the bed and slid it over his beautiful body. He turned back towards me, not daring to make eye contact. "I'm—" he started to say but paused. "I'm sorry for… that," he finished. He moved to the door and opened it without even looking at me. "You should go."

"Good idea," I said, bolting for the exit.

Before I could cross the threshold fully, he grabbed my arm, pulling me back. He held me in front of him as he peered down into my eyes with desire or lust, I didn't know which. His gaze trailed from mine down to my mouth. I watched as he slid his tongue between his lips.

"Please," I whispered. "Let me go." He instantly released me, slamming the door shut as soon as I made it across.

I walked as fast as I could towards my room locking myself in once I knew I was safely alone. I was still panting as I fell back onto my bed, not knowing what the heck had just happened. The way he looked at me. The sound of his voice. The way his body felt against mine. How my magic reacted to him.

"No!" I screamed, sitting upright. No, no, I was not going to do this. He was my cousin's fiancé. A cousin I had just found. Who I happened to love. I was not going to do this to her, to Tony, or to myself. Whatever that was meant nothing. A fleeting moment.

My head was spinning as I moved to the balcony. I needed fresh air. I needed to go for a drive. I need to get out of here, that's what

I needed. As if God had been listening, a knock came at my door. I looked back at it, hesitant to discover who was on the other side.

I opened the door slowly, to see Antonio's handsome face on the other side. He smiled at me, leaning against the frame.

"Now that I am no longer wet—" he said, before I interrupted him.

"Teach me to drive," I demanded.

"What?" he asked with confusion.

"You said when I first arrived you would teach me to drive. Now that I can walk, and swim, and do magic, it's time for a driving lesson," I said, pulling him along with me towards the exit.

"I suppose we can work on your driving skills."

"Great, I can't wait to take your Jag for a spin."

"Uh, no one is touching my baby except for me. We'll start you off with something a little more kid friendly," he said, catching up to me as he flashed me a smile.

I beamed back at him, feeling my affections awaken. He was where I wanted to be. He was what I needed. No one else mattered but him.

CHAPTER ELEVEN

"I think teaching you to drive may take longer than rehabilitating you to walk," said Tony as we strolled back into the castle.

"Ha, ha, ye of little faith," I said, smiling back at him.

"And now do you see why I won't let you touch the Jag?"

"Oh, I'll drive her. One day soon," I said winking at him.

"Once someone is insane enough to issue you an actual driver's license we will buy you your own car to wreck. Just leave my baby out of it."

"And here I thought you prided yourself on being such a great teacher," I mocked, as we entered the main hall.

"Some things are better left untaught."

I elbowed him in the arm as we both began laughing. I turned my focus ahead to find my nonna walking arm in arm with Orion. I stopped, dead in my tracks as they headed straight for us. Tony, looked back at me and then ahead at who was approaching.

"Bambina," said nonna. "I'd like to introduce Orion Camerino. Orion, this is my granddaughter, Seren De Salvo, daughter of Annalise De Salvo.

Orion took my hand, bowing to kiss it. His lips lingered a little too long for my liking while he locked eyes with me, in a taunting fashion. "It's a pleasure to meet you, little dove," he said, smiling.

I snatched my hand away instantly, moving closer to Tony. "You as well, Orion," I replied. "Now, if you'll excuse us, we were just on our way to train."

"Actually," nonna said before I could escape. "This was the trainer I was telling you about last night. Orion is one of the most talented weapons master and fighter I have ever had the privilege of knowing. He will be training you in that area while he is here."

"I can assure you," interrupted Tony, "that Seren is getting the best training possible during our sessions."

"Yes," said nonna in a very smug and sarcastic tone. "I have seen the type of lessons you have been giving my granddaughter. If the pool situation is any indicator of your talents." Orion's eyes snapped to Tony as the two of them stared each other down in a silent war. "I have decided. Seren will begin to train with Orion after the ball tomorrow night. I appreciate all the support you continue to give my granddaughter, Antonio. This is nothing personal. I hope you understand."

"Of course, Elder Salvo," Tony said with a small bow.

"Simonelli," said Orion with a small nod.

"Camerino," replied Tony, pulling me around the two of them.

We got back to my room, putting as much space between Orion and myself as possible. I turned to face Antonio, noticing the worry streaked across his face. I went to him, placing my hands on his arms.

"Not a fan of the horned god?" I said playfully.

"Not when the horned god is looking at you all horny like," he replied. I couldn't help but laugh at the play on words. I pulled him to sit with me at the edge of my bed.

"He's destined to be with my cousin, remember? Not going to happen," I said reassuring the both of us.

"He has to marry her. It doesn't mean he can't take others after... or before, for that matter."

"First of all, I have discovered I don't like to share, especially that," I said making a disgusted face. That got a laugh out of him. "Secondly, if you haven't noticed, I've been a bit distracted lately by a tall, dark, and charming warlock from the Luna Coven."

He turned to me and smiled. "Is that so?" he said reaching out to move a strand of hair from my face. "And what if I told you, that certain someone has noticed your distracting behavior and returns your interest?"

"That would make me more than happy," I whispered, biting the side of my lip as I processed through what I was feeling. "Tony..."

"Yes, beautiful?"

"I've... I've never done this before... obviously with me almost being a nun and all."

He laughed, which caught me off guard. "Sorry," he said. "I

just sometimes forget that little detail about you. It's hard to ever imagine you—"

"As what?" I interrupted. "I am not that unhinged."

"No, that's not what I meant. I am just saying, I feel like I've known you forever. Longer than these two months."

"Probably because normal people don't spend every waking moment together like we have."

"Very true. Now, what were you saying?"

"I was wondering... I was wondering if you were okay with waiting for me... to be ready to take things further? This is all very new for me and though I have developed an interested in you, I am not sure where that is going to go or when I'll be ready, if you get my drift."

He smiled, taking my hand in his, kissing it gently. "You take all the time you need, beautiful. I'm not going anywhere."

God, how I adored this man. Everything about him. His patience. His kindness. How gentle and caring he was. Just as I lost myself in his eyes a knock came at the door.

Frankie came barging in with a garment bag. "It's here! It's here!" she exclaimed. She looked at me and then to Tony who still sat at the edge of my bed. "Oh, uh, I can come back later if—"

"Oh, stop," I said, walking over to her and pulling the bag out of her grip. Tony stood, joining the two of us.

"Do I get to see?" he asked.

"Absolutely not," snapped Frankie. "If you wish to see her in it, you will have to wait till tomorrow night like every other thirsty male in this building."

Tony laughed, putting his hands up in a surrendering manner as he backed away towards the door. "Alright, alright. I am confident it will be worth the wait," he said, winking at me.

"You heard the moon goddess," I said, smiling at him. "No peaking."

"Well, can I at least reserve a dance?" he asked.

"Hmm, I believe my dance card is already full. Sorry, Simonelli, you'll have to be put on the waiting list."

"I'll wait all night if I have to," he said in a deep voice. My heart swelled. "See you later, beautiful. Frankie," he said with a nod as he left us alone.

Frankie turned her gaze back to me with her mouth open. "Oh, my Aradia!" she said, pushing me playfully. "You have him wrapped around your little finger, don't you?"

I laughed, unsure of how to answer that. "We have... an understanding."

"And what pray-tell is this understanding?"

"We're seeing where things might go is all."

Frankie squealed, literally. "Does my little cousin have her first boyfriend?"

I shrugged, not wanting to put a label on it.

"Oh, this calls for a celebration. You, me, and the girls are going out tonight for sure."

"Shouldn't we be getting rest before the ball?"

"That is small potatoes compared to this." She wrapped her arms around me, pulling me in close for a hug. "I am so happy for you, cuz. And look at you, bagging one of the most desired and eligible bachelors on the market. A Salvo through and through."

We laughed as I let my excitement and joy overwhelm me. I jumped up and down with her, letting go of any worry I had. "Okay, fine, let's do this!" I replied, silencing the cautious, rule abiding nun that still lurked beneath my skin.

"That's my girl. Now, tonight, you are going to wear the sluttiest thing in that closet. Meet me in my room at ten sharp. This is going to be a night we most likely won't remember."

I smiled, looking upon my cousin's beautiful face. "I love you, Frankie. Not just because you're my family, but because you're... you."

Her face softened. "I love you too, Seren. I couldn't be happier that we found each other." She pulled me in for a hug. "Now get a cat nap in because I am going to have you on that dance floor all night."

Chapter Twelve

*K*nock, knock, knock.

I felt a warm sticky substance pool under my face. Drool. I was drooling. *Knock, knock, knock.*

"Go away," I called out, weakly, unable to pull myself from the pillow. I felt like I had been hit by a semitruck. My head was still spinning, and my stomach felt horrid. *Knock, knock, knock.*

"Ugh, what?" I yelled, pushing myself up for only a moment before falling back to the bed. Damn you, gravity.

I heard the lock rattle as someone opened and entered my room. I didn't care, as long as they let me sleep. *Whoosh.* The curtains flew open, allowing the bright sunlight of the July day to fill my room.

"No," I whined, smashing a pillow over my face. "We're from the Étoile Coven. We like darkness. Not that damn sun."

"Oh, I heard all about how the lot of you enjoyed your evening last night," boomed my aunt's voice. It was as if someone had handed her a megaphone. "The entire town was talking about it this morning. 'Boy those Salvo girls know how to bring down a club.' Or my particular favorite, 'Did you see all the party tricks the

Salvo cousins preformed at the club?' Ah, and then the one that would make any caregiver proud, 'Wow, what I wouldn't give to bed the two Salvo cousins—'"

"Alright, alright," I interrupted, wishing she had a mute button. "I get it. We were bad." I pushed myself up, running my hands through my rat's nest of hair. My aunt came and sat on the side of my bed, looking at me with her judging eyes. She held out a glass of water and ibuprofen. "Thank you," I said, taking both.

She watched me for a moment before breaking out into laughter. I smiled at her, not knowing where this was going. I thought the lecture was far from over.

"You disgraced our family last night," she said in a more serious tone. My smile fell in shame. "That was the responsible Elder Thora talking," she leaned in and whispered. "As your fun, loving, aunt... I am so happy."

"What?" I said with confusion.

"You and Frankie. You remind me so much of your mother and me. Though, somehow, I birthed your mother's spirit and you got more of mine. Your mother was always the life of the party. Pulling me into so much chaos. Nonna use to get so furious with us, but that never stopped us. We lived for the night. Aradia, how I miss those days. What I wouldn't do to have your mother back at times like these. Just so we could sit back and laugh at the two of you together."

I smiled, finishing off the water as my eyes adjusted. "Well, one thing I will say, is that your daughter is very, very hard to keep up with. I thought I was going to die of alcohol poisoning, and I'm pretty sure Frankie drank twice as much as I did."

She laughed, brushing my hair from my face. "My daughter has many talents." She brought my eyes up to hers. "My heart is so full. Thank you Seren." I smiled back at her. "Now, for all our sake, get your culo in that shower. It's already three in the afternoon. Get something to eat and then ready yourself for the ball. Tonight's a big night for all of us. Our family is finally whole." She pressed a kiss on my forehead before leaving me to swim through my hangover.

After a long shower and a few more ibuprofen pills, I sat in front of my mirror feeling like an absolute mess. A knock sounded at the door. I looked back in the mirror to see nonna enter with a cup and saucer on top of a small box. She placed it down in front of me as the coffee scent filled my nostrils.

"Strong, Italian espresso. Best thing for a hangover," she said, pulling up a seat next to me. I looked at her curiously. "What? I was young once. Me and my sister used to get into all sorts of trouble in our youth." She paused, looking down at her hands. "You know, it's almost like fate knew your mother would die and so would Thora's Dominic. Salvo sisters always come in pairs. You and Frankie... you're kindred spirits. Ying and Yang. Two halves of a whole. Funny how fate corrects the worlds mistakes."

"I didn't know that," I replied, picking up the espresso. "About the sister pattern in our family."

"It will be up to you to carry on the line now," she said, looking back up at me in the mirror.

"What do you mean?"

"Frankie. Once she goes through with the ceremony, she will be barren. There has never been any record of the moon goddess and horned god bearing a child. This world is their child, their life's work."

"And how does Frankie feel about that?" My heart sank for my cousin. To not have the option of ever becoming a mother.

"She doesn't really talk much about her duty. She's always been good at putting her responsibility to the covens first. That is why I think she chooses to express herself like she does. All the parties and the drinking. It's the only thing she has control of. Though I give thanks that the gods chose our family for this blessing, my heart breaks for Francesca at times. To not have a choice as to how her future plays out. As to who she loves."

I watched emotion flood over my nonna. Not since the first night that we met had I seen this side of her surface again. She loved her family dearly. I knew she would do anything for us.

"She is a strong woman, nonna. She knows what's expected of her and where her duties lie."

"Yes, she is. I just wish... I don't know what I wish anymore," she said, looking at me in the mirror.

"You look beautiful, by the way," I whispered, admiring her

perfect and elegant updo. She wore a stunning cream dress that was off the shoulder and trailed to the floor. She looked like starlight itself.

"Thank you, bambina. That is why I came in here in the first place. I was hoping to help you prepare for your first ball."

"I would love that."

For the next two hours, nonna groomed me to perfection. My hair was straightened and slicked straight back falling well below my bottom. The dress Frankie had picked for me was made of black and gold fabric. It had an elegant organic neck piece that stopped at the top of my chest bone.

My shoulders were exposed, along with more cleavage than I had ever allowed to be seen. My sleeves started midway down my biceps and continued to my wrists. The top of the dressed formed around my breasts, pushing up my full chest. The rest of the fabric hugged my body firmly. It was hard to breath, but I was in awe of the craftsmanship.

I stood in front of the full-length mirror admiring the mixture of black and gold and how it complimented my skin perfectly. Nonna laid on the makeup, using eyeliner to dramatize my eyes and mascara to lengthen my lashes. A red lip drew attention and finished off the ensemble.

Nonna stood behind me with tears in her eyes. "You look stunning my bambina, just like your mother. A picture of perfection."

She went over to the small box and pulled out an extravagant gold mask. She brought it over to me and placed it across my face. It matched perfectly.

"It was your mothers," said nonna. "The first time she attended the summer solstice ball, she wore this. I thought you might like to have a piece of her with you tonight."

I turned around, embracing her with so much joy and love. "Thank you, nonna. For everything. I love it," I said, pulling away from her. "I love you." She laughed with joy, placing her hands on either side of me head.

"And I love you, bambina. Now, let's get you out there so you can make that Simonelli boy drool." My face fell, not knowing how to respond. "Oh, you didn't think I noticed? I have eyes and ears everywhere, my dear. And after that pool situation, I walked in on. Woohoo," she said, waving a hand, fanning her face.

I began laughing. "And you approve?"

"The verdict is still out. I am still trying to figure a few pieces of this puzzle out myself."

"What do you mean?"

"You will know in time. Now, no more talk of business. I want you to have a magical night that is unforgettable. Time to be introduced as a true Salvo," she said with pride, taking me by the arm as we headed towards the ballroom.

Chapter Thirteen

We waited behind the two large iron doors of the ballroom as the announcer began to address our guests. My aunt and nonna would be escorted out first. Next, my cousin would be announced, descending the staircase as Orion waited for her at the bottom. Then, since it was my first public event, I would be announced last, leaving me to walk the intimidating staircase on my own.

My hands were beginning to sweat, and I felt nauseous. Was it my nerves or the pounds of liquor I had consumed the night before? Did it matter now? No. All that mattered would be the judgy people and their beady little eyes peering at me as I was introduced as the newest member of their most rivaled coven.

"Hey," whispered Frankie, as we waited for our grand entrance. "You look absolutely gorgeous."

"Really? You think?" I said hesitantly, running my hands down my body. "The dress isn't too much? Like I'm trying too hard?"

"You look perfect," interrupted my aunt.

"Like a true Salvo," added nonna.

"You'll be fine," said Frankie. "Just remember to keep breathing so you don't pass out."

"Right," I said, as they opened the doors to introduce my aunt and nonna. "You look beautiful by the way, moon goddess," I whispered as she elbowed me.

"Oh, shut up. You are totally out showing me tonight, but don't get used to it. I like the attention too much," she replied with a smile as the doors opened and her name was called.

I couldn't stop shaking. I took a deep breath in and blew it out. "Get yourself together, Seren," I said, pepping myself up. "You are a witch. A powerful one at that. You've overcome everything so far. So what? Who cares what they say or think? You are a Salvo. You have a family who loves you. Screw them all. Set your power free."

I took another deep breath as I heard the announcer on the other side of the door. "And now, presenting from Coven Étoile, for the first time, daughter of Annalise Amore De Salvo, Seren Lucia De Salvo."

The doors opened, and I let go. Darkness and stars sprang from me as they mixed with the levitating balls of white light placed throughout the room. The crowd gasped as they watched my display of power. Let them see. I no longer cared what anyone thought. I descended the staircase taking one step at a time. I held my head high as my aunt and nonna stared up at me with pride.

At the bottom of the landing stood Antonio, looking devastatingly handsome. I smiled at him as everyone and everything else faded away. He extended his hand, leading me to the dance floor.

We never took our eyes off each other.

The orchestra began to play as he led me across the floor. His eyes traveled across my face while his hands slid down my body. Every part of my being was awakened by this man. Nothing else mattered but him.

"You look—" he said, unable to finish his sentence.

"Is it too much?" I asked, suddenly self-conscious.

"You are perfect, in every sense of the word," he said, pulling me in closer to him.

"You are rather dashing yourself," I replied smiling up at him.

"Want to see a party trick?" he asked, leaning his face against mine. I closed my eyes, relishing in the contact.

"Yes," I whispered.

"Hold on, beautiful." He wrapped both arms around me as the music continued to carry us along the dance floor. Suddenly, I felt weightless, like a feather floating in the air. I heard the crowd around me gasp and begin laughing.

I opened my eyes and immediately tightened my grip onto Tony. I looked beneath us, seeing the floor of the ballroom at least a dozen feet below. All around us, couples danced in the air, weightless. I lightened my hold, smiling at the magic that was my new world.

"You're doing this?" I asked in amazement.

"Ya know, Luna coven and all. We can manipulate gravity."

"You mean levitate?"

"In other words," he said, taking in the joy of my face.

"You're amazing... you know that?"

He leaned his head against mine, pulling me in closer towards him. "Did you not witness that beautiful little astrology show you blew the covens away with a few moments ago?"

"Hm, no, I missed it. My attention was focused on something much more beautiful," I replied, looking up into his breathtaking eyes.

There was a moment of silence between us that lingered. "I want to kiss you, Seren." My heart swelled and that fire inside of me burned just like it did that day in the pool. I had been waiting for this moment for weeks. "But I don't think your nonna would appreciate the public display of affection."

I smiled at him. "Do you trust me?"

"Yes," he said looking at me curiously. "Why?"

"Leave the privacy to me," I said, allowing my magic to well inside of me before releasing it into the air around us. Darkness incased the two of us acting as a barrier between our joined bodies and the outside world.

"Amazing," he said, reaching out to touch the fog.

"Now, you were saying?"

He turned his attention back to me, sliding one hand behind my head and the other behind my back. He pulled me in, ever so slowly rubbing his bottom lip against mine, testing the waters. I couldn't wait another minute to know what he felt like, to taste him. I intertwined my fingers through his hair, pulling his face to mine.

Lust, passion, desire, all of it overtook me. His mouth moved so sensually against mine, claiming me as his own. I came up for breath, only for a second before going in for another kiss. This time, his tongue tested the seam of my lips. I parted for him, welcoming everything he wanted to give. Every part. God, what this man did to me.

He pulled away slowly, kissing the edges of my lips and then my cheeks. I looked up at him with sated eyes. He smiled and chuckled, turning his focus back to the dark fog around us.

"I think if we stay in here any longer," he whispered against my ear, still holding me close. "People are going to begin to talk."

"Let them. They are already," I said.

"Very true. But we always have tonight. When we're *fully* alone." I frowned, allowing the fog to dissipate. "Nah ah," he said, pulling my face back up to his. "One more." He pulled me back into him as we drifted down to earth, completely consumed with each other. He pulled away as my shadows fell.

"Can we just skip this whole thing," I said, feeling the attention of the audience return to us.

"I would love nothing more, but it would be a shame to let the dress go to waste," he said, stepping away to look me up and down. He twirled me once, pulling me into him. "Just so you know," he said, whispering against my ear. "I know it is custom for the hosting family to accept dance requests from other covens, but if I see another man touch you in any way, I deem unfit..." he nipped my earlobe, which sent a thrilling sensation through my entire body as he pulled away. "I will kill them."

"I'll make sure to warn them ahead of time. For their own safety," I said, pulling away from him, heading towards my family.

I felt his eyes on me the whole way until I got to Frankie. "Well, that was some fucking entrance," Frankie laughed, pulling me in for a hug. "Damn girl, you gave one hell of a light show and then all but had a quicky up on the ceiling."

"Francesca Rose," snapped Aunt Thora. My aunt straightened herself, as she tried to hide her laughter. I watched as her eyes focus on me. Her face became smug and ornery. "A Salvo woman through and through," she said sending us all into a fit of laughter.

The surrounding guests looked our way, but we didn't care. This was my family and I loved it. Frankie and I entered the dance floor, not caring who was around us or what her station was. When we were together, it was only the two of us. Ying and Yang. Two halves of a whole.

Magic began to fill the ballroom. Balls of light and fire. People were dancing in the air, drunk off wine and power. Frankie exploded the room with a brilliant white light. I created a ball of water, watching it grow as we danced and laughed as one.

Frankie clapped with joy, leaning in towards me. "Make it rain, cousin," she whispered. I shot the ball of water into the air as high as it could go. I slammed my arms down, sending a vibration of power throughout the room. Rain began to fall from thin air.

The crowds clapped and laughed in awe of what we could do. Of the power we possessed. We were unstoppable. Frankie latched onto me as we spun and twirled in the rain. Glass after glass we drank, living out the best moments of our lives… together.

As I swayed, I took a step back, knocking into something broad and hard. I turned to see Orion, staring down at me in a gold mask. He wore a beautiful black suit with a golden trim. His hair was tied back, with only a small strand falling to the side of his face.

"Looks like we had the same opinions on attire this evening," he said, looking down at me with those deep, dangerous eyes.

"Would seem so," I replied, reaching for Frankie. "Here she is," I said, pushing his fiancé towards him. "Have fun."

"Oh no," Frankie said, swaying back and forth. "I think I'm… I'm going to be sick." I watched as her face turned green before she took off towards the restrooms.

I was once again stuck with Orion. Not knowing what to say or what to do. "I should… go check on her," I said, moving to follow her before he gently caught me by the arm.

"Is one dance going to kill you?" he asked, not daring to make eye contact with me.

"Well, according to the rules of the hosting coven, I can't deny a dance with you, even if I wanted to, so ." I turned back to him.

"You can simply say no, little dove. I would never force you to do something you didn't want." I looked up at him, allowing myself to fall into those deep reach eyes of his. Even with Tony on my mind, something inside of me, in the smallest corner of my being wanted to be near him.

"I'll give you one dance, Orion. Then I need to go check on Frankie," I said, placing my hands on his shoulders. He was so large I felt like he was going to trample me with one wrong step. But to my surprise, he was graceful and considerate. "You're a surprisingly good dancer," I commented, following his lead. "For your size and all."

"And what's wrong with my size? Most women seem to enjoy it," he said, looking down at me with one eyebrow cocked.

"Nothing. And I am sure they do. I am just saying."

"Your power is very unique," he said, thankfully changing the subject from his size to something more practical. "No one in your family has possessed a gift like this before, am I correct?"

"Not that I've read. My mother was a syphon like my grandmother. Aunt Thora's gift is omnikinesis. And Frankie... well obviously you know hers."

"Interesting," he said, plainly. "Maybe you should look into that."

"Maybe. It's new. I am still learning how to control it."

"We can work on that when we train."

"Yeah, about that," I said, fully aware of his hand on my lower back. "Maybe you can talk to my nonna about choosing someone else to train me."

"And why would I do that?"

"Well, for starters, you're engaged to my cousin."

"I am."

"And I don't feel that what almost happened between us the first time we met is appropriate. Nor should we be training alone, in close proximity to one another after that little... mishap."

"For starters," he said in a sarcastic tone. "I already apologized for that and don't pretend you didn't feel whatever was there between us. Your power called to me as mine did to you. Maybe you should put that on your little 'to look into' list. Secondly, I am fully capable of controlling myself. You should be worried about your control when it comes to me. And thirdly—"

I pulled away, feeling rage erupt inside of me. "How dare you insinuate that I want—"

"What?" he said, taking a step towards me, plastering his body against mine, while holding me firmly in place. "Tell me, *little dove*, what is it you want?"

I froze, for some reason unable to answer his question. I was locked in his stare, unable to break myself away. Safely tucked in his arms. Being around him felt was so familiar and comforting and I couldn't figure out why.

I heard a man's voice clear next to us as Orion dropped his hands from my waist. I turned to see Antonio standing between us assessing our interaction. "Sorry to interrupt," he said, looking at me with a questioning stare.

"You weren't interrupting," I replied. "The music ended. We are finished."

"Thank the gods," Orion said, stomping away without another word.

Antonio watched him leave until he exited the ballroom. He turned back to me, taking me gently in his arms. We swayed to the slow tempo without a word. I didn't know what had just happened or why I reacted to Orion the way I did. I clearly was falling for Antonio. But the way my mind and my power reacted to Orion. It didn't make sense.

"Seren," said Tony, softly. "Am I missing something here or is there something between you and Orion? It seems—"

I pulled away, shocked at his accusation. "What? No, of course not. He is going to be my cousin's husband. And, frankly, I can't stand the asshole."

I felt Tony laugh as I looked up at him. "Did you just say asshole?" he asked.

I stopped, thinking back to what I said. "I guess I did," I replied, laughing along with him. "You warlocks are something else."

"Hey, don't group me into the same category as Mr. Horned God, over there. All manly and brutish."

"Yes, you do appear to be the more sophisticated of the two, don't you?" I said, running my hand down his chest in an insinuating manner.

"Beautiful," he said, taking my hand and kissing it softly. "As much as I want you tonight, this isn't going to happen."

I stumbled back, feeling disappointed and embarrassed. "Why? Did I do something? Is it because of Orion?"

"No, you did nothing wrong. It's just... you're a bit intoxicated. And though I am impressed you somehow managed to outlast your cousin, I'd rather not have the first memory of anything we may decide to do or not do tonight involving alcohol."

"Well fudge nuggets, if I would have known that I would have just stuck with water."

He laughed, taking me back into his arms. "Watching you have fun with your friends and family makes the wait well worth it. I think even Aunt Thora had a little too much fun tonight. I saw her being escorted back to her room about thirty minutes ago."

I laughed, running my hand down his face. "I wanted... more," I admitted, running my fingers across his lips. "Of this."

He kissed my fingers softly. "We have all the time in the world. And remember what I told you earlier this week. I will go at the pace you set. You are not obligated in any way. I will take the parts of you you're willing to share."

I looked up at him, feeling the need to fist his hair in my hands. All I could think about was his body on mine and how good it felt to finally feel his lips. Mm, and that tongue.

Antonio exhaled and moaned. "The way you're looking at me... you're not making this easy."

"Good. Because I was just thinking about what I would like your tongue—"

"Ah," he interrupted, pressing a finger to my lips. "Let's get you to bed. Then, tomorrow we can re-assess what you would like me to do with my tongue." I laughed as he ushered me safely to my room. Nonna was right. Tonight, would be an evening I would never forget.

Chapter Fourteen

The next morning, I woke early, not able to sleep a moment longer. I showered and dressed before rushing to Tony's room. The halls of Castle Salvo were still sleeping. Most likely thanks to the overindulgence of wine and substances thanks to the summer solstice ball.

I got to his door and knocked twice. Nothing. I knocked again, feeling the anticipation and excitement swell inside of me. Finally, I heard the latch rattle as he pulled the door open. His dark black hair was tousled from sleep. He wore a black pair of silk pajama pants that hung off his hips right as his hipbones veered into a V disappearing underneath his pants. His black robe was left open, revealing his tan and lean body.

Cord after cord of muscle rippled making up his abs. My eyes trailed up to his chest, noting the crescent moon on his left pec. He pulled the robe shut, tying it at his waist. I whimpered a little from the loss of his beautiful physique.

"Is everything alright?" he asked, in a deep, slumbering voice.

I went to open my mouth to form words, but my mouth was suddenly dry. "I didn't know you had a tattoo," was all I managed to get out.

He laughed, leaning his sleepy head against the door. "You woke me to comment on my body art?"

"I... no... I'm sorry. I'll just... go," I said hesitantly, turning to head back to my room so I could burry myself under my blankets and embarrassment.

"Beautiful," he said from behind me. I stopped dead in my tracks. I turned back to see him smiling softly as he stepped back, opening the door. He nodded towards his room. "Get in."

I beamed, trying not to move too anxiously. His room was still dark, with only a bed lamp illuminated next to his dark black sheets. I heard the door shut behind me as he moved back to his bed, sitting casually on the side before checking his text messages. Finally, he placed the phone down, turning his attention back to me with a tired smiled.

"Now, what can I help you with?" he asked. "Frankly, I'm surprised you're even up at this hour."

"I'm... I'm sorry I woke you," I said, still stumbling over my words.

He smirked, rubbing his hands down his face. "It's okay. I had my alarm set to go off thirty minutes from now anyways." He paused, looking at me with question.

He stood from the bed and walked towards me. He peered down into my eyes while he ran his hands up my arms, until one of them found the back of my neck. Ever so gently, he tilted my eyes up to meet his.

"Beautiful," he said, deep and sensual. "How can I be of service to you this morning." The sound of his rich voice set fire to every nerve ending in my body. My toes even curled as my breath caught in my chest. His lips were so close to mine I could almost taste him.

"I'm... I'm not drunk," I whispered.

He pulled back, looking slightly confused. "What?"

"I'm not drunk. You said last night, you wouldn't continue with things... between us... if I were intoxicated. Well, I'm not. So here I am." My cheeks flushed from the admission. I didn't want to appear too desperate, but God did I want to feel him again.

He paused, staring at me for an awkward moment. I watched as he smiled again, allowing a small laugh to escape before he slammed me up against the wall sending a picture that hung nearby shattering to the floor. His mouth was on mine in an instant as his hands roamed cautiously over every curve of my body, making sure not to cross a line we hadn't discussed.

He picked me up, leveraging me against the wall. I wrapped my legs around his waist and tangled my fingers through his loose hair. His hands slowly moved up my thighs until they ended at my bottom. He squeezed either side of it and moaned with what I assumed was delight. I laughed against his lips, allowing my hands to scan the bare skin of his neck. I pushed gently on the edges of the robe forcing it to open, revealing his magnificent body.

His skin felt like silk. I made sure to take my time, exploring every fine-tuned muscle that I came across. He finally released my mouth, moving his lips to my jaw and then my neck. I arched back, taking in deep breaths as I encouraged him to continue to explore me. I wanted his mouth on every inch of me. I needed it. I needed him.

Knock, knock, knock. We both froze, me still pinned up against the wall. "Ignore it," he said, moving his lips back to mine, this time with more force and aggression. I nipped at his bottom lip, feeling all control leave my body. Whatever he wanted, in this moment, I would give him. I would give him everything.

Knock, knock, knock. "Dammit," he snapped as he pulled away, placing me gently down to the floor. He re-tied his robe, running his hands through his hair taking a few deep breaths in.

I was barely able to stand from our little... tryst. I pushed my hair back and straightened my clothes. My lips felt swollen and bruised but I couldn't wait to do it again. He looked at me, with a smile before he took my face in his hands, kissing me softly.

"You good?" he asked with a nod.

"Yes, just... whoever it is, get rid of them," I begged, pushing up on my tiptoes to take his mouth with mine one more time. He laughed, pulling gently away from me.

"That's the plan." He moved to the door as I watched him, fully aware of every inch of his magnificent body. As he pulled the door back his smile faded. He didn't say a word before he took a step back, allowing whoever was there to enter the room.

Nonna walked with grace and sophistication across the threshold as she examined his room. Her gazed scanned each wall, until she found me standing near the bed.

"Nonna," I said, with surprise. "What are you doing here?"

"Not the same thing you are, obviously," she said in a snarky tone, looking Tony up and down in a judging manner.

"I can explain, Elder Salvo," Tony said, taking a step forward.

She held up her hand and he froze in place. Not because of her power but just because she was... her. "No need for that, young man. I'm old, not dead. Why does everyone assume I am ignorant?" she said locking her eyes onto me. "Come Seren, it is time for your training session. I will escort you."

I followed her to the door. Tony grabbed me by the hand, pulling me into him and kissed me one last time. "Later," he said, against my lips, "we need to talk about all of this."

"Or we can just pick up where we left off." I wiggled my eyebrows up and down in a playful manner.

He chuckled. "I love the sound of that, but talk first, play after."

"Deal," I whispered, kissing him one more time before he closed the door.

Nonna walked casually down the hall, hands in front of her, face expressionless. I didn't know what to say or how to act after what she had just walked in on. I was a grown woman, though around her, I felt like I child.

"Nonna, I—"

"Why didn't you tell me about the shadow magic you possess?" she interrupted, saving me from myself.

"It's fairly new. It's only happened twice before and until last night, I had no control over it. I don't know where it came from. It just shows up whenever it wants," I admitted.

"When did it appear the last two times?"

"Once, when I was at the abbey. It sent me to the ground it was so powerful. Then, the second time was—" I stopped, not wanting to finish retelling that particular memory.

"Bambina," nonna snapped.

"The most recent occurrence was when I met Orion for the first time," I forced out.

"No, I was there for that. There were no shadows or stars that day," she recalled with confusion.

"That... that wasn't the first time we met."

Nonna stopped in the hall, pulling me over to one of the opened arched windows. "Continue," she insisted.

"I went to return some books I borrowed from Frankie. She told me just to put them back in her room. When I got there, Orion was inside, which I was unaware of. I tripped. He caught me and boom, stars."

"And what were you feeling during this... explosion of power?"

"Nonna," I said uncomfortably.

"Answer the question, child."

"Uncomfortable," I spat with frustration. "I was uncomfortable that I was alone in a room with a half-naked stranger who just happened to be engaged to my cousin whom I love very much and would never do anything to hurt." I felt anger well inside of me at any insinuation she was trying to make.

She looked at me blankly, and then turned, continuing to walk towards the training rings. I followed, unsure of what was going on.

"Bambina," she said calmly. "I only want what is best for you."

"I know, nonna," I said softly.

"What if we made a mistake," she continued. "What if yo—" she stopped moving, trying to make the words come out of her mouth. She snapped her lips shut, taking a deep breath in. "What if you ar—" she strained, but the sentence never came.

I put my hands on either side of her shoulders. "Nonna, are you alright?" I asked.

"What in Aradia's name," she said, looking away from me deep in thought. "I can't—" she said. "I can't fi— Dammit!" she spat, walking with a bit more speed down the hall.

"Should I call for a healer?" I asked, catching up to her.

"No. I don't need a damn healer," she snarled, clearly pissed. "Go to your training and pay attention. You will need the skills Orion can provide. Regardless of your personal life, learn from him. He is the best there is and you need to be prepared."

"Yes, nonna," I answered, following behind her.

"Again," Orion demanded. I pushed myself up from that mat. That was definitely going to leave a bruise. I held the long stick in my hand, trying not to show my fear. Without warning he struck. I was able to block one swing before he nailed me in the thigh, hip, and shoulder, ending in a swift knock to my legs, sending me back to the mat.

I panted, trying to catch my breath. My skin was burning all over. I raised my hand in the air. "Question: how is this benefiting me in anyway shape or form?"

"You are learning to anticipate my attacks. You are becoming aware of your surroundings and the diameter around your personal self. Two hours ago, you couldn't block a single hit. Now, you just blocked one."

I sat up, still catching my breath. "Yea, but when are you going to teach me how to attack?"

"First, you need to be able to survive in order to attack. If you can't get close enough to land a blow because you can't protect yourself, what's the point?"

"Okay, I see your train of thought."

Orion tossed his stick down to the ground without looking at me. "That's all of this for today. I want you to spend an hour a day in the gym building your muscles. Loriana Classet is from my coven. She will be waiting for you. Then, after dinner, we will spend an hour with firearms. This will be your new routine."

"Four hours a day training?" I asked in shock.

"Four hours a day training your physical abilities, then your nonna will spend two hours with you on magic. The rest of the day will be spent educating yourself. Will that be a problem?"

"No, not at all," I replied, not wanting to poke the bear.

"Good. Loriana will be waiting for you. Probably should get a move on."

Without another word I left, not sure about the awkward encounter that just had been the last two hours of my life. There was no flirting, no smiling, no teasing. Not that I was complaining. Every interaction with Orion since he arrived had been... uncomfortable.

I found my way to the gym, not sure exactly who I was looking for. The floor was vacant. Not crowded like usual, but I was thankful about the emptiness. I had never set foot in a gym before and had no clue what half of these intimidating machines were used for.

"Salvo?" said a deep female voice behind me. I turned, plastering on my usual, friendly, smile. The woman before me was an amazon warrior come to life. She had long jet-black hair, flawless chocolate skin, and the most piercing eyes I had ever seen. She was jacked, but still had a feminine look to her.

"Yes. And you're Loriana?"

"That's me," she said, chewing a piece of gum as she circled me. She returned to the front and scoffed. "Fucking Camerino gave me a doe to train. You don't look to have an ounce of muscle on you."

"Well, to my defense, I was poisoned the last eleven years of my life, so there's that."

She smirked, chewing her gum between her front teeth. "You're cute, let's get this party started." She moved into the gym, bringing me to what I believed was called a squat bar. "Leg day. We'll start light, but every week to two weeks we go up in weight. You will run for an hour uphill every morning before you meet with Orion. Then, after we finish our workout you will walk another thirty minutes to burn the lactic acid from the strain on your muscles."

"What's lactic acid?" I asked, completely lost.

"It's an acid your body uses to break down carbohydrates that we will be burning during your workout. Walking it out will help your muscles recover faster. You're also on an eating plan from this point on. We need to get some meat on that bony ass of yours," she said, loading the weights onto the bar.

"Well, this is going to be fun," I whispered.

"You're damn straight it is. Let's go. You will start with 15 reps and then we will work down from there. Get to it, Salvo."

I braced myself under the bar as she fixed my form and instructed me how to properly lift so I wouldn't hurt myself. With a single thrust up, I began my fitness journey.

CHAPTER FIFTEEN

Barrel, slide, clip, cock. I was exhausted, but here I was, yet again with Orion, learning how to field strip weapons. I hadn't even gotten to shoot a single gun yet. He told me that in order to understand the power I held in my hands, I first had to understand how guns work.

My eyes were heavy, and my body was tired, but I kept going. I had been so busy today that I hadn't had time to think about Tony, and our upcoming conversation about our romantic life. Now, with the clock ticking down each moment until I would be free, the thoughts of what I was going to say to him became overwhelming.

I finished putting the Glock together and set it on the table before Orion. He picked it up, examining my puzzle mastery.

"Very good," he said, placing the gun back on the table. "A little slow, but with some practice we will get you there."

"Is that a compliment?" I asked in a snide tone.

"I give compliments when they are due. How did you do with Loriana this morning?"

"Oh, you mean the warrior princess you have training me? Yeah, that was great. I most likely won't be able to walk tomorrow, but hey, you gotta start somewhere."

"That's the spirit," he said, ignoring my sass. "Seren," he said, with his back turned towards me.

"Yes, torture master," I replied.

He huffed a laugh before turning to face me. "I am sorry about the way I spoke to you last night. I didn't mean for our interaction to turn into... whatever it did. My intentions were honorable. I assure you."

I froze, looking at him for what felt like the first time. "Thank you for that," I replied, grabbing my jacket from the chair. "Since we're going to be working together for the foreseeable future, can we just... start over maybe? Forget all the awkward first encounters and maybe try to become friends? We will be family after all in a few months."

He smiled, dropping his eyes down to the clip of bullets in his hands. "Yes, little dove, I'd like to be your friend very much."

"Good. Now that we're back on neutral ground I am going to go soak in a cold bath and pray that I can walk tomorrow."

"6 o'clock sharp," he said, turning back to the table of weapons.

"Yes, master."

I heard him laugh softly and repeat, "master," as I walked back to my room.

I showered as quickly as I could and put a very formfitting blue dress on before heading to Tony's room. I unlatched the door as quietly as I could and slid in, not wanting to draw attention to myself. He was standing in front of a golden mirror with his hand on the edge as if he was closing the frame like a cabinet.

Click. The latch gave me away as the door locked shut. He turned around instantly, and his smile stretched from ear to ear.

"Well, well. After hearing what they put you through today, I am surprised you can even walk," he said, moving slowly towards me.

"I can as of right now. Not so sure about tomorrow." As soon as he got close enough, I wrapped my arms around his neck, pulling his lips into me. He kissed me passionately as he held me close to him. I pulled back, looking into his beautiful multi-colored eyes. "I've been counting down the minutes till I could get back to this."

"Oh, really? This morning was that good, was it?"

I pulled away, looking at him concerningly. "I mean, I thought it was. Was it not for you? Did I do something wrong or not to your liking?"

He started laughing, pulling me back into him until we were forehead to forehead. "It was perfect. Like always, you were perfect."

"Oh, good. Because I really don't know what I am doing here. So, any pointers or suggestion would be greatly appreciated."

"Why don't you just focus on doing what feels comfortable to you when it feels right. Can we agree on that and just continue to explore where this can go?"

"You're so wise," I said, looking up at him in an admiring gaze.

"And you are stunning," he said, gently kissing my lips again. He held my hand, leading me out to the balcony where a spread of food was waiting. A full moon lit our scenery, incased in the mountains of Triora.

"Ugh, I could kiss you again," I said, as my stomach groaned.

"I won't reject that offer. I noticed you didn't come to the dining hall for dinner. Figured you'd be hungry after all the training today." He pulled out a chair for me and I took a seat. He placed a napkin on my lap and filled my plate with chicken, vegetables, and a rice dish. "Now... tell me all about your training."

As we ate, I told him about my day. How training had kicked my culo. How envious I was of Loriana and all her muscles. I told him how excited I was to field strip my first gun. We talked about my magic and how I was making progress in leaps and bounds every day.

"Sounds like your days are full now," he said, sipping on a glass of white wine.

"Tell me about it. Though, I am excited to see if I can learn how to fight like the rest of you. Being able to defend yourself gives you a sense of power, ya know?"

"I agree. Hopefully, you will never have to use what you learn out there," he said, gesturing over the balcony.

"If the war is coming like nonna says, we all will."

He paused, looking down at his glass, swishing the liquid in a circle. "Speaking of, I was assigned another cleanup mission to-day."

My heart dropped. "What? Where?"

"North America. New York to be exact. I'll be gone for two weeks."

I felt as if a bundle of bricks had come crashing down on me. We were exactly where I wanted us to be and now, we would have to put whatever this was on hold. "When do you leave?"

"Tomorrow. They don't really give us any real notice. Obsidian strikes randomly and without an obvious pattern. Once we figure out what they're after, we can begin to anticipate their moves and stop them before they make a mess of things."

I got up and walked over to his chair. He looked up at me with a soft, yet sad smile. "May I?" I asked, gesturing to his lap.

"Of course," he said, opening his arms to me. I gently slid against his body.

"I hate this," I whispered, nuzzling my head underneath his jaw. "I was hoping we would have more time."

"Hey," he said, lifting my chin softly so our eyes met. "We will have our time. These two weeks will fly by. You need to focus on your training and getting stronger. Who knows, by the time I return, maybe you'll be able to kick my ass."

I laughed at him. "I would never." He nuzzled his nose against mine before kissing my cheek. I held onto him, never wanting to let go. "Do you... do you think nonna assigned you this mission because of this morning?"

"No. This order came from my father directly. We have a lot of businesses in New York. It's only fitting I go and handle the cleanup. I'll be checking in on our investments while I'm there."

"I didn't see your father at the ball last night," I said, sitting up to look at him.

"He wasn't in attendance. He is currently in China handling another mishap."

"Hmm, what is New York like? I've never been anywhere outside of Italy before."

He smiled, brushing the back of his knuckles down my cheek. "When all of this is over, or at least calmer, I promise, we will get on my jet, and I will take you anywhere you want to go."

"Should I start making my list now?"

"Most definitely." He stood with me in his arms, taking my mouth against his. I relaxed, enjoying every touch and every taste. He set me down on the bed, hovering over me as his eyes filled with lust. "Stay with me tonight," he whispered.

My eyes widened. "Here? In your bed?" I asked, feeling my heart begin to hammer against my chest.

He chuckled. "Yes, here, in my bed. I just want to be with you. To sleep next to you. My plane leaves early in the morning, and I will be gone by the time you wake."

I felt my cheeks blush as I diverted my eyes. "I'd love to," I whispered. His smile reached his eyes as he pressed his body against mine, kissing me more passionately. I fell back to the bed, allowing his weight to engulf me. He pulled away, too soon for my liking.

"As much," he paused, kissing me down the side of my face, "as I would like to do this the entire night, we both need our sleep."

I let out a whimper. "Five more minutes," I pleaded with him.

He laughed, flipping me on top of him. "Alright, beautiful. If you insist." Five minutes turned into an hour, but he was true to his word. That night, all we did was sleep. When my alarm went off at 4:30 a.m., he was already gone. My hurt sank as I sent up a little prayer to keep him safe.

I returned to my room and changed into my workout clothes. I ran for an hour just like Loriana had instructed. I met Orion after, and our training began.

The next week I slept, ate, and trained. With 7 days already under my belt I could feel myself getting stronger, faster, and wiser. I practiced how to field strip every weapon we had in the castle. Even after my lesson with Orion was done, I would stay late after, training myself to be faster... to be better.

I stuck to the eating regiment Loriana created for me and forced myself to work past her set goals. I wanted this. I wanted to be like them. I wanted others to fear me. I wanted to be good. I wanted to be better.

Jam. Dodge. Slam. Smack. Every punch I threw into Orion's mitts I did so with intent. By week two we began to incorporate offensive moves into our steps. I was still getting my culo handed to me, but I was learning how to use my weaknesses to my advantage. I was naturally small, and in a real fight there was no way I could ever overpower Orion, but I could outrun him.

I would use the thing I once believed was lost to my advantage. My legs. I worked on my endurance and stamina. I now was able to outrun Gabby during our morning cardio sessions. The challenge and the thrill invigorated me.

Chapter Sixteen

Two days till Antonio returned home, I thought to myself as I got ready for the day. It was Friday which meant Frankie would want to go out this evening. Especially because the city's annual wheat festival celebration began tonight. *I could use a little fun*, I thought to myself.

I went to open my door and froze as Orion appeared with one hand up as if he was about to knock. He was in a causal pair of jeans and a tight black crewneck shirt that hugged his godly body. His hair was tied back in a short ponytail away from his face.

"Good morning," he said, straightening himself.

"Morning. I was just about to go on my run. Want to join?" I asked.

"Not today. I was coming to let you know you have the next three days off."

"What? Why?" I asked.

He smiled. "Is that disappointment I hear?"

"A little. I mean, I like learning all... whatever this is."

"Well, I'm not going to stop you from training, but take it easy. You've been going nonstop for two weeks straight. I don't want you to burn out."

I leaned against the door frame, looking at him with suspicion. I folded my arms over my chest and glared. "I know you well enough, horned god. One day off, I get, but three? What's really going on?"

He huffed, running his hand over his head. "My mother is coming for a visit tomorrow morning and insists we spend time together. She wants my undivided attention."

I laughed, trying to hide my mouth with my hand. "That is the sweetest thing I've ever heard."

"Yeah, yeah, laugh it up. You think your nonna is bad, just wait."

"There's nothing wrong with a strong woman. Do her and Frankie get along?"

"Ha, sure. As well as a cat and mouse like to play together."

"Ouch, that bad, huh?"

"Let's just say my mother has ridiculously high standards."

"I would too if I was a mother. Someday, when I have little ones, I hope to be just as scary and protective as my nonna and your mother." I watched as his face filled for a moment with something like grief.

"Anyways, take the next three days, enjoy the festival and don't drink too much."

"Is it a party if there isn't alcohol?"

"Suit yourself, but Monday is going to be hell," he said as he walked away from my room.

"Yes, master. Okay, master. Whatever you say, master."

I heard him laugh as he shook his head.

Even though I had officially gotten the day off from my drill sergeant, I still went on my hour run and hit the gym before breakfast. Everyone was busy today even though it was a holiday weekend. Nonna was training Frankie, which gave my schedule another free slot. Aunt Thora was helping local members of the town with the festivities. Gabby and Bella had gone on a road trip for the weekend, which left me alone.

Surprisingly, the silence was a welcome change of pace. I hadn't had this type of solitude since the abbey. I sat on my balcony for an hour, studying the Bible. I rolled the beads of my rosary between my fingers, taking comfort in the familiar action even though the string of balls were only symbolic to me now. Even with the hours I dedicated to my training, I still found the time to continue this part of my life. The life that I thanked God for each and every day.

I slipped on a yellow floral patterned summer dress and a pair of open toed flats and hit the town around lunch time. This was my first festival and I wanted to experience it as if I was just a normal girl, in a normal town, living a normal life.

Venders were set up on every corner. Fresh baked goods littered every surface. The harvest had been plentiful this year. Tourists filled the cobblestone streets, here to celebrate one of the towns oldest festivals. Families with children ran from booth to booth, tasting and admiring the artistry of the bakers and chefs.

Luscious flower arrangements and potted plants lined the sidewalks. A little girl caught my eye as she held a small pink tulip in a pot between her little hands. I looked around for her parents but didn't notice any one particular adult paying her attention.

I walked over to her and knelt to her level. Her eyes were full of tears as she sniffled. Her curly little pigtails blew in the wind as her nose wrinkled. She couldn't have been more than three years old.

"Hello there. My name is Seren, what is your name?" I said softly.

"Josie," she sniffled.

"Nice to meet you, Josie. Where are you parents?"

She shrugged, looking down at her broken flower. She held it out to me. "I broke it. I made it die."

"Oh, sweetheart," I said, taking the pot from her. I looked around, making sure we weren't attracting any attention. "Can you keep a secret," I whispered. Her big brown eyes looked up at me as she nodded her little head. "Watch."

I focused on the broken stem, waving my hand slowly around the flower chanting, *"restituet vitam, restituet vitam, restituet vitam"*. The stem sewed itself back together until it was strong, and the tulip stood tall, full of life.

The little girl's eyes grew wide, as did her smile. She began to clap, jumping up and down while she giggled. She took the pot from me, stuffing her little button nose into the center of the tulip. She looked back at me with a wide grin as her eyes caught on my pentagram necklace. She laughed and pointed before saying,

"Witch". I looked around, making sure no one heard.

"Shh, remember," I said, leaning in towards her, "our little secret."

She nodded, wrinkling her cute little nose as she hugged the pot.

"Oh, thank God, Josephine Renee," said a woman, rushing towards her. She wrapped her arms around the child, kissing her head profusely.

"Look, mommy. Flower," said Josie.

"Yes, sweetheart, it is a beautiful flower. What did we tell you about running off without one of us?"

"I wasn't alone, see," Josie said, pointing towards me. The mother looked at me with a tapered smile.

"Thank you, for staying with her," she said shortly.

"No problem at all," I replied. "You have a beautiful daughter."

"Thank you. We must be on our way," she said, pulling Josie along with her. Josie smiled and waved back at me. I did the same, giggling to myself. The innocence of a child was something to cherish. I turned around, sliding my purse back onto my shoulder when my view was interrupted by a familiar form.

"You're not supposed to do party tricks out in public, little dove. I heard about the last time you and Frankie got a little too generous and overshared," said Orion.

I laughed moving around him. "Stalking me now, *master*?"

He caught up with me with one long stride. "Might want to pick a different nickname. People might get the wrong idea."

"I stopped caring what people thought about me the moment I found out I was a witch."

"Eh," he said, without any context.

"What?"

"You and I both know that isn't completely true."

"Are you presuming to know me better than I know myself?"

"Yes," he replied shortly.

"Arrogant aren't you?"

"Yes, that too," he chuckled.

"What do you mean by that?"

"You care what people think. That is why you train so hard. Why you push yourself past your breaking point. You're trying to prove to the rest of them that you are one of them. But you're not."

I stopped dead in my track. "And what is *that* supposed to mean? What? Just because I wasn't born here and training since I could walk, I will never amount to the same worth as the rest of you?"

"No little dove, that isn't what I meant. If you would have let me finish, what I was going to say is that you are more than they will ever amount to. You are better in every sense of the word," he said, continuing to walk forward into the crowd of people.

I was taken off guard. What was he playing at? I caught up with him. "What are you doing here anyway?"

He shrugged, "I like the festivals Triora throws. The townspeople are friendly, and the food is something I look forward to."

"You're a foodie?" I asked, surprised to learn something personal about him.

"And what if I am?"

"It's just surprising is all."

"What? That I have likes and interests beyond weapons and fighting?"

"Yes."

He laughed, flashing that blinding white smile. "Surprise, I'm just like everyone else."

"Well, not exactly. Horned god and all," I whispered.

"Right, I almost forgot."

I grinned, looking down at the road. "I like to cook," I shared.

"You do? What do you like to cook?"

"All kinds of things. Pastas, gnocchi, cakes, lemon tarts."

"Mm, lemon tarts are my weakness."

"Really? The big strong god has a weakness?"

"Don't tell anyone," he said, winking at me.

"Well, maybe I will bake them for you sometime. They're one of my favorites, too."

"I would like that," he replied as we came to a group of people dancing in the courtyard to lively music. They laughed and twirled one another, not seeming to have a care in the world. Orion held out his hand to me, looking down in a tender manner. "Would you honor me with a dance, little dove?"

I was hesitant, but something inside of me couldn't resist. This was a part of being normal. A part of experiencing life. "I'd love to," I said, placing my hand in his. He pulled me into the crowd of people as we laughed and danced like we were children.

Orion took me in his arms, leading us ever so gracefully across the cobblestone floor. He spun me out and then caught me as he pulled my body into his. He had perfect rhythm and footwork. I looked up into his carefree face. For the first time, I saw Orion for who he really was. Not a leader, not a god reincarnated, not a warrior, just... Orion.

He smiled and laughed, and I did the same. My heart was full, and my mind was without worry. Everything in that moment fell away. As the music came to an end, he pulled me in one last time from a spin and the world stilled. It took everything I had to keep my shadows in check. My magic hummed when he was near, and I didn't understand why.

He looked down at me with what I could recognize as longing. He didn't make a move, but neither did I. Something inside tugged forward as if it recognized him.

To my surprised, Orion pulled away first, taking in a deep breath. My attention snapped to a faint glow on his skin where my hand had just been. "Orion," I whispered, grasping his arm with my hand, not wanting the light to fade.

He turned back, his eyes following mine to where we touched. "I'm not losing my mind, right?" I whispered, watching as the yellow glow slowly faded.

"No, I see it," he said smiling in astonishment.

"What was that?"

"Hmm," he said, straightening in front of me before leaning down casually to my ear. "Maybe add that to your 'to look into' list and get back to me," he said with a smile.

"You're worthless, you know that?" I spat in aggravation.

"Ouch, that was hurtful," he replied, covering his heart as if he was wounded.

I smacked him in his oversized arm. "Whatever."

"Oh, I see. You're hungry."

"Are you accusing me of being hangry?"

"Yes, now stop talking and follow me," he instructed, taking me by the hand and leading us into the crowd.

We entered a packed little bistro at the corner of town. There wasn't a free table in sight, but that didn't stop Orion from pushing through the crowd, with me still in hand until we got to a door in the back. We entered a stairway, ascending to the top until he opened the metal exit to a beautiful rooftop garden.

The owners had planted every vegetable imaginable in garden boxes. There was a trellis with grapevines intertwining throughout the sections. Exquisite flowers and small fruit bushes lined the edge of the roof. At the front, underneath a gazebo was a small table for four.

"This is—" I began to say but couldn't manage to find the words. This little restaurant was every chef's dream. Orion looked back and smiled.

"Mr. Camerino," said a man, coming behind us from the stairwell entrance. "We were only expecting a reservation for one. Glad to see you've brought a friend."

"I hope it won't be too much trouble," Orion said, pinching me in the arm as we followed the man to the table.

"Not at all," replied the man. "Quite the opposite. I always enjoy cooking for a beautiful woman."

"This is your restaurant?" I asked with excitement.

"Why, yes, it is. Filippo Biondo, at your service," the older man said with a small bow.

"This place is breathtaking," I said, reaching out my hand to shake his. "Seren De Salvo."

The man looked shocked. "Another Salvo?" he asked, taking my hand as if I was a celebrity. "It is an honor. I wasn't aware there was another Salvo in the city."

"Neither were any of us," I laughed. "I am Annalise De Salvo's daughter. I only recently connected with my family."

"Oh, Annalise," he said as his face fell. "I haven't heard that name in many years. She was a bright light in this city... truly. Though, I see that trait has passed from mother to daughter."

"Thank you, Mr. Biondo," I said, feeling proud I was doing my mother's memory justice.

"Please, please, take a seat," he said, pulling out a chair for me. "Today's special is a rich and creamy pesto pasta with sundried tomatoes and fresh mozzarella."

"Sounds delish," I said.

"Make that two," Orion added. Mr. Biondo poured us two glasses of white wine before re-entering the restaurant.

"So, this is your little secret hideaway?" I asked.

"Yes, so don't tell anyone," Orion replied, taking a small sip of the wine.

"Do you take Frankie here often?"

He focused his attention on his wine before looking at the landscape of the city. "I'd feel more comfortable if any questions you have regarding Frankie and I, you refer to your cousin."

"Right. Sorry. I didn't mean to be nosey. You just... you just never mention her. I find it... odd."

"There's not much to say. Your cousin is... fun, beautiful, and has claimed the title of the moon goddess. What more would you like me to say?"

"Frankie is much more than that," I said, taking a large sip of wine.

Orion laughed, refilling my glass. "I wouldn't have chosen this," he admitted, not bringing his eyes to mine. "When I was young and lived here, I could feel the power inside of me beginning to grow but I fought it. I fought it so hard until I couldn't. The power began to pour from within me like a pipe had broken free.

"The covens rejoiced, but I knew my life... any chance I had at choosing a life of my own, free from rules, regulations, and traditions, was gone. I am honored that the gods found me worth, but I also wish it had been someone else. Someone with more of a mind for this type of role."

I reached across the table, feeling my heart swell for him. "I'm so sorry, I didn't know you felt this way. I couldn't imagine what it must be like to have such a burden on your shoulders."

He looked up at me and smiled. "Thank you."

"Let's focus on the perks. What about all the magic you have and will have once the ceremony is complete?" I said, trying to look on the bright side.

"That is a perk, but it puts a large fucking target on my back."

"So, what power will you have?"

"Most witches and warlocks spend their entire lives honing one specific type of magic. I will be able to master every type of magic, including the ability to control life and death."

"Wait, wait, wait. You mean to tell me you can bring someone back from the dead?"

"Not exactly. I will be able to heal someone from internal sickness. The healing abilities that I will have thanks to Cyrus are endless. The horned god is also the god of the hunt. This ability will help when it comes to finding Obsidian. I can tap into that power a little now if I know the person I am looking for but since we don't have a lead, it makes things more difficult."

"What else?" I said fascinated with what he would become.

"I'll be able to control animals and even transform into some. And lastly, I will have the power of the sun."

"And what is that exactly?"

"Still unsure about that one myself," he laughed.

"And what about Frankie? What will she get?"

"The moon goddess will be able to channel power the same as I will. She will have the power and influence over the sea and the moon. Her power comes from the darkness. The are records of moon goddesses communing with the dead, but not a lot to go off. I believe this cycle; the covens will insist that we keep better records of our powers and what we experience for future generations to gleam from."

"Interesting. Well, I can't wait to see what you both do together. I know you'll be a great leader. The both of you."

He gave me another small smile before our food arrived. The aroma was delicious. I bowed my head, saying a quick prayer before I stuffed myself like a pig as Orion told me about what it was like growing up with the other witches and warlocks his own age. We moved onto the subject of his mother and how overprotective she was of her only child. His father had passed away when he was ten, killed by a dark warlock.

I filled him in on my little and unextraordinary life back in Montecassino. Retelling my life's story to another opened my eyes to how many warning signs there had been. How couldn't I have known that nuns were poisoning me my entire life?

We took a long time walking back to the castle, retelling small parts of our lives to one another. I could feel my guard falling away brick by brick. With every laugh and every smile shared, something inside of me craved more. I made sure to always keep a layer of awareness around us. Afterall, he was my cousin's fiancé, and I was falling for Antonio. A part of me couldn't help but wonder what could have been between us if it weren't for our stations. I buried that thought deep inside.

That night, Frankie and I hit the town. The city was even more beautiful in the moonlight than in the day. The people of Triora never slept. It was a constant party and celebration. I made sure to control my drinking, not wanting to do too much damage to my body; I was still planning on training in the morning.

Frankie was a mess. I managed to get her to her room and was surprised when I didn't find Orion asleep in the bed. After I tucked my cousin in, I noted that her room contained none of his belongs. It was evident they weren't sharing a room, let alone a bed.

CHAPTER SEVENTEEN

O ne hour run. *Check*. Lifting for an hour. *Check*. Practicing with firearms. *Check*.

I was drenched in sweat, but I didn't care. It felt good. My body was working, and I was improving. That was all that mattered. I had my headphones in, listening to my newfound obsession, rock music, as I scrolled through my phone. I needed to grab a shower before heading to breakfast.

Antonio still hadn't reached out. I didn't know if he was okay, or hurt, or dead for that matter. The time apart drove me insane. He wasn't allowed to contact anyone when he was away on a mission. Something about not leaving a paper trail, blah, blah, blah. I flipped to my photos, looking through some funny pics he and I had taken a few days before he left. I couldn't help but smile. God, I missed him.

Smack. My face slammed into something hard sending my phone tumbling from my hands. My nose stung from the impact. I looked up at Orion's broad figure standing in front of me.

"God, Camerino. Ever think about moving those annoying muscles of yours before—" he began laughing, bending down to pick up my phone from the floor when I saw a small redheaded woman standing behind him. She was shorter than me, no more than five feet tall.

How on earth she gave birth to Orion I had no clue. Her face was elegant and beautiful, yet stern like nonna's. She didn't smile while she roved her eyes from my head down to my feet and then back up again. I subconsciously smoothed my hair back, knowing I must have looked like garbage.

Orion knocked me in the shoulder with my phone, but I was trapped by his mother judging glare. "Little dove, your phone," he said, finally snapping me out of her intimidating stare.

"Oh, yes, thank you. Hi," I said to his mother, holding out my hand to her. "You must be Mrs. Camerino." She didn't move to take my hand. I nervously pulled it back to my side. "It's wonderful to meet you. Orion has told me so many wonderful things about you."

"Like what?" she asked flatly. I was taken off guard by the question.

"Um, well," I started, looking at Orion for help but he was useless. He just smirked, with one eyebrow raised as if he was entertained by my discomfort. "He has told me how wonderful of a mother you are and how he admires your strength and resilience as the matriarch of your family." I smiled, hoping that was enough.

She allowed a long, awkward pause to fill the air.

"Mother," Orion said, standing between the two of us. "This is

Seren De Salvo."

His mother made a scoffing noise while her face soured. "Another Salvo?" she spat. "Like three wasn't enough."

My face froze in shock. I didn't know what to say. Orion covered his mouth, fighting the laughter I could clearly see trying to escape.

"This one is different," Orion continued. "She was raised by nuns."

"Oh, triple goddess save me," his mother said, forcing her way past me. "By the looks of her, there is nothing different. I can smell the arrogance rolling off her, just like the others." She continued to walk down the hallway, leaving me firmly planted in shock.

Orion leaned down against my ear. "I think she likes you," he said, chuckling softly.

"Oh, that's what you call liking someone?" I asked, still baffled. "I'm assuming she isn't a fan of any of my family then?"

"Nope. Bad blood from when your nonna and her were younger. Rumor has it my mother was fond of your nonno, but he favored Lucia. Female rivalry and all that."

"And how does that reflect poorly on me?"

"It doesn't," he said, pinching my cheek as he walked after her. "Don't worry, little dove, she'll warm up to you," he said with a wink. "Oh, and good job with the training. I'm proud of you," he called back.

"Thank you, master," I yelled back.

After a relaxing bath I made my way to Frankie's room to see how she was recovering after her bender last night. Without thinking, I opened the door. To my utter shock, I was greeted with the image of Frankie up against a wall as Joseph Dialgo had his way with her. She saw me, eyes going wide before I slammed the door shut.

I hurried off to the breakfast hall, trying to force the visual of the two of them from my head. My God, she was going to be so pissed at me. I didn't even know they were a thing. Up until yesterday I thought she and Orion were madly in love. What in the hell was going on around here?

I sat at a table with my coffee and croissant. I opened a book, trying to distract my mind. I must have read the same sentences ten times, not remembering a single word. The chair in front of me pulled out as Frankie took a seat, her own mug of coffee in hand.

I closed the book, running my hands over my face. "Frankie, I am so sorry," I started. "I should have knocked. That was so—"

She held a hand up, stopping me before I could continue to ramble on. "Knocking would be appreciated moving forward," she said taking a sip. We sat there, just staring at our coffee mugs.

"All I care about is your happiness," I finally said, breaking the awkward moment of silence. Her eyes met mine. I could tell they were full of pain.

"I can't imagine what you think of me," she said, holding back tears. "I'm engaged and I—"

I reached across the table, taking her hands in mine. "I don't think anything. That isn't my place, and I am not here to judge you. I love you. But I... I don't understand. I thought you liked Orion."

"He's great. Amazing, in fact," she said, wrapping her hands back around her warm mug. "He's everything I wanted in a man. He's strong, smart, powerful, kind, and sexy as hell, but... it's just... it's not there between us. And believe me, I've tried everything I could think of to ignite a spark. I've tried romance, seduction, taking an interest in what he likes... everything. It just isn't working."

"But what about the whole 'fated mates' thing with the gods?"

She shrugged. "I'm hoping once we marry and complete the ceremony everything will click into place as it should be. That we'll be so madly in love that it makes all this waiting worth it."

"It will. It has to," I said, giving her a reassuring smile.

"But until then, Joseph is a welcome distraction. He desires me in a way I've always wanted. And praise Aradia, he is amazing in bed."

I choked on my coffee as a laugh escaped. "Good to know," I said, wiping my mouth with a napkin.

She leaned back, arms crossed as she examined me. "You and Tony haven't done it yet, have you?"

My cheeks blushed. "No, we're taking things... slow. Ya know, with my lack of experience and all."

"Who in the hell cares? You two are obviously crazy about each other. Rip the band aid off and get to it. I thought for sure you were going to the night of the ball."

"Believe me, I've thought about it. I want to make sure—"

"Oh look," said a deep familiar female voice. I looked up to see Orion's mother standing above us with a cup of coffee. "A gathering of whores."

Frankie rolled her eyes. "Good morning, Evaline. Didn't realize you were going to be arriving so early this morning," Frankie grumbled.

"You would have if you were by your future husband's side, as you are supposed to be," Evaline said in a snarky tone.

"Your son does just fine without me," replied Frankie, finally bringing her eyes up to Evaline's.

"That he does. And it appears, by the looks of you, you're living up to the family name. Out all hours of the night drinking and whoring. I can't help but be comforted in the fact that our bloodlines will never be mixed. It would be a shame to have a grandson or granddaughter I would be ashamed of thanks to their mother's poor choices."

I felt my blood begin to boil. Not only was this woman insulting one of the kindest women I have ever known who just happened to be my family, my blood, but she was rubbing the fact that Frankie would never get to have a child of her own in her face, as if it was a blessing.

My hands tensed as I tried to calm myself, but I was failing miserably.

"Why the gods have chosen to punish my poor son by binding him to you for eternity is beyond comprehension," Evaline continued. "My son is an honorable man and deserves a wife that is a reflection of his power and goodness. Not some tramp that he must worry about, who enjoys spreading her legs for whatever male looks at her twice."

One minute, I was taking a deep breath in, then the next *Boom!* Evaline's mug shattered in her hand, sending the hot coffee splashing through the air. I stood from my chair, now face to face with her. The dining room went silent. All eyes turned towards us. Evaline didn't flinch. Her face was cold as stone.

"How dare you insult a woman you clearly know nothing about," I said, aggressively. "If you were capable of getting past your own jealousy issues you would see that Orion is the lucky one in this arranged marriage. Francesca is one the kindest and compassionate people I have ever known. She is more than worthy of the goddess's blessings and for you to come into our home, under our roof, and insult our family and the future moon goddess shows just how completely ignorant and foolish you are.

"You sit here and speak down to my cousin as if she has no class but in reality, Evaline Camerino, you are the one who is without an ounce of grace." I took Frankie by the hand before Evaline had a moment to rebut and lead us out into the hall.

Once we got back to my room, Frankie slammed the door behind me with the largest smile on her face. "Oh girl, that was priceless," she said, rushing me. "I cannot believe you just told that she-devil off like that. And when you exploded the coffee mug in her hands, I just about lost my shit."

I laughed, feeling a bit embarrassed. "Yes, well, I am sure Orion is going to make me pay for that in my next training session."

"Oh, don't worry about him. I'll handle that side of things," she said, pulling me into a bear hug. "Thank you for defending me. I am so glad you came into my life when you did. I needed you and I didn't even realize how much."

I hugged her back, feeling a sense of strength when I was near her. "You'll have me forever. You're the Yin to my Yang, as nonna describes us."

She laughed, pulling back to look at me. "Very true. Salvo sisters forever. The women in our family always come in pairs. I'm just happy I found my other half. Geesh, could you imagine the havoc we would have made if we had grown up together? Maybe the gods separated us so Castle Salvo would remain standing."

We both started laughing. "I can see your point." A knock came at the door. We both froze, looking at each other, daring the other to answer it. I walked over, expecting to see Evaline on the other side so she could let us have it but instead Orion stood with a stern look on his face. I stepped back, allowing him to enter the room.

He looked between the two of us as I went and stood next to my cousin for support. "Frankie," Orion finally said. "I am so sorry for the way my mother spoke to you in public. I have spoken with her, and she promises me she is going to work on her behavior."

"Thank you," Frankie said. Orion stood, looking between the two of us once more.

"Can I please speak to Seren alone?" asked Orion. Frankie looked to me for direction.

"It's fine. I'll find you later," I said, as we kissed each other on the cheek. Once the door was shut, Orion moved further into my room, assessing my belongs.

"I have a feeling the two of you are going to cause me many headaches in the future," he said playfully.

"You're blessed to be surrounded by such strong and independent women," I teased. He huffed a laugh. "I'm sorry about the exploding coffee mug," I finally said. Regardless of what the evil witch said, she was still Orion's mother, and I cared about him. "I didn't intend for it to explode. I just got so mad about how she was talking to Frankie it... it just happened."

"I understand the anger you both felt from her words, but in the future, can you please try and refrain from burning my mother with scolding hot liquids?"

"Is she okay?"

"She's a healer, she'll be fine," he said, making his way over to the doors of my terrace as he peered outside. "Beautiful view you have." I joined him, still feeling a bit awkward.

"It is," I whispered. His gaze found mine while his expression softened. The longing reappeared in his eyes I had come to recognize. Ever so slowly, he lifted his large hand until he gently cupped the side of my face, now turning fully towards me.

My breath caught in my chest. I was completely paralyzed, unable to move. His thumb brushed my skin while his eyes scanned every inch of my face. Without knowing it, I had stepped closer towards him, needing his warmth, wanting it.

"You never cease to impress me, little dove," he whispered, leaning his head lower towards me. "Your power is strong. Maybe that's something you should add to your 'to look into list'." He was now only inches from my lips.

"Orion." The only word I was able to get out. He closed his eyes, allowing a deep groan of pleasure to escape.

"Say my name again, Seren," he whispered. His voice now heavy with seductions and desire. I felt his other hand find its way around my waist. His fingers splayed on my lower back, pulling my body into his. Every part of me now pressed against him. My hands found their way to his arms as I admired every large and firm mound of muscle he possessed. God he was huge.

Something deep inside of me yearned for him. Every inch of my skin was aware of where we touched. My breath was now ragged and unsteady. My heart felt like it was going to beat out of my chest. Then, there was a warmth low in my stomach, between my legs that began to throb, needing to be touched.

His eyes were hungry. His hands slowly exploring my body. I leaned back, exposing my neck to him. Before I could think twice about what I was doing, his lips pressed firmly against the tender column of my neck. His teeth, gently scraping against the more sensitive parts sending shockwaves of pleasure throughout my body.

My hands found their way to his untamed hair, fisting it, forcing his mouth to press harder against my flesh. I wanted more. I needed more. I need him. In this moment I—

"No!" I screamed, pushing him away from me with every ounce of control I had left. What in the hell was I doing? I ran my hands through my hair, trying to calm myself. I looked back up at him, seeing the disappointment in his eyes. "Orion," I whispered. "This can't happen. Whatever this is, it has to stop."

He took two large steps towards me, placing a hand on either of my arms. "No. This is right. This *feels* right," he said, pressing his forehead into mine. "Seren, open your eyes. See what is right in front of you," he pleaded.

"Stop. Just stop. Regardless of the issues you and Frankie have, you are still engaged to my cousin and I'm... I have feelings for Antonio."

Orion's eyes went deadly at the mention of Tony's name.

"I'm sorry, but this isn't right and neither Frankie nor Antonio deserve this."

"This has nothing to do with them," he said firmly. "You and I... we're—" he stopped, trying to force the words out but couldn't. He looked confused and aggravated as he tried again to speak but couldn't.

"Orion, I care about you. More than I should. Whatever this is, it's dangerous. It must stop," I said, leaving him standing on the terrace.

Chapter Eighteen

I kept my distance from everyone the rest of the day. The next morning, I continued with my normal routine and then hid in my bedroom until my appetite got the better of me. As I headed towards the dining room, I saw Orion approaching from the opposite direction. I took a deep breath and gave him a small smile as we stopped in front of one another.

"Good morning," he said, looking down at me in a soft manner.

"Morning," I replied, shortly.

He looked down at his hands, appearing as nervous as I felt. "Listen, about yesterday—"

"Can we just forget about it," I interrupted, not wanting to venture down that road.

"No, we can't, because even though it meant nothing to you, our moment meant something to me. I am not going to lie about that. But—" he said, taking a deep breath, "at the same time, I respect you and what you want. So, in sight of that, I am sorry for my behavior and if I made you feel forced or uncomfortable in anyway."

"You don't have to say you're sorry, Orion. We were both responsible for what happened yesterday. It just... it can't happen again," I said, softly.

His head fell in disappointment. "I understand. I'll refrain from now on. Until you tell me otherwise."

I smirked at him, unable to control myself. "Arrogant, are we?"

He walked to my side, leaning his lips down to my ear. "Not arrogant, little dove. Just confident," he whispered before walking away. Something inside of me lit at his words. I snuffed out the ember of hope.

I ate my lunch in peace, studying some new spells and earth magic nonna had assigned me before returning to my room. When I entered, the terrace doors were open causing the curtains to flutter freely in the wind. I approached the opening cautiously, unsure of who had invited themselves into my space.

Antonio stood at the edge in a dark washed pair of jeans and a buttoned up pressed shirt. His hair was cleanly brushed to the side. I smile stretched across my face. He peered back at me over his shoulder.

"Hello, beautiful," he said, seduction already lacing his words.

I hurtled myself forward, needing to feel him, needing to taste him. He was where I belonged. This was what I wanted. He was what I wanted. Our lips met, with a vicious kiss, laced with passion.

"I've missed you," I whispered in between kisses.

"And I you," he said, picking me up as he led us back into my room.

The next two months flew by. With each passing day I got stronger and more knowledgeable about my people and our history. My magic seemed to have no bounds. Now that the poison was completely out of my system, I felt invincible. I worked with nonna almost every day. I learned how to concoct potions and use elements and crystals found in the earth to boost my magical abilities.

I could make things levitate. I was able to control the elements around me with ease. Fire was still kicking me in the culo, but I was determined to conquer it. My favorite spell was 'calling cast'. I was able to imagine any object and call it to me through a spell. It would magically appear in the palm of my hand.

In the gym, Loriana continued to find new ways to torture me every day. On the mat, Orion did the same. I met his friends Roric, Tyler, and Adrianna. I began to train with them learning various weapons and how to anticipate my opponent's moves. They were deadly and fierce, but with every bruise I accumulated I reflected on where I had gone wrong and fixed it the next time I was back on the mat.

Orion was true to his word. He didn't make another inappropriate move regarding he and I. Though, he wasn't the one I was worried about. Even though things were beyond amazing with Antonio, I still found my mind wondering to 'what-if' scenarios regarding Orion and me. To make things worse, I was constantly in close proximity to him. A good portion of my day was spent just him and I, hot and sweaty, slamming into each other over and over again until one of us pinned the other to the mat. I always lost, but I didn't mind. Feeling his strong, massive body against mine was something that felt... natural.

Sexual tension aside, he and I had become close friends. He was all the things Frankie had described and then some. He was funny and intelligent. He was patient and kind when it came to our training. Especially when it came time to teach me how to shoot, which quickly became my favorite part of the day.

Every gun they had, I practiced with. I honed my skills and familiarized myself with each firearm I shot. How it felt loaded and unloaded. What to expect when it came to the kick back of each weapon. I learned how to pack my own bullets and which bullet went to which gun.

Antonio and I continued to explore our relationship. We even started training together in the gym just to spend more time with one another. Nonna didn't seem thrilled about our relationship, but I was happy and that's what mattered. He continued to leave for short cleanup missions which I was kept out of the loop on;

nonna's orders.

Frankie's twenty first birthday finally came mid-September. Even though Aunt Thora and I worked endlessly to make sure she had the most glamorous and extravagant birthday bash any twenty-one-year-old could hope for, it did nothing to raise her spirits. Now that she was of age, the ceremony uniting the horned and moon gods could take place at any time. Nonna assured her it was still scheduled after the new year and would not be moved ahead of schedule.

To Frankie, it was a death sentence. Something she couldn't escape. No matter how many others she was with, at the end of the day, Orion would still become her husband. I tried to be there for my cousin as best as I knew how, but this was a situation I couldn't understand.

On one hand, I chose Antonio. I was happy. On the other, I envied Frankie. How could she not desire Orion? Though, their relationship was different than he and I's. He didn't flirt with her or try to make her laugh like he did me. It was more business casual than hot and tempting. I could see where her hesitation was born from. I was sure the ceremony between the two would change that soon enough. Two star crossed gods, together, after being separated for 300 years. How romantic.

October arrived sooner than I had expected. I wasn't complaining. The weather and colors had always been my favorite. Now that I knew I was a witch, it all made sense. My birthday was quickly approaching. The first one I would celebrate with my family. Sister Odette would always bake me a small cake and bring it to my room the night of October 16, but that was the extent of my celebration.

After a long and extraneous training session, I returned to my room, skipping lunch. Instead, I soaked in a warm bath. After I was rid of the sweat and grime, I planted myself into one my reclining chairs on the terrace. The fall sun was still warm. I wore a thin, loose black cotton dress and my favorite gray cardigan.

At some point, I had dozed off, comforted by the silence and warmth of the sun. I felt someone rubbing my cheek softly. When I opened my eyes, Antonio smiled back at me, sitting on the side of my chair. I turned and kissed his hand.

"Well, hello, sleepy head," he said in his deep and sensual voice.

"Hi yourself, handsome," I replied, with a small stretch and yawn. Tony pulled a plate of food from the side table, placing it next to me.

"I figured, since you missed lunch, you'd be ravenous after all your training," he said.

"You're so thoughtful. What did I ever do to get so lucky?"

"I'm the lucky one," he whispered, leaning down to kiss me tenderly. "Now, eat up."

I obeyed, as he sat silently, watching me nibble on the food. After I was finished, I stretched back out on the lounge chair, taking in the last few hours of the sun.

"This is heaven," I said, closing my eyes. I felt his hand gently lift my leg as he positioned it on top of his lap.

"Yes, you are," he replied. I watched while he massaged my calf as if he was a professional. I let out a little groan.

"God, that feels good. How did you know today was leg day?"

He laughed, continuing up to my knee. "Just lay back and relax, beautiful. Let me take care of you."

I did as he commanded, allowing my muscles to get some much-needed TLC. I felt him move his attention to the other leg, taking his time. His hands gently rubbed my smooth skin, pushing the dress further up. I became aware of where his hands were headed.

He caressed my inner thighs with his fingers. My entire center exploded with heat. I licked my lips, arching my hips ever so subtly forward. His warm lips pressed a kiss to my left thigh, breaking any control I had. I let out another moan, gripping the side of the chair cushion.

He had never ventured this far in our physical relationship.

Though, the way my core was heating and the desire that was beginning to spread throughout my entire body, I wasn't about to start objecting. One of his hands slid up my dress while he continued to kiss the other leg. His fingers played with the edge of my panties causing my bundle of nerves to swell with anticipation and need. I felt the warmth begin to seep from me as everything inside pulsed with desire.

So damn slowly, he pulled the side of my underwear back, testing to see if I would stop him. When I didn't, he took his thumb and slid it down the center of my slick sex. I gasped, feeling as if I was going to explode. I felt his warm breath against my skin as he let out a deep laugh.

He then took his first two fingers, doing the motion over again, yet this time, he paused at my opening, gently caressing either side. My body began to move, begging him for more. I opened my eyes to see him on his knees in front of me. As we locked eyes, he slid his hands under my dress, slowly sliding off my underwear.

My breathing was uncontrollable. My breasts became heavy as my nipples pressed against the thin fabric of my dress. He placed a hand on either side my legs, sliding them up my skin, pressing my thighs open. His eyes, now focus on the swollen bundle between my legs. He bit the side of his lip with a devilish grin in the sexiest response I had ever seen.

His eyes found mine again as he lowered himself in between my legs. "Lay back beautiful. Let me take care of you." His voice was laced with sex. He began kissing up my skin, allowing his tongue to do most of the work. He sucked on my inner thigh gently, cause my insides to twinge.

I felt his silky hair, brush across my skin as I reached down, running my fingers through it. He finally reached the top of me, continuing to kiss and lick the insides of my hips. One of his hands trailed up my dress, sliding over the plains of my stomach until he cupped my full, aching breast. I could have cried at the sheer pleasure it sent through my body.

I began to quiver as I felt his lips gently kiss down the seam of the most sensitive part of me. Once he got to my entrance, I felt his tongue circle the hole. My entire body went frantic. He held me down by my chest while his other hand found my bottom, cupping my ass while bringing me further up to his mouth. His tongue slid all the way back up zigzagging across that damn bundle of nerves.

My body was no longer my own. As he licked, and sucked, and kissed the center of me, moans, and cries of pleasure and ecstasy escaped from deep inside. The heat and the moisture of his mouth taking this part of me inside of him was too much to bear.

With one hand, he held the lips to my sex open as he worked my clit with his tongue. His other hand, found my entrance once more and gently slid one finger inside, making sure to take his time. My body instantly clenched around him, wanting this feeling to last forever.

"Yes," I panted.

"Is this what you want, baby," he said, plunging his finger inside of me again.

"Yes. I want more," I said in between breaths. He added a second finger, pumping me as his tongue continued to flick the very tip of my clit.

"Come on, beautiful. Come all over me. Let me hear those pretty lips moan," he whispered, before he took me fully in his mouth. He began pumping harder and faster until all I could hear was the sound of my own blood coursing through my veins.

"Antonio," I yelled, feeling my body build with a pressure I had never experienced.

"Let go, baby."

At his command, my body released. Everything inside of me ignited from the pleasure of what he had done. My insides clenched around him as I arched my hips, riding the orgasm until I finished. I screamed out, with one hand buried in his thick head of black hair and the other wrapped around my own breast. My body shook and spasmed while the release ever so slowly drifted me back down to reality.

I was shaking and my heart was pumping fast. Antonio kissed my thighs gently, pushing himself up on his arms before crawling on top of me. He was smiling with pride. I could still see the shimmer of my orgasm on his lips. He kissed my chest, working his way up to my neck and then my lips.

"Are you... satisfied," *kiss*, "my beautiful," *kiss*, "powerful," *kiss*, "little witch?"

"And to think, I was about to sign my life away and never experience that type of pleasure," I said, followed by a laugh of pure joy.

He laughter joined mine, before allowing his body to rest on top of me. "I'm glad to hear that was worth breaking a few vows for."

"You are very good at that. How much practice have you had Mr. Simonelli?"

"Hmm, funny. I can't seem to remember any other women before you. Have you spelled me, little witch?"

I chuckled, leaning up to kiss him. "I think I'll keep you."

"Well, I'm hoping so."

I drew the back of my knuckles down his face, tracing his lips with my fingers. "What can I do for you?" I asked. "Tell me, and I'll do it. I want to give you the same kind of pleasure you gave me just now."

He took my hand, kissing my fingers softly. "I want today to be only about you. We will have time to explore each other further, but right now," he said, turning his attention back to my leg. He took a hand, sliding it up slowly along the sensitive skin until he got to my entrance. He plunged two fingers inside. This time, it wasn't soft or hesitant. It was rough and passionate. "I just want to watch you," he finished, kissing my lips softly as he pumped his fingers in and out of me.

CHAPTER NINETEEN

Nonna had assigned me a pile of homework, but all I could think about was Antonio and what he had done to me the day before. It consumed me, just like he had consumed me on the terrace. Just thinking about it lit my entire body on fire. I had researched what to do in order to pleasure him, but I was still hesitant. What if I did something wrong or it didn't feel good? Would he be comparing me to other women who had more experience?

I slammed the book shut getting up from the table in the library. I was exhausting myself stressing about it. I had to focus on my tasks at hand. I still had so much work to do. But... the image of that dark head of hair, buried between my legs was too beautiful not to picture.

As if he knew I was thinking about him, Antonio rounded the corner, smiling ear to ear. He walked straight up to me, not caring who was in the hall or who saw. He slid his hand into my hair, tilting my lips up towards his and kissed me with passionately. I moaned against his mouth, dropping the books I was carrying, preferring my hands to be on him instead.

He pulled away, looking into my eyes as the heat flared between us.

From behind, I heard someone clearing their voice. I turned to see Frankie and Orion, standing there. Orion's eyes were locked on Antonio as if he was about to gut him alive. He was breathing so fiercely you could see his massive muscles rise and fall. His jaw was locked.

Frankie smiled, wiggling her eyebrows up and down. "You two love birds better not make nonna wait," said Frankie. "She will set both of you on fire."

With a confused look, I turned back to Tony for answers.

"Right, I almost forgot," reaching his hands around my waist, pulling me back into him. "Your nonna has requested all of us in the meeting chamber. That's why I was on my way to find you, but then I saw you and I—" he stopped, making a move to kiss me again before he stumbled back, catching his balance.

"Let's go," grumbled Orion as he pushed past Tony.

Tony chuckled, fixing his shirt. He landed a small kiss on my head before mouthing the words, 'later' to me. He bent down, picking up my books before he made his way to the meeting chamber.

Frankie looped her arm around mine and pulled me forward towards the others. "So," she whispered in her devious voice. "You two are hot as fuck. What haven't you told me, little cousin?

I blushed. "Actually, I could use your... insight on a few things later, if you wouldn't mind," I whispered.

She pulled away, clapping loudly, laughing with joy. I stopped her, trying not to draw more attention than she already was. "Aradia, I have been waiting for this moment," she said, pulling me back down the hall. "Yes. Absolutely. Whatever you need."

I chuckled. "Thanks... I think."

Nonna was seated at the head of the table along with my aunt. Twelve other witches and warlocks were seated in attendance. Two members from each coven, as was custom. Chairs were set in rows for us. I looked around, noting Adrianna, Roric, Tyler, Loriana, Joseph, George, Bella, Gabby, and about ten other young people I didn't know.

The doors behind us shut and locked as two guards stood in front of them. Frankie and I looked to each other, both confused about what was happening. Nonna stood, her face expressionless.

"Please, sit with your coven members so we can begin," instructed Nonna. Frankie, Bella, Gabby, and I sat front and center as the others filed in around us. Aunt Thora nodded at me with a small smile. "You all have been asked her today because the threat to our covens has been publicly declared for the world to see. Our way of life, as we know it, is in danger."

An elderly man, tall and thin, yet still handsome with his salt and pepper hair stood. Frankie leaned over, "Torrian Astra, Terra Coven leader. Next to him, his daughter, Aris," she whispered.

Torrian took the floor. "The information you will learn here today stays between those in this room until we have determined the appropriate timing to inform our covens as a whole. We must warn you—" he paused, taking a moment to swallow and refocus. "What you will see and learn today is very graphic and inhuman on multiple accounts. It goes against what we believe as a magical community and as a people."

"Some of you," nonna said, "have already had to face what you will see head on in the field. Your sacrifice and service does not go unnoticed. Now, if you would all turn your attention to Elder Mystic, we can begin."

"Marriana Mystic, Vento Coven leader," whispered Frankie. "Her daughter, Delphine, doesn't like me. She's Orion's ex."

I nodded, matching faces with names.

Elder Mystic stood, walking over to the tv as the debriefing began. The first image appeared on the screen. It was of an abstracted eight-pointed star laying on its side, encased in a circle. "This," said Elder Mystic, "is the symbol of the dark coven Obsidian. Over the past fifteen years this group, who we knew very little about, has surfaced, making their presence and organization known. At first, we were able to contain their reign of terror, but as of last night, they have captured the attention of every nation, every country, and every political power on all seven continents."

The next slide appeared, with images more horrific than I could have imagined. "Russia," said Elder Mystic. A picture of seven naked and decapitated children nailed to a Russian political building appeared.

"Japan." Another imaged flashed of 7 more children, naked, hanging from a bridge.

"Australia." A photo of what I assumed was seven children hacked to pieces on the steps of the Sydney Opera house.

"America." Seven dead and naked children impaled onto the White House fence.

"Germany." Seven children skinned, nailed by their hands to the Brandenburg Gate.

"Rome." Infants. Seven of them, nailed to crosses lining the front entrance of the Vatican. Tears fell from my eyes silently as I heard others behind me sniffle and whimper in pure shock. My heart was shattered. My mind couldn't comprehend, and my body was enraged.

"There are more. We have accounts in Mexico, Canada, Scotland, Britain, Spain, Kenya, and Nigeria all reporting the same type of brutality. We are still waiting on more reports from South America. The United Nations have called an immediate meeting of all world leaders. They will meet in two days' time to discuss the actions you have seen here today.

"There are live feeds and pictures of these tragic, heinous acts that have gone viral." She clicked to the next slide, showing seven sigils burned into various corpses. Each brand represented one of the seven covens. "It's been reported that our crests were found burned into the corpses of the victims in every country. We can only assume that this is a direct message from Obsidian that they plan to eliminate each of our covens.

"We do not know what they are planning, and we don't know how they will execute their plans. We have spies on the ground, but we have come up empty handed."

Nonna stood, "There are some of you in this very room that have come face to face with the horrors this dark coven has orchestrated." Elder Mystic clicked the next slide, revealing a video. As it began to play, I could see Tony in the background. The main subject, one of Obsidian's witches, stood bound in a circle of magic as it fought to get out. Female by the looks of it, though most of its human features were distorted.

The creature was missing teeth. The ones it had left were sharpened into pointed needles. Its eyes were dilated, with blood vessels busted throughout the remaining white parts. The skin that we could see was broken and oozed with blood and what looked like yellow puss. The witch was missing patches of hair. Claw marks stretched along its arms, neck, and chest. Blood dripped from its dry and chapped mouth.

It moved unnaturally, making loud screaming and hissing noises throwing itself repeatedly into the magical cage, causing it to bust its head wide open. But it didn't stop. I watched as our witches began to chant. It was a spell of undoing. What they were trying to undo, I didn't know.

The creature began to claw at its own skin, causing ribbons of bloodied flesh to litter the ground. It pulled at its hair and flung itself around as if it was on fire. Then, suddenly, it stopped. In a calm fashion it locked eyes one the witch holding the phone that was recording.

The creature walked over, slowly, and confidently, in a predatorial manner. It snapped its head back and forth. You could hear the cracking of its bones. It stopped, just inches from the phone and leaned in as close as it could get. The camera began to shake still capturing the creature's eyes shifting back and forth as if it could see who would be watching.

"I see you, little moon goddess," it hissed in a deep and demonic voice. It began to laugh. "Give her to us, and we will stop our displays of... love. If you refuse—" the creature reeled back, slamming its fingers into its eye socket, pulling its eyeball out and then popping it into its mouth.

It leaned back down towards the camera, smiling in the most disturbing manner I had ever seen. "The innocent will suffer. The world will rain with the blood of your kind. And the original seven will cease to exist." It pulled its head back once again and then without warning, it shoved its long fingernails into its throat, pulling out its jugular. It remained standing, glaring at the camera before it impaled its own chest, ripping the heart out, falling lifeless to the ground.

My breathing was ragged as I fought to steady myself. Frankie and I were holding hands, both trembling. I had never seen something so horrific in my life. And Tony was there. He was out in the world, risking his life trying to fight these things. And the children... I wiped the silent tears I had been shedding for them.

My nonna stepped in front of us, looking long and hard at each witch and warlock. "We did not heed their warning," she said, her eyes snagging on me for a second longer than I liked. "And those children have now paid the price... our price. Make no mistake, we will not be giving up the hosts for the horned god or the moon goddess. We now must prepare ourselves for what comes next."

"And what does that include exactly?" asked a man with a darker complexion that I didn't recognize.

"War. By now, the countries have begun to point fingers at one another. They will be researching our coven crests and will find nothing more than folklore. Most likely, they will conclude these murders a result of some new homicidal cult. But if Obsidian continues to push boundaries and begins to perform larger displays of magic, we will all be exposed.

"We have some time, but not as much as I we had hoped. Thus, your involvement. The 22 of you have been handpicked by the covens. Each bring unique qualities and gifts to this group that our people need. Briefing will begin tomorrow. Training will continue. After, you will be broken up into two separate regiments. One will head to the America's. The other will stay here on this side of the world."

I rose my hand, daring to speak.

Nonna nodded at me.

I took a deep breath. "It isn't going to be enough," I whispered. I felt Frankie's eyes snap in my direction. "The covens need to know... they need to know all of this."

"As we clearly stated at the beginning of this meeting, the information shared in this room today and any information moving forward stays here. Is that going to be a problem Seren?"

I swallowed hard. "No, Elder Salvo," I replied.

"Good," she continued. "Now, if any of you are not up for this task, now is the time to get out." She paused, looking at each person. "Perfect. You will receive more information tomorrow morning. That is all."

The chairs screeched on the floor as the other 21 cadets marched out of the room. I rose slowly, unsure of what I had just signed up for. All I knew was that keeping this from the others was a mistake. We were more powerful together than divided. Plus, they deserved to know what was coming.

Frankie grabbed me by the arm as soon as I exited the meeting hall. "What in the hell were you thinking?" she said, pulling me alongside her. "Questioning Nonna like that. You are lucky she didn't slap you in front of everyone. I know you are new to this cousin, but no one questions nonna... ever. She is, by far, the most powerful witch the covens have and the most knowledgeable."

"But that doesn't make her decision right," I said, pulling my arm away from her. "If your coven, if your family was in danger, don't you think you should have the right to know? To have time to prepare? We are throwing a very small percentage of our arsenal at this enormous threat. Why?"

Frankie looked at me as if she was a deer in headlights. "It doesn't matter what we think. Nonna knows best," she said softly.

"That doesn't mean this is the right choice," I replied, walking towards Tony who was waiting for me. He gave me a small smile as I approached. My heart became heavy, knowing the burden he had been carrying and unable to share with anyone.

"Now you know everything," he said, taking my hand, leading us to his room.

CHAPTER TWENTY

The rest of the day we spent in bed. Tony told me about his travels and what he had encountered along the way. As he detailed the attacks, and the murders he had witnessed, the friends he had lost, all I could do was listen. We fell asleep somewhere in the early hours of the morning.

A knock came at the door. Tony answered, still dressed in his clothes from the day before. He handed me an envelope, keeping one for himself. We both held our breath as we opened them. I read my letter silently and then watched as he read his.

"I'm staying on the continent," he said.

"Oh, thank God," I replied, throwing my arms around him, both of us smiling with relief. I pulled away, looking into his beautiful hazel eyes. "Well, at least we'll be facing Hell together."

"I wouldn't want it any other way," he whispered, kissing me softly. "I'm going to grab a quick shower. Care to join?"

I felt the heat swell under my skin at the thought of seeing his body completely soaked and naked. "As tempting as that is—"

"Wrong time," he said, kissing the back of my hand. "I know. I saw an opening and I took it. Can't blame a guy, can you?"

I laughed. "Clever warlock."

"More like hopeful," he said, kissing me again. "I'll meet you at your door in fifteen?"

"Sounds like a plan." I got up, reluctantly leaving the warmth of his bed as I headed back towards my room. I had so much on my mind I didn't know where to begin. Hopefully, today in our briefing, I would get most of those answers.

I turned the corner, stopping abruptly. Orion was hunched in the corner by my door holding his envelope. He stood slowly, assessing me as I approached. I opened my door to my room. "Good morning," I said, moving past the doorway.

"May I come in?" he asked.

I nodded. "What can I do for you?" I asked.

"Did you receive your placement?"

"I did."

He stopped, staring at me. His face was tense and full of what looked to be anxiety "And?"

"I'm to remain on the continent."

He exhaled, running his free hand through his thick and unbound hair. "Thank the goddess."

"Antonio is staying as well," I added, making sure he was aware that I wouldn't be available.

"I don't care," he replied flatly. "As long as you remain close."

"Shouldn't you be worried about keeping Frankie close?"

He turned towards me, hands on his hips. "We are safer together," he said softly.

"I can protect myself now, Orion."

"You are strong, and a quick study, but there is still so much you haven't even explored, little dove. Don't be arrogant. That will get you killed."

"Me, arrogant? And what are you?" I paused, waiting for him to answer. "Showing up to my room, barely before the sun has even risen. We have had this conversation, Orion. You are engaged and I am with—"

I didn't have a moment to think, or breath. One minute he was ten feet across the room, the next, he was in front of me. One hand on my waist and the other tangled in my hair. He pressed his lips to mine, tenderly, yet full of desire and passion.

Everything in my body woke and then I exploded. Darkness surrounded us as the stars and universes spiraled helplessly through the air. I felt the warmth seep off Orion while my hands betrayed me, finding their way along his ripped and chiseled torso and arms. My fingers tangled through his hair. I used it as leverage to pull myself harder against him.

He tasted of sunshine and spring. As his lips moved across mine, everything around me ceased to exist. It was only the two of us. Something inside of me recognized him. It was comfortable. It was safe.

He pulled away from me slowly. The air returned to my lungs as my eyes opened softly. Orion was glowing. His entire aura surrounding him beamed golden yellow. I looked at my own arms. My aura was shades of silver and white. It was as if he was the sun, and I was the—

Bam! I heard the fist make contact before I saw who it belonged to. Orion stumbled back, fire erupting from his hands readying for a fight. Antonio stood in front of us, seeping with rage, his eyes locked onto Orion. I stumbled back, feeling an overwhelming flood of emotions.

"What in the fuck do you think you're doing?" yelled Antonio to Orion.

Orion extinguished the flames that wrapped around his arms. "None of your business," he said coldly.

"None of my business?" snapped Antonio, taking a step towards him. He pointed towards me without removing his eyes from Orion. "She is my business. She is mine."

"The hell she is," replied Orion, manning up to Antonio. I couldn't take this.

"Stop!" I yelled, making my way in between them. "Orion leave," I demanded.

Orion looked down at me in shock. "What?" he asked, his voice laced with hurt.

"Leave, now," I repeated myself, moving to Antonio's side.

Orion looked at me for another moment before shifting his eyes to Antonio. Another awkward moment passed before he finally left, leaving me alone to cleanup our mess.

I ran my hands down my face, feeling the shame and embarrassment from what Antonio had seen. "Tony, I am so sorry. I don't know—"

"I am going to ask you this one more time, and *only*, one more time," he said, unable to bring his eyes to mine. "Is there something going on between you and Camerino? And please, for everyone's sake, be honest with me this time."

I paused, feeling the tears well inside my eyes. It didn't matter if there were feelings between Orion and me. He was marrying my cousin. He didn't have a choice. And then there was Antonio. I couldn't deny that I was falling in love with him. I did want him, but a part of me was drawn to Orion. Something I couldn't explain.

"He is marrying my cousin," I replied softly.

"That wasn't my question, Seren. Do you want Orion? Be honest, because if you do, I will walk away right now, no questions asked."

I rushed to his side, wrapping my arms around him. "No, Antonio, that isn't what I want. He isn't what I want. I want you. I do. I want you," I cried.

His gaze finally met mine. He exhaled and I could feel his whole body shiver with relief. "What was that then, beautiful? Why was he here?"

"He came to ask where my placement was. One minute I was telling him to leave, and the next thing I know, his face was shoved against mine."

"It didn't seem like you minded very much."

"Tony, please. I don't know what that was, but I do know I want you. I am falling for you. He and I will never be, but this... you and I... it's real. I want this. I want you."

I felt his hands on my face as I sobbed, afraid of ruining something that brought me so much joy. "Okay," he whispered, kissing me on my head.

"I'm sorry. I'm so sorry."

"I know. But from now on, if he ever kisses you again, you tell me immediately. And I don't feel comfortable with him training you anymore. I know he is talented and revered for his experience but after this—"

"Deal," I said, not letting him finish. "Whatever will make you more comfortable I will happily do."

Tony smiled softly at me, taking another deep breath. "Go get in the shower. We're going to be late," he said, pulling away, heading for my balcony.

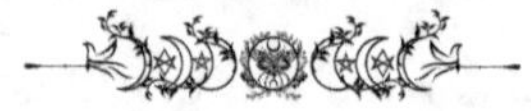

My hair was still wet from the shower as we entered one of the debriefing rooms. I looked around, noting I was surrounded by people I already knew. Seemed like nonna kept all our friends and acquaintances together. Though, I wasn't sure if that was a good or bad thing. Surely not all of us would be surviving this.

I sat by Frankie while Tony took the seat next to me. I made sure to keep my face unfeeling and faced forward, trying to focus on the mission at hand. Frankie nudged me, leaning in so only I could hear.

"What is going on?" she asked. "Your aura is crazy."

"I'll tell you later," I whispered.

"Over drinks. Just you and me," she winked as nonna cleared her throat to begin.

That morning was a crash course in all things Obsidian. We learned that the coven had somehow made a deal with demons. In return for power, the witches would freely give themselves as hosts so the demonic beings could once again walk the earth. Two consciousnesses sharing one host. Though, we didn't know what their shared goal was. This was our mission. To discover what the dark coven was really after and why.

Obsidian had tried for centuries to harness the power of Hell but failed time and time again. What made this time different? What had changed? Nonna educated us on the earliest accounts of the dark coven. No one knew when they began or who broke away first from the original seven, but they had never obtained enough power to become a real threat. Not until now. As always like in history, they wanted more power, more control.

After three hours of information being poured down our throats, nonna finally released us. My head was swimming, and my stomach was growling. Antonio followed me out of the room just as Orion stepped in front of me.

"See you in the ring, little dove," he said, ignoring Tony behind me. I froze, unsure of what to do or say.

"Not anymore, Camerino," intervened Tony, stepping in front of me. "She will be training with me from now on since you seem to have a problem keeping your hands off what's mine."

Orion's face tensed with rage while Tony remained calm and collected. "Our training order came from Elder Salvo directly," rebutted Orion.

"Seren is a big girl," replied Tony. "She can decide who she trains with from now on."

"There you are," said Frankie, rushing to my side, interlocking her arm through mine. "Time for breakfast!" she paused looking between the two men while they remained glaring at one another. "Just us girls, boys." She pulled me out the door before they had a chance to protest.

"Thank you," I exhaled, as we took off as fast as we could down the hall.

"Hey, what is family for? Though, you have a lot of explaining to do missy. I am beyond intrigued as to what that little masculine display of possessiveness was back there."

We made our way out of the castle and into town. After we settled into a small little café and ordered a pitcher of mimosas and a few espresso shots I sat back and exhaled. Frankie leaned forward, resting her head on her hand while her foot twitched back and forth with anticipation.

"So..." she said, bringing her espresso to her lips.

"Please don't be mad at me," I blurted, putting my hands over my face.

"Hey, hey," she said reaching across the table to remove my hands. "There's nothing you could ever do that wouldn't make me not love you. No matter what, we're family first. That's all that matters. Now spill."

"Orion kissed me this morning," I blurted, needing to be rid of this secret.

Frankie choked on her espresso as she coughed to clear her windpipe. "Excuse me?"

"I wasn't expecting it, nor did I ask for it. And to make matters worse, Tony walked in on it happening and clocked Orion in the face."

"Oh, my Aradia," she gasped. "I need to start randomly showing up to your room it seems. No telling what I would be walking in on."

"It's not funny. I don't know what Orion was thinking. I have explained to him multiple times now that nothing is ever going to happen bet—"

"Wait," Frankie, interrupted, pausing to process the words that had just escaped my mouth. "You mean, he has propositioned you before this?"

My eyes dropped to the flute glass in my hand. "Please don't be mad at me."

"I'm not, I promise. I'm just... shocked is all. He hasn't shown any interest in anyone since I was named the other vessel. He broke up with Delphine that same day in fact. Probably the reason why she hates me."

"God, Frankie. I am so sorry about all of this. I don't know what I did to make him think this was okay."

"It's not your fault, Seren. And I am not mad, really. Just surprised is all. You know Orion and my situation. There just... there just isn't anything between us. Not like that at least. Even if there was something that developed between the two of you, I wouldn't be mad. I have Joe, remember."

"Oh, like that's even a possibility. I am sure as soon as the ceremony takes place you and Orion won't be able to keep your hands off each other. I've read up plenty on the god and goddess to know that nothing and no one is going to stand in the way of your all's passion."

"Yes, you've read accounts from hundreds of years ago. We don't know what is going to happen and if things are going to change. But, if they don't, would it be fair to deprive him of having a relationship? A real love just because he was randomly chosen by some cosmic destiny?"

I froze, thinking through her reasoning. My heart broke for Orion in that moment. The thought of never knowing love. I had just found it and already knew I never wanted to go without it again.

"And I would never do that to you," she continued. "Deprive you of the happiness your heart craves."

I just stared at her, not knowing what to say.

"Is that something you want? Is Orion who you truly desire?" she asked.

I opened my mouth but struggled to find the words. "There's... there's something there between us, I can't deny that, but I've fallen for Antonio."

"So, Antonio is who you want... you're certain?" she asked.

"Yes," I whispered, feeling my heart strain.

"Then it's settled," she said as our food arrived. "Now, onto more exciting topics, like that little question you asked me about the other day regarding a specific male body part."

I blushed, finishing off my glass. "Do you really think this is the right time to be discussing that?" I asked. "After everything that has happened?"

"Oh, any form of makeup sex is amazing. Just you wait." We both laughed while we ate breakfast together under the cool October breeze.

After breakfast I met Loriana in the gym and trained with Adrianna on the mat. Orion was nowhere to be found. After dinner, I went to the kitchen. The staff was finishing up with their cleaning. I found empty counterspace and began to collect the ingredients I needed. Flour, sugar, baking powder, vanilla, chocolate coco powder. All the ingredients to make Antonio's favorite dessert, a chocolate fudge mousse cake.

I opened the fridge to gather the heavy whipping cream and eggs when my attention snagged on the bowl of fresh lemons in the middle shelf. Orion.... His favorite dessert was lemon tarts. I pushed the thought far from my mind and began baking.

Once the cake was cool and the mousse was set, I assembled the layers and headed to Tony's room. I knocked this time, holding the cake nervously. We hadn't spoken since this morning, and I didn't know where his head was now that he had time to ponder over what he had seen.

The door opened, revealing a topless Tony in black cotton pajama pants. He looked at me with surprise, his hair tousled as he held a book in one hand.

"It's almost midnight," he pointed out. "And what are you doing with a cake?"

"I... I made it for you. As an apology present," I admitted.

He looked down at me, finally allowing a small smile to spread across his chiseled face before stepping aside to let me enter. I placed the cake on his small round table on the other side of the room, standing there, unsure of what would happen next. He walked over to me slowly, tossing the book on a dresser.

"You made me a cake? At 11:30 at night?" he asked.

"Yes."

"So, every time you need to apologize, I can expect some type of baked item?"

"Probably."

He stopped in front of me, sliding his hands around my waist, pulling me in closely. "Well then, I hope you need to apologize often because that cake looks almost as delicious as you do."

I let out a laugh of relief. "I'm so happy to hear you say that. I've been worried all day."

"I asked you what I needed to know, and you answered. All I need is for you to be honest with me. I trust you, beautiful," he said, leaning down to kiss me.

"And I meant what I said. I do want you, Tony." I pushed up on my tiptoes, taking his mouth with mine more forcefully this time.

"Good, because I only want you. And lucky for us practices and meetings have been canceled for tomorrow."

I pulled away. "What? Why?"

He laughed. "Well, according to my sources, Elder Salvo has a soft spot for her youngest granddaughter and tomorrow just happens to be a very special day for that granddaughter."

"Oh... right," I said, remembering my birthday.

"21 years old. No longer a child."

I hit him on the arm playfully. "And when did you ever look at me as a child? And if you did... well, you are very disturbed."

He swept me up in his arms, carrying me to his oversized bed, laying me softly in the middle of his black silk sheets. He laid down next to me, brushing his fingers down the side of my face. I smiled up at him, happy to know everything was okay between us.

His fingers trailed down my chest and abdomen. His fingers slid across the top of my pant line before he undid the button. I stopped him from proceeding. His eyes narrowed on me with confusion.

"I thought we'd start the celebrating a few minutes early," he said, bending down to kiss me.

"I would be up for that, but there's something I'd like to do first."

"And what is that?"

I pushed him against the bed, setting myself on top of him. I began kissing and caressing his body. His hands trailed down the length of my waist, cupping my bottom as I moved grinded my hips, feeling him already hardening. I continued to trail my lips down his throat, to his defined chest and mounds of abs.

Once I got to the spandex of his pants, I stopped, allowing my tongue to glid across the border, teasing the soft skin I had yet to explore. Slowly, I hooked my fingers on either side of the waistline pulling the fabric down away from his hips. He stopped me, sitting up before he pulled me against him.

"What?" I said in a confused tone. "Was I doing something wrong?"

He kissed me tenderly, pressing his head against mine. "I'm not expecting anything. You don't have to do that because... because of this morning. I told you, we're okay. You can stop."

I pulled away, looking into his eyes. "Do you not... do you not want me to do... that to you?"

He chuckled softly. "Beautiful, I can't tell you how many times I've imagined those innocent, full, and delicious lips wrapped around my cock. Mm, and how that tongue would feel, sliding up and down me."

I blushed, looking down at my idle hands, trying to hide my smile, but he forced my face back up to his. "But, as I told you in the beginning, we move at your pace. I don't want anything we ever do to be rushed or for it to be forced."

I nodded, pushing him back down on the bed before kissing him. "I want this, Antonio. I want you," I said, sliding my hand underneath his pants. I wrapped my hand around his cock causing him to hiss. He threw his head back into the pillow. The skin was so smooth and silky.

I moved my hand up and down, watching him while he closed his eyes and breathed in deeper with every stroke. I began to kiss down his abdomen again, only removing my hands from him to slide the fabric away from his legs. His hardness sprang free. I curiously examined him trying not to make it too obvious.

I worked him again with my hand, exploring his legs and his balls with my fingers. He began to moan while he slid his hands over his face. Then, I slid my tongue around the tip of him, tasting and exploring the area for the first time. I placed the tip inside of my mouth and sucked gently, allowing my tongue to do circular motions around his head.

"Fuck," he groaned. I continued to pump him. I took a breath and allowed him to enter my mouth fully. I held onto the base, moving my head up and down while his hips pressed towards me, begging me to go deeper. I relaxed, taking as much as I could. I continued at a steady pace. I made sure to trail my tongue along the long vein that extended down the bottom of his penis, circling to the top as I sucked and pumped him.

His breathing was unsteady. He buried his hand in my hair. I quickened my pace, feeling the need in him grow. His body lit up with small gooseflesh as the moans spilled from his mouth. I felt him gently try to press me away, but I didn't allow him to move me from where I was.

"Seren, I'm going to cum," he whispered in between breaths. I felt his hand try to remove my mouth, but I remained firm, wanting to finish what I had started. His hips arched. I felt his penis throb inside of my mouth. Warmth released. He roared loudly, his body flexing and tensing from the action. I stilled, slowing my strokes like I was instructed to do, until he collapsed from pleasure.

I pulled away, wiping my mouth with the back of my hand. He was sated, breathing heavily, laying against the bed. I smiled, proud that I had been the one to do that to him. As powerful of a witch I had become, this was a different type of power all together. The power to make a man fall to his knees before you. To make him helpless and vulnerable. To take his strength and power with our sexuality. This was our true magic.

I laid next to him, circling my fingers along the rows of muscles on his chest. "I'm waiting for my review," I whispered, watching his chest rise and fall. He turned his head, mouth slightly parted from his rigorous breathing.

"I'm beginning to doubt that was your first time doing that," he finally said.

I laughed. "Not too bad then?"

He rolled over, laying his beautiful naked body on top of mine. I went still, unsure of what would happen next. "You were amazing," he whispered, sliding his hands under my shirt.

He tugged the fabric away from my body before pulling my pants away from my legs, leaving me in my underwear and bra.

My breath caught as nerves began to stir inside of me. I closed my eyes and bit the bottom of my lip, trying to calm myself. I felt him pause, removing himself from me completely. When I opened my eyes, he stood at the edge of the bed, pulling his pants back on.

"I'm only going to do what we've already done," he said, crawling back on top of me. "If I have your blessing." I nodded, laying back allowing his fingers to graze my skin. "I do have a request."

"And what might that be?"

"I want to see you... all of you."

I trembled a bit at the thought of being completely exposed to someone, but I nodded, wanting to share myself with him. I had thought long and hard about these moments. About what I wanted to share... to give to Tony. The truth was, I loved him. I wanted to give myself to him. I had made peace with my decision regardless of my upbringing.

I sat up, reaching behind me to unhook my bra. The straps fell slowly, as I tossed the fabric to the floor. I laid back down, watching while his eyes devoured me.

He leaned down, kissing me softly on my lips allowing his hands to trail across my bare skin. He pulled back, sliding my lace underwear from my body, leave me completely exposed. He sat up on his knees and just stared. I didn't know what to do with my hands. Should I cover up or... or just lay there?

His chest began to rise and fall more heavily. "I will wait as long as it takes to have you, Seren, but just know... I have never wanted something more in my life than I want you in this very moment." Without another word, he slid his hands up my legs, parting them before placing his mouth right where he knew I liked it. I gasped with pleasure at the first swipe of his tongue, allowing myself to relax around him as he licked and sucked me to orgasm, not once, not twice, but three times that night. My favorite birthday yet.

CHAPTER TWENTY-ONE

"Good morning, birthday girl," I heard a deep voice say. I forced myself to open my eyes. I stretched, feeling the soft material of his shirt slid against my skin.

"Can't I just sleep for a few more hours?" I whined, pulling the pillow into me.

"I suppose your presents can wait," said Tony.

My eyes popped open. "Presents?"

He laughed, leaning over me from the side of the bed. He pressed a firm kiss to my lips. "Happy birthday, beautiful."

"Thank you." I sat up, seeing the room completely littered in candles. There were even some suspended in the air above us. The table was filled with breakfast foods. Champagne sat in an ice bucket off to the side and three presents were stacked at the end of the bed. "You did all of this when I was sleeping?"

"Well, you were out pretty hard. Snoring away and all," he said, taking me by the hand as he helped me out of bed.

"I snore?"

"You couldn't hear yourself?"

"Oh, gosh. I am so sorry. I'll figure something out."

He chuckled. "Don't worry about it. I'm a pretty heavy sleeper myself. Now, come and sit. Time for presents."

He placed the first one on my lap. I unfolded the wrapping eager to see what was inside. I pulled out a beautiful black leather-bound book with my name carved into the front along with my coven's crest. I flipped through the blank pages, smelling the fresh sent of new paper and leather.

"It's beautiful."

"I figured it was about time you had your own grimoire to start documenting all the wonderful things you're going to do with your powers."

I bent over and kissed him before he slid a smaller box onto my lap. It was a beautiful diamond necklace with matching earrings. The third present was an envelope. I opened it slowly, unsure of what was hiding inside.

I pulled out an itinerary for New York. It was labeled for the day after Christmas. I looked up at him with excitement as I read through the list of things we would do and see while we were there.

"You're taking me to New York?" I asked. "Just us?"

"If that's alright with you."

I nodded, unable to stop smiling.

"There's nothing like New Years in Time Square."

"Tony this is all... this is all too much," I said, my eyes filling with tears of joy.

He pulled me to the floor and onto his lap, wrapping his arms around me. "Are you happy?" he whispered, pressing his forehead against mine.

I nodded. "More than happy."

"Then I've done my job."

I pressed my lips against him so hard that he tumbled back against the floor. God, I wanted him. I wanted all of him, right here and right now. My hands slid down his hard body, our kiss deepening, causing me to lose control of myself. Before I could slide his pants off his hips a knock came at the door twice before it flew open. We scrambled upright as Frankie barged in, hand over her eyes.

"Yoohoo," said Frankie. "It's just me. Your dear old cousin, here to steal you away for your birthday."

"Dammit Frankie," Tony muttered, sliding a shirt on.

Frankie peeked between her fingers, noting the coast was clear before she dropped her hand to her side. "Now, now," she said, "no need for hostility. You need to learn to share. She was my cousin first." I couldn't help but laugh. She rushed forward, wrapping me up in her arms. "Happy birthday, sister."

"Thank you," I replied, feeling genuinely happy.

Frankie took my hand, and lead me towards the door. "Shower and be ready in thirty," instructed Frankie. "We have big plans for today."

"Like what?" I asked.

"You'll just have to wait and see," she replied with a smile and a scrunched nose. "Sorry about the blue balls, Tony."

"Yeah, thanks for that," he replied, running a hand through his hair. I broke from Frankie, rushing into his arms, pressing a kiss to his lips. I pulled back, admiring the smile that formed.

"This morning was more than I could have asked for," I whispered so only he could hear. "Thank you. For everything."

"You're very welcome, beautiful. Now, go have fun with you cousin and I'll see you tonight." He pressed a kiss to my head before I returned to Frankie.

Frankie went all out. Bella, Gabby, Loriana, and Adrianna joined us as we took the Étoile's jet to the Amalfi Coast. From there, we boarded a private yacht and took off across the beautiful sea. We danced, drank, sunbathed, and swam the day away.

For a moment, I wasn't a witch. I wasn't in the middle of a war or worrying about my training. I was just a 21-year-old girl celebrating her birthday with her closest friends. I had a man who I adored waiting for me back at home who couldn't have been more perfect if he tried. How could life get any better?

When we returned around 6 that evening, I rushed to my room to shower and ready myself for dinner. Frankie said that nonna had prepared something special for just our family. I ran through the shower, allowing my hair to remain wavey and loose. I slipped on a deep wine-colored silk dress and applied minimal makeup. I put on the jewelry Tony had bought for me before I walked over to my dresser.

I looked at the pictures of my mother that remained unmoved. I slid my fingers across her face wishing this day could be spent with her. As I turned to head to the door, my attention caught on a small yellow box at the edge of the dresser. I picked it up slowly, already knowing who it was from.

I held my breath, opening the top tenderly. As soon as the lid was removed a beam of light shot out from inside, revealing images of a moon and a sun, orbiting one another. A beautiful melody accompanied the images. An array of doves, starting small as seeds, began to grow before they flew around the image. I couldn't help but smile while watching the beautiful display.

A few moments passed before the images faded. I returned my attention back to the box. Inside, contained a breathtaking golden bracelet. A waxing crescent moon, a full moon, and a waning crescent moon sat at the center of the dainty chain. An extraordinary opal stone was set in the middle of the full moon. I picked it up, completely in awe of the craftsmanship. I placed it on my wrist, sliding my fingers across the smooth stone.

A knock came at my door. My heart skipped a beat, wondering if it was the person whose gift I had just opened. The door cracked slowly. Tony's head peaked inside. I took a deep breath and relaxed. He stepped inside, scanning me from head to toe. I gave him a little twirl, feeling silly for doing so.

"I mean," he said, rubbing his chin with his hand. "Just... wow."

I laughed, walking over to him, wanting to feel his lips against mine. "Thank you, I think."

He picked me up, twirling me around as he buried his head in my neck. "Would you protest to us skipping dinner and just staying here, in your bed?"

I pulled away, looking astonished. "Wait," I said. "You mean nonna actually invited you to the family birthday dinner?"

He shrugged. "Guess I'm wearing her down. I mean, can you blame her though? Look at me," he said, splaying his arms to the side in a sarcastic way.

I hit him before moving towards the door. "Arrogant warlock."

He caught up to my side. "So, I'm guessing that's a no to the whole bed suggestion."

"Nonna supposedly worked very hard on this night. I don't want to disappoint her. But there's always after," I smiled up at him. He pulled me into his side.

"After it is, beautiful."

We made our way up to the top of the castle where everyone else was waiting. Nonna, Aunt Thora, Frankie, and Orion.

"Happy Birthday!" they all shouted at once. Fireworks erupted in the sky for miles. I looked up and watched in awe. Laughter filled the air. My loved ones surrounding me. Nonna and Aunt Thora hugged me, kissing me on my head. Frankie tackled me, smacking a kiss on my cheek. Orion was the last to approach. He walked over slowly, with a small and unsure smile.

Tony was off to the side, talking with Aunt Thora while the fireworks continued. "I can leave, if that is what you want," Orion said.

"No," I replied, a little too fast for my own likely. "You can stay. We're going to be family after all."

He huffed, shaking his head. "Happy birthday, little dove."

I touched the bracelet gently, never allowing my eyes to leave his. "Thank you for my gift. It was absolutely breathtaking."

He leaned down, keeping his hands buried in his pockets. "And so are you," he whispered, before returning to Frankie.

Nonna clapped, gathering our attention. We gathered in a circle. "Come, come. Off to dinner we all go," demanded nonna. "Hold hands, that's it."

I looked at Frankie with questioning eyes. She shrugged

"Close your eyes now," nonna demanded.

The air began to thin as the wind whipped and lashed around us. Our circle felt like it was spinning. My stomach flipped and turned forcing me to tighten my grip on Frankie and Tony's hands, but I didn't let go. In one breath, we were on the roof, wind lashing around us and in the next a massive force slammed into me before the air returned and the wind steadied.

I stumbled back, heading for the ground, but Tony caught me before I made contact. I opened my eyes, greeted by a beautiful, tropical scenery. Birds of extraordinary colors and sizes flew overhead throughout a thick and luscious canopy of leaves and branches.

We were in the middle of a rainforest. A path was cleared, lined by balls of firelight, leading towards a beautiful pool, fed by a small waterfall, reaching at least twenty feet high. A round table was set, filled with bright and vibrant floral centerpieces, tall candle sticks, and gold place settings. Small diamonds and crystals twirled above the table, creating a beautiful ambience.

I looked back at my nonna and aunt. "You two did this... for me?" I asked, trying to hold back my tears of joy.

Nonna stepped up next to me, wrapping her arm around my shoulder. "This is the first time in two decades that our family has been complete," she said, with a small tear falling from her eye. "And it's because the goddess has brought you back to us. Back to your familia."

I hugged her as my aunt joined in. "We love you, sweetheart," whispered Aunt Thora.

"Awe, hell. Make room for one more," cried Frankie, joining in.

Nonna pulled back, looking at the three of us. "This is where our power comes from," she said. "Right here. The four of us. Our family. Our blood ties. If we are united, nothing stands a chance." She paused, rubbing Frankie's and my faces. "I am so proud of each of you. You are truly a testament to our family's name. Our ancestors have blessed the Salvo women once again."

"Thank you, nonna," we both replied.

Nonna turned to Aunt Thora. "And you, my dearest daughter," she whispered. "I couldn't have wished for a stronger daughter or a better leader to become the next matriarch of this family. You will surpass me in all things, I am sure of it."

"Thank you, mama," Thora said, hugging her tenderly.

"Well," nonna said, wiping her face and straightening her clothing. "Now that the wretched emotional part of the night is over, I'm ready to eat and drink. What do the rest of you say?"

We agreed, laughing with one another, arm in arm as we walked back to the boys.

"Four beautiful and strong Salvo women," commented Tony.

"Stop the flattering, Antonio," said nonna. "I invited you here, didn't I? Enough with the brown nosing."

Frankie and I started laughing as I wrapped my arm around Tony's. He just shrugged, making our way to the table. Once we were all seated, nonna waved her hand, magically making the first course appear. The rest of the night we spent eating, drinking, and laughing amongst the tropical trees of the rainforest, surrounded by the people I love the most.

Chapter Twenty-Two

The next day, briefings and training continued. The team selected to travel to the America's were sent on their way. We waited, unsure of when and where Obsidian would attack next. The anticipation was killing me.

During my training with Adrianna and Roric, nonna came and retrieved me without any explanation. I followed her farther under the castle into a dungeon area I had yet to explore. She stopped at a door with hesitation. She looked back at me, holding a pad of paper and pen.

Nonna took a deep breath. "Frankie is—" she said, unable to finish. She grunted. "You are—" Another exasperated groan. "Orion and— ah!" she screamed. A surge of energy rippled from her slamming into the wall of weapons and tools behind me, sending them rattling to the ground.

"What's going on, nonna? Are you feeling, okay?" I asked, concerned with her odd behavior.

"Fine, bambina, just fine," she replied, clicking the pen against her lips. She stopped, looking at the pen and paper for a moment before she began to write something down. She ripped the paper and handed it to me. I looked down at the paper I had just seen her write something on.

It was blank.

"What?" I asked.

"Do you see?" she asked. I handed her the empty paper. She yelled again, crumbling it up and throwing it to the floor. The ball instantly lit on fire, turning into ash a moment later. "Come," she said, pushing open the door to a dark room.

I followed her, not sure of what in the heck was going on. She flipped the light switch on. The sounds of rattling chains and screams filled the air. I took a step back, looking at a wall of re-trained Obsidian witches. There were six of them.

They were even more hideous than the one we saw in the video and photos. Their skin was peeling away from their muscles. Their teeth were yellow, broken, and jagged. Bile slid from their mouths. Open sores and wounds littered their exposed flesh. Their eye sockets sagged. It was as if they were decomposing right in front of our eyes.

"Hideous, aren't they?" noted nonna, walking over to a table of weapons.

"Speak for yourself, elder," spat one of them, laughing and shaking against the wall.

"Oh, brought us a little witch, have you?" said another.

"Pretty little thing."

"Powerful too."

"Enough!" yelled nonna, throwing her hand forward casting a silencing spell. They thrashed and shook against their chains, moving their mouths but nothing came out.

"What is going on?" I asked.

"This is your lesson for today," replied nonna. "I'm assuming you've never killed anything?"

My heart dropped, completely unprepared for this task. "That is correct."

"I figured you should probably get your hands dirty before you're sent on an actual mission. Killing isn't for the faint of heart. Now, you will be killing them in three different ways. The first, with your power; second with a firearm; and third up close with a knife. Any questions?"

I paused for a moment, processing through what she was asking me to do. Finally, I shook my head in response.

"Good. You remember how to kill them?"

"Removal of head or piercing the heart."

"Excellent. Off you go," she said, folding her hands behind her and taking a step back. I walked to the other side of the table looking at the first Obsidian witch.

I grounded myself, calling on my power as I sent a tendril of darkness towards the witch. It moved slow, as I focused my control. It snaked around its neck, wrapping twice. I held out my hand, tightening my fist until the black fog severed the head of the witch.

I watched the head fall to the ground with a thud, rolling a few inches forward. Though they no longer looked human, they were once just like me. I took a deep breath, trying not to focus on the blood or the stench. I closed my eyes, turning my head away.

I felt cold fingers yank my chin forward with force. "Look at it," nonna demanded. I opened my eyes, doing as she instructed. Nonna strapped a knife belt to my waist and then placed a Glock 19 in my hand. "How many rounds does this weapon hold?"

"15 bullets," I replied, still staring at my first kill.

"Correct. Three in the head and then two in the heart. Begin," she said, stepping back towards the door.

I loaded the weapon, taking my stance and aimed. *Bam, Bam, Bam.* Three in the head. I moved the weapon lower. *Bam, Bam.* Two in the heart. The creature stopped moving. I lowered the weapon, looking back at nonna for my next set of instructions.

"Good, now take a deep breath," she said, nodding slowly. She raised her hands and twisting her wrists. I heard the chains rattle and fall from the witches. My attention snapped back to the wall of demons. They were free. Their sounds returned as they shook like dogs, snapping their joints and necks from side to side.

I took a step back, unsure of what was happening. Two of them leaped onto the walls, crawling up the vertical surfaces as if they were spiders. Another darted to the side and the remaining warlock tilted his head, staring at me, smiling with his bloody gums. He snapped his fingers, and the lights went out. Only the red glow of the exit sign remained.

My heart pounded out of my chest as I tried to steady myself. I squinted my eyes, begging my vision to adjust. I held the gun up, trying to quiet the rushing blood that pounded through my skull. *Thump, thump, thump.* I heard to my left. I swung my gun towards the sound. *Thump, thump, thump, boom.* Came from behind me, I swung as fast as I could.

My breaths were unsteady. I began to well my magic inside of me before whispering the word, "*luxire.*" A ball of light appeared over my head, just as one of the creatures came flying off the wall, teeth bared and claws out. It made a high-pitched screaming noise before that was made my blood chill. It slammed into me, forcing me to the ground. The gun went flying across the floor. I held its oozing, rotting neck in my hands as it lashed, snapping its teeth in my face.

Its claws scratched into my sides, cutting through skin. I let out a small cry of pain. I heard another one land somewhere near me, along with the footsteps of the third. Panicked, I reached down to my belt, pulling a small knife from its sheath as I reeled my arm back and slammed the blade into its head over and over again. Blood squirted from the gashes, but I continued to stab, screaming in rage until the thing fell, lifeless on top of me.

I flipped it over, shoving the knife into its heart just as another one jumped onto my back, sinking its teeth into my shoulder. I pulled another dagger from my belt, shoving the blade into the creatures eyeball, forcing it to release me. I turned around, readying to deal another death blow into its heart when I heard chanting coming from behind me.

My body froze no longer heeding to my command. An icy feeling spread throughout my veins, making it impossible to move. I angled my eyes down, watching as the blood in my veins turned black, spreading throughout my body like a virus. The three remaining creatures were chanting, holding their hands towards me as I began to levitate off the ground.

I fought to regain control but couldn't seem to muster a single ounce. I looked to where nonna had been, but she was gone. She left me…. I was on my own.

I could feel the icy pricks of death reaching towards my heart. If I didn't do something, I would be dead in a matter of seconds. Tears of pain… of fear, ran down my face. This wasn't how I ended. Not after everything I had endured. Not after I had finally found a life worth living.

I closed my eyes, thinking of my family. Thinking of Tony. Even Orion. I felt a passion inside of me come to life as rage and anger took over. I remembered the pictures of all those innocent children. Their poor bodies mutilated. These things were responsible. They deserved death. They would die.

In an instance, I felt a pure, burning fire light within me, unable to remain contained. I relaxed, allowing it to grow until I couldn't hold it any longer. My body tensed and extended outward. A powerful white light exploded from inside of me. The force threw the creatures back, freeing me from their magic. As soon as I hit the floor, I called the gun to me, sending three bullets into one of their heads.

The fourth one charged me faster than I could aim the gun. I took the remaining dagger left on my belt, slamming the tip into its heart before putting two bullets into its skull. The last one remained calm, standing by the wall, watching me with something like curiosity.

I walked over to it, still hearing the blood dripping off the edge of the dagger I held. It looked me up and down before smiling. "You are exactly as we hoped," he said in a deep and demonic voice.

"And who, exactly, is *we*?" I asked, standing before the creature without fear.

"You will soon meet us. You're in for a treat, I can promise you that."

"You must have me confused for someone else."

"No, little one. We know exactly who you are, and we like. We like very much," it said, licking its lips in a slow and vulgar manner.

"Well, I can promise you one thing," I said, smiling at the thing. "*You* won't be meeting anyone." *Bam, bam.* Two bullets in the head. Then, I emptied the rest of the clip into its heart. I dropped the gun. My hands were trembling from the shock. I took a moment, gathering myself. I looked down at my hands. I was covered in blood. Without another thought, I left the room in pursuit of my dear nonna.

I walked through the halls, feeling the deepest sense of betrayal I had ever endured. Sister Odette's offenses were nothing compared to this. Nonna had left me to die. She released those things on me and just left me there.

The people I passed, stopped, staring and gasping, but I didn't care. Let them see. Maybe they would start asking questions. I walked towards nonna's quarters, not caring who saw. Frankie was in the hall, talking with Gabby. She saw me and did a double take, her mouth falling to the floor.

"Oh my, Aradia! Seren, are you okay?" she asked, but I didn't answer.

I continued forward until I go to nonna's double doors. Without knocking I pushed them open, revealing her and Aunt Thora sitting at her table. Nonna was in tears, holding her head in her hands. Aunt Thora was by her side, consoling her. Frankie followed me in, closing the doors. Nonna and Thora's attention turned towards me.

"Oh, thank you, moon goddess. Thank you," nonna cried, standing from her chair.

Aunt Thora rose, laughing in relief as she wiped the tears from her eyes. "I told you, mama. I told you she would survive."

"What in the hell was that?" I yelled. I walked over to my nonna, standing face to face with her as the blood continued to drip off my skin to the floor. "Why would you do that? Why leave me there to die? Were you trying to kill me?"

"No bambina," she cried, reaching for me, but I recoiled away from her. "Of course not. It was a test you needed to pass. You needed to do this on your own or you would have been as good as dead in the field."

"So, you lock me in a room with four Obsidian demons and just left?" I yelled.

"You did what?" interjected Frankie, now standing at my side.

"What if I hadn't survived?" I continued. "How long where you going to give me until you found my dead body in that room?"

"I knew you would survive," said Nonna, taking a step towards me. "You are a survivor. It's in your blood."

"Seren," interrupted my aunt, "please try to understand. Nonna was only doing what was best for you. What you needed. In the field, they wouldn't have been chained."

"No," I replied. "But I would have had backup. I would have had my team."

"And what happens when they are all dead?" nonna said, no longer crying. Her stern demeanor returning. "What happens when they all sacrifice their lives to save you and you are the only one left standing? What will you do then, Seren?"

"That's not going to happen," I snapped back.

"It might. Then what?" She paused, her bottom lip quivering. "I hate that I had to leave you in that room to kill those demonic things, but it was the only way to test you. To see if what you have learned these past months is enough to keep you alive. Those creatures weren't even at full strength."

I stopped, looking at her with confusion. "What?" I asked.

"I fed them an elixir that took their power down by half. They haven't been fed or seen daylight in weeks. They were weakened to give you a fighting chance. When you are in the field, they will be at full strength. There will be stronger ones then those four, I can promise you that."

I froze, not knowing what else to say. Nonna came over to me, taking my face in her hands.

"Bambina, I love you and wouldn't think twice if it came to your life or mine. Everything I do is for you and this family." She looked at me with love in her eyes. "If I didn't think you could survive, I would have never left you in that room alone. I promise you that." Nonna pulled me into a hug. I stood there, unable to comprehend what had just happened.

Aunt Thora and Frankie left the room. Nonna pulled away from me and kissed my dirty cheek. "I thought you left me to die," I whispered, still in shock.

"I would never."

I began to sob as I fell to my knees, my nerves finally getting the best of me. She held me, while my emotions to took over. I felt her hands running over my hair in a comforting manner. She pulled away, wiping my dirty face with her hand.

"I was so scared," I admitted.

"And that is completely normal," she assured me. "Those things are not of this world. They are pure evil, created my Lucifer himself, but you rose to the occasion, and you overcame them. I am so proud of you." She pulled me to my feet, returning to her desk in the corner. She picked up a book and walked back, holding it our towards me.

I took the book. It was bound in brown leather and looked ancient. "What is this?"

"Some more homework I need you to read." I nodded, turning towards the door. She reached out, taking my arm in her hand. "It is important that you read that book, bambina."

"Yes, nonna."

Her face softened. "I love you so much, Seren. You will never know just how much."

I forced a smile, feeling the exhaustion of the trauma settling into my bones. "I love you too, nonna."

I returned to my room, placing the book down on my nightstand. I peeled the blood-soaked clothes from my body. I stood in the shower for what felt like forever, allowing the blood to burn off my skin. My sides and shoulder were killing me from the wounds. I put on an oversized t-shirt and crawled into bed.

I tried to force the images of those demonic witches from my head, but I couldn't. The way their skin pulled away from their bones. The sounds each of them made. The cracking noises of their joints as they bent and moved in such an animalistic way.

How was I ever going to get used to this? To killing? It didn't matter. I needed to find a way, or I would die.

Chapter Twenty-Three

I felt a light caress along my cheek causing my skin rise in responses. The touch trailed down my neck towards my chest but stopped as it neared my shoulder wound. "Seren," I heard a deep voice say. "Seren, wake up now."

I opened my eyes to see Tony leaning over me, pulling back the edge of the blood-soaked t-shirt. Oh yeah; I had forgotten to bandage my wounds. He pulled back the covers, revealing trails of blood along my sides, now staining my sheets.

"What in the hell happened?" he said, standing over me, whipping out his phone and beginning to dial.

"Tony, I'm fine. Really. I just forgot to bandage myself."

"That," he said, pointing to my shoulder, "is not fine. Hey, Celeste, are you at Salvo Castle? You are? Great. Can you please come to Seren De Salvo's room immediately. Yes, it's an emergency. Fantastic, thanks so much."

"Tony, there's no need. I will heal, it's not even that—" I pulled my shirt back, revealing the chunk of bloodied flesh hanging off the side. "Oh," I said, all the sudden feeling lightheaded.

"You were saying? Now, tell me what in the hell happened before I start killing people."

I exhaled, swinging my legs off the side of the bed. My body protested in pain. "Nonna took me down to the dungeons today. When we got there, she had six Obsidian witches chained to a wall. She wanted me to experience killing before I went out into the field so I wouldn't freeze up when we were on a mission. I killed the first on with my magic and the second one with a gun.

"Before I could kill another, nonna released the rest, leaving me alone and trapped in the room with them. I had to fight my way out."

Antonio's face and demeanor went deadly still. It was as if he was another person entirely. I had never seen this side of him. "She did what?" he asked in a cold and unfeeling manner.

"She said it was to make sure I would be ready in the field. That I had to overcome this on my own. Believe me, I was livid when I got to her, but after hearing her out, regardless of how messed up the whole situation was, I believe her."

His jaw tightened. His hands straining into fists. "I am having a very hard time finding a reason not to kill your nonna at the moment."

I smiled, pulling him towards me. "Because it would hurt me. Because she's an elder. Because we need her to fight whatever is coming."

"I don't care who she is. No one puts you in that kind of unnecessary danger and just walks away."

"I know it was completely messed up, but I see her reason behind it, really. At first, I was scared. I couldn't control myself or my emotions. It was as if my body wasn't responding to my own commands. Then, once I found my center, the fear dissipated. All my training, physical and magical, came into play. In the end, I felt strong."

He sat down next to me. I could still feel the rage rolling off him. "You took on four demon possessed Obsidian witches on your own?"

"Well, their powers were dampened, but... yeah, they're all dead." I smiled with pride.

He huffed. "You never cease to amaze me, beautiful. But I hate this."

"I know, but I'm okay. And now I know what I am actually up against. What I've been training all these months for. I know what I have to do. What I have to become."

I watched his eyes trail to my side table, landing on the book nonna gave me. His brow furrowed. "What's that?" he asked.

"More homework curtesy of nonna."

"So, she tries to kill you, and in the same day she assigns you a reading lesson?"

I shrugged. "She was very adamant I read it. Who knows."

A knock came at the door. Tony left the bed to answer it. A small young woman with short blonde hair, cut to her scalp walked in.

Here eyes were as blue as the ocean, her features dainty and cute.

"Well hello there, cutie," she said to Tony, strolling into the room. "How can I be of service?"

"Hello to you too, Celest," Tony replied, pulling her in for a side hug. "This one over here needs some mending."

"Of course," she said, walking over to the bed. She noted all the blood on my sheets and then my t-shirt. "Let's have a look." She pulled up my shirt, examining my sides and then my shoulder. "Ouch. That one is going to take some time to heal, but I can help. Lay back and let's get started."

For the next forty minutes, Celest mended my sides and then worked on my shoulder. My torso had small, raised, rash marks that were tender to the touch once she was done. My shoulder would need to be worked on throughout the next few days until it healed completely. She mended the deeper layers of muscle back together, but the wound was still open on the surface and would need to remain bandaged until it was completely healed.

I thanked her before she left, moving to the bathroom to take another shower. When I finished, Tony was still waiting for me. He pulled me in close, planting a passionate kiss on my lips. I pulled away, looking up at him, knowing why he was here.

"You're leaving, aren't you?" I asked.

"Yes, but this time, it's only for business. I have to go to Japan to check on one of my father's investments. I will only be gone for two nights. Enough time for you to heal up and be ready for me when I return."

I exhaled, relieved he wouldn't be out in the world fighting those things. "Promise me you will hurry back."

"Always," he said, pulling me into him. "And promise me you won't be going anywhere alone with your nonna anymore." I laughed, pulling away from him.

"You think you're funny, don't you?"

"I am. Funny, smart, handsome, extremely rich... and a master in the bedroom," he said, laying his head on top of mine.

"Oh, is that so?"

"It is."

"And when do you think I'll get to... experience... that specific talent of yours?" I asked, feeling the blood rush to my cheeks.

He pulled back with a look of confusion on his face. "What are you saying, beautiful?"

I bit the side of my lip, thinking through what I was about to say. I had thought about this a lot the past few days. The way I felt for him. They way it was when we were together. How I wanted a future with him. He was everything and then some that I could have ever hoped for. I now understood what love was. I just hoped he felt the same.

"I'm saying I'm ready to take that next step. To take that next step with you," I whispered.

He froze. I watched as a small smile stretched across his face. It reached his eyes. "You tell me this now? When I have to catch a plane in thirty minutes?"

"I mean, obviously not right now, but when you get back."

"And how in the hell am I supposed to focus on anything when I'm away knowing this is waiting for me when I return home?"

I laughed, stretching up to kiss his cheek. "I'm sure you'll find a way. Now, off you go," I said, pushing him towards the door. He stumbled back still looking at me with a big goofy smile.

"You're sure? This isn't some kind of joke?"

"Why would I joke about that?"

"I... it's just.... You're just too good to be true, Seren," he said, walking back over to me. "Truly, I don't deserve you. I don't deserve that gift." He took a deep breath as his face fell. Something like uncertainty or guilt flashed behind his eyes.

"Is... is this not something you want?" I asked, confused.

His eyes found mine again instantly. "You are *everything* I want. Everything I never even knew I wanted. Before you.... It doesn't matter. We're here now," he said.

"Well, like I said before... hurry back."

He laughed. "Abso-fucking-lutely," he replied, kissing me passionately one more time before he left.

I crawled back into bed, obeying my bodies request for sleep. Tonight, I would heal, but tomorrow, I had work to do, and I knew who I needed to ask help from. I wasn't going to like it, but if I had any chance against Obsidian, I needed help and I needed it from the best.

The next morning, I woke, feeling the pains of my body, forcing myself out of bed. I pulled on a pair of black pants, a loose t-shirt, and my combat boots and headed towards a decision I hoped I wouldn't regret later.

I stood in front of his door, inhaling deeply before bringing my knuckles up to the barrier. I hesitated for a moment but then, I closed my eyes and knocked three times. I took a step back, waiting for the door to open.

Orion came to the door, standing in nothing but a pair of jeans, just like the first time I had met him. His hair was long and loose, still wild from sleep. Every muscle glistened from the light that poured into his room.

"Can I help you?" he asked, holding a cup of coffee.

"Yes. I came to ask you for a favor," I said, trying my darndest not to stare. God, it was an effort. Even if I was in love with Tony. I was still human. Oh, dear heaven, Orion was a sight.

"Eyes up here, little dove," he said, bending his head down to look at me. He smiled and huffed a little laugh. "What is the favor?"

"I need your help with my fire element," I admitted. "I discovered a new power yesterday, and it resembles fire. I know that fire is your coven's strength so I was hoping you could help me tame it."

"What's the new power?"

"I'm not sure, but I believe it's some sort of white flame, but… it doesn't burn…. It felt… cold."

He leaned against the doorway taking a sip of his coffee. "Really? No one else I know has a 'white, ice flame' power. What makes you so special?" he asked, sarcastically.

I stared at him, trying my best not to just say forget it and walk away. "Are you willing to help or not?"

He arched an eyebrow, looking down at his coffee. "Does your boyfriend know you're here, asking for my help?"

"No," I admitted, "but I will tell him if you agree."

"Hmm, and what's in it for me?"

I rolled my eyes, not able to take this banter any longer. "Forget it, I'll just ask someone else," I said, turning to leave. I felt his large hand wrap around my arm instantly. I smiled to myself, knowing exactly what I was doing.

"Fine," he grumbled, pulling me back to face him. "I'll help. Just let me get a shirt on." As he turned around, I noted the large black tattoo of antlers residing along most of his back. The tips of the antlers stretched all the way to his shoulders and extended down to his lower back, stopping right before his pant line. They were intricate. Delicate. Beautiful.

A memory surfaced from my time at the abbey. The night when Sister Odette had drugged me so effectively, I was paralyzed. The dark, shadowed figure in the corner of my room... watching me. But that figure didn't have antlers. No, it was a bull, then... a ram before changing into a man. And those red eyes. Something about those red eyes was so alluring and comforting. They made me feel like I was... home.

I forced my eyes away from him, reaching into my pocket and pulling out my phone. I quickly texted Tony, letting him know what I had asked of Orion. The three little dots popped up immediately in the bottom corner of our message window.

I don't like it, but I trust you. And if he so much as looks at you the wrong way, I will kill him this time. Make sure that is clear.

I smiled, texting him back, *Done.*

Orion returned with a shirt on this time and shoes. He put on his leather jacket and then exited his room. "Where are we going?" I asked.

"Out."

"Out where?"

He looked back at me while I basically had to run to catch up to him. "We're dealing with fire... wouldn't be smart to have an untrained witch light the oldest castle in town on fire, now would it?"

"First of all, I am not 'untrained'. All I have done is train since I stepped foot through these doors."

"And the second?" he asked.

I rolled my eyes, already annoyed with him. "You piss me off, you know that? More than anyone here, you are the one that gets under my skin the most and I hate it."

He laughed, heading for the front door. "Maybe add that to your—"

"Yeah, yeah, I know. Add it to my 'to look into' list. There are too many things to count. I might need you to write them down for me after all."

He huffed. "I would if I could."

"What's do you mean?"

"Never mind." He held the door open for me. I followed him to his black truck. I had to all but take a running jump to get into the damn vehicle. It was monstrously massive, just like him. I buckled, looking around at the luxurious vehicle.

"This thing is huge. How do you drive it?"

He smiled, tilting his head to the side, looking at me with mischief in his eyes. "Want to find out," he said in a low a seductive voice before winking at me.

"God, I am already regretting asking you for help."

He laughed, pushing a button as the car roared to life. "I'll let you drive it on the way back, deal?"

"I'm not very good at the whole driving thing."

"I doubt that. You just need the right teacher," he said, pulling out of the driveway. I didn't respond while he drove us out of the city and onto some back roads I had never been before. The car finally came to a stop about twenty minutes later.

I hopped out, looking around at the empty field. There was a rundown house in the distance, but nothing for a few miles. Orion made his way around the car.

"This is where we're practicing?" I asked.

"Not exactly, but for this next part, I'm going to need permission to touch you."

I took a step back, looking at him suspiciously. "That's not a good idea."

"Why? Don't you trust yourself?"

"I trust myself fine, thank you."

"Then what seems to be the problem?"

I huffed. "What are you going to do?" I asked.

"I'm going to shift us somewhere else."

"Shift?" I asked.

"Yes, like I did for your birthday."

"That was your power? I thought that was nonna."

He laughed. "No, little dove. No one else can shift except the horned and moon gods."

"Frankie can do that?" I asked, astonished.

His face fell. "Not yet. Now come, before we lose anymore daylight." I walked towards him hesitantly. He opened his arms, and I wrapped mine around his large torso. I placed my head against his chest, only coming up to the top of his abs. He softly folded his arms around my shoulders and waist, securing me against him.

That familiar smell of sunshine and spring intoxicated me. I closed my eyes, allowing my body to take his in. The wind picked up around us forcing me to tighten my grip. He placed his head on mine while his strong arms held tight.

Within moments, the wind calmed, and the sound of water and birds filled the air. I opened my eyes and was greeted by the most beautiful and tranquil scenery I had every laid eyes on. Tunnels of water and cave walls surrounded us with beautifully colored vegetation spread throughout the landscape.

"Breathtaking, isn't it?" he asked.

"Where are we?"

"Ligurian Alps. It's one of my favorite places. It's also far away from civilization just in case you lose control."

"Smart," I replied.

"I know," he winked, walking forward. "Now, onto training."

For the next four hours we tried to summon the white fire but failed. Eventually, we moved on to just normal fire. I incinerated a tree, then the ground around us at least a dozen times. Orion was able to put it out no problem. He walked me through smaller exercises I could do in order to control myself when I unleashed the unpredictable energy.

He was a good teacher; I'd give him that. Over and over again we summoned the flame. With each cast, I felt my powers draining, something I had never experienced before. Orion explained to me that the draining feeling was normal. No matter how powerful you were, each witch or warlock had their limit. The more powerful you were, the longer battery life you had.

He encouraged me to reach the end of my battery life so I would know the feeling of burn out. It was smart. Around six we finally called it a night. I was exhausted, barely able to lift myself into the car after we shifted back to the empty field. Driving would have to wait.

As we drove back, I noticed Orion stealing glancing in my direction.

"Yes?" I finally said, uncomfortable by the attention.

"Your shadow gift. I've been thinking on it."

"And..."

"Since you can grasp things with it, I think you can also weaponize it."

"How so?" I asked, now intrigued. That would have come in handy yesterday with the Obsidian witches.

"Forging it into weapons. Spears, knives, small needles. Things that are sharp and long like arrows. If you compact the energy enough, it can act as a physical object that could penetrate anything. If you learn to control it, you could even potentially dematerialize it to go through walls and then rematerialize it to strike an enemy on the other side of a surface. The possibilities would be endless.”

"Interesting," I replied, now thinking on it.

"It's just a theory, but we could work on it as well during some more training sessions if you would like."

I paused, unsure about the aspect of us spending time together. The gain was worth it though. "Yes, I'd like that."

He smiled softly. "Great."

CHAPTER
TWENTY-FOUR

The next day, Orion and I returned to his little oasis and trained until I walked the steep edge of burnout. I felt completely exhausted and weak, but I had already made so much progress in just two training sessions. Regardless of how I felt about the match up, I needed Orion.

On the way back to the castle, Orion trusted me to drive his massive truck. I felt like an ant in comparison to its size, but I took it slow and got a feel for how it handled. Orion coached me through the turns and how to anticipate when to press the break.

Once we arrived, I thanked him for his help and then rushed to my room, readying myself for Antonio's return. Tonight, was the night. I hadn't told anyone, including Frankie. I didn't want to psych myself out. If it was going to be like anything else he and I had already done physically, I had nothing to worry about. I trusted him completely.

I had a meat and cheese board with fresh fruit arranged in my room along with bottles of wine and candles. It was now eight in the evening. He'd be home any minute. I slipped on a black lingerie piece Frankie had forced me into buying months ago along with a matching silk robe. My hair was down, curled into big waves. I had put on a small amount of makeup, not wanting to overdo it.

I paced the length of my room, anxiously waiting. It took everything in me not to call or text him. Finally, a little before nine, a knock came at the door. I held my breath. My nerves were beginning to get the best of me. I cracked the door open, just enough to see who it was. Antonio.

I smiled, stepping aside as he walked in slowly. "I was beginning to worry," I said, shutting and locking the door behind us.

He looked around the room, taking note of the little touches I had added in lieu of our special evening. "Nothing was going to keep me from you," he said, trailing his eyes along my body ever so slowly. I felt the heat inside of me erupt from his attention.

"You must be hungry," I said, moving towards the table.

He grabbed my arm as I passed by, pulling me into him. "You're sure?" he asked, searching my face for an answer. "We can wait. I don't want you to feel pressured."

I shook my head. "I don't. I want this. I want you."

He held me against him, trailing his fingers down the side of my neck while he pushed me back towards the bed. His fingers slid underneath the silk robe, following the seem down to the belt that held the fabric closed. He untied the knot, pushing the robe away from my shoulders until the it pooled at my feet.

The back of my knees hit the mattress as his eyes drank me in.

His hands skimmed the fabric of the lingerie, carefully assessing each curve of my body. His mouth parted and his breathing became heavy. "You are so beautiful," he whispered, leaning down to take my mouth with his.

I smiled, moving my fingers to unbutton his shirt. Before I could finish, his hands lifted me underneath my bottom, throwing me onto the bed. I scooted back, towards the headboard as he placed a knee on the edge of the mattress, continuing to unbutton his shirt, never allowing his eyes to leave my body.

He tossed the shirt to the side and then began unfastening his belt, pulling it from the loops. I bit my lip, watching my very own strip tease. He unbuttoned his pants, leaving them on while he crawled towards me. He slid his hands up my bare legs, kissing the inside of my knees before he towered over me.

I laid back, allowing him to take the lead. His lips found mine. His fingers slid the dainty straps down my shoulders and arms. He pulled the lacy fabric down my chest and then my torso, his lips, following the trail of newly exposed skin. I arched up, meeting every kiss that he pressed against my body. His mouth hovered over my nipple, scraping his teeth against it, teasingly.

I could feel his warm breath against the sensitive skin causing me to let out a little moan, begging him to continue. His tongue circled the throbbing area. His hands cupped each breast, squeezing them gently before he finally took it into his mouth. My insides ached in reaction. My legs felt like Jello and the center of me throbbed.

As if he could read my mind, he pulled the small piece of lingerie from my body with his free hand and slid his fingers right over my slick opening. I gasped, allowing my hips to move up and down. He moved his mouth, continuing to kiss down my abdomen until his lips pressed against the opening of my sex.

An instant rush of pleasure overtook me from his tongue lashing in and out, circling and teasing the bundle of nerves. I buried my fingers in his dark hair, allowing my body to move up and down, reveling in the feeling and passion. He squeezed my butt, pulling my body harder against his mouth.

I let out a cry of pleasure while his tongue continued to circle my opening, finally pressing its way inside. With one final stroke, I found my finish, crying out as I came. I laid completely wrecked on the bed, unable to move from the intense orgasm he had just delivered me.

He sat up on his knees, sliding his pants and underwear down his hips. My eyes scanned his body, enjoying every single inch of him. Once he was completely bare, he positioned himself over me, kissing my face softly while his hands trailed over my body ever so gently.

His eyes found mine as we laid naked on top of one another. "You're sure this is what you want?" he whispered.

I smiled and nodded, pulling his mouth to mine. I felt his hands move in between our two bodies as he took hold of himself, dragging his tip along my wet slit. My entire body shivered at the motion. He pulled back from the kiss and watched while he hovered his head outside of my opening. His other hand brushed my face and hair gently.

My breathing was deep and unsteady. I licked my lips, waiting to feel him press inside of me. Slowly, I felt the head of his penis pushing, gently going in and out as he stretched me open. I let out a little whimper as he continued to watch my expressions.

Once his head was in, he continued to pump, working the rest of his length inside. I was so wet he had no problem sliding into me. He removed his hand from himself, now using it to trace my nipple with his thumb, returning his mouth to mine once again.

I could feel his body shaking while he worked to remain in control of his actions making sure not to hurt me. There was a slight burning sensation at first, but he was gentle. That feeling soon was replaced with one that was more sensual and pleasurable. My breathing steadied as my breaths became deeper and more passionate. I closed my eyes, laying back against the pillow allowing myself to take him fully.

His pace began to pick up as I felt him reach the top of me. He began to moan into my neck while his mouth sucked on the thin skin below my chin. My hips began to move in sync with him, demanding more. I allowed my hands to trail down his biceps and back as my insides tightened around him, never wanting this sensation to end.

His pace quickened as he began to lose control. I felt his hips drive into me, causing my entire body to come to life. His hands became ravenous, as did his mouth. His kisses became rough and untamed.

I grabbed hold of his hips, pulling him harder into me. The feeling was so intense, I cried out, allowing my body to feel every part of him. He reached out, grabbing the headboard, pulling himself deeper into me. I could feel the warmth seeping from in between my legs.

His body was slick with sweat as his muscles gleamed in the moonlight that swept into my room. With one deep, controlled thrust, I watched as he shattered inside of me. He let out a deep groan, continuing to pump slower inside of me before relaxing against my body.

He pulled out slowly, trailing kiss down the side of my face. He sat up, running a hand down my body. His lips turned up into a small smile. "Are you okay?" he asked.

"I'd say better than okay," I replied turning towards him. He chuckled, continuing to tickle my skin with his fingertips.

"You're not hurt?"

"A little sore, but nothing to complain about."

"Good."

As we laid, facing each other, I looked into his beautiful multi-colored eyes and felt an overwhelming sense of emotion I wanted to share with him. I had never been in love before, but something inside of me told me this is what love was. To share this with some-one who cared so deeply for you. To completely trust someone with every part of your being.

He sat up, noting my mind was elsewhere. "What's wrong?" he asked.

I shook my head. "Nothing. It's just... I want you to know how grateful I am to you. For everything."

"You don't have to—"

"No, please, let me finish." I paused taking a deep breath. "You saved me Antonio. From death, from a life not worth living. You brought me here... to my family and my destiny. And you showed me what—" I felt the tears spring from my eyes. I took another breath, meeting his eyes once more. "You've shown me what trust truly is. I trust you with every part of myself. And I've... I've fallen in love with you."

I exhaled, relieved that I finally said it out loud. He looked at me with something like confusion or guilt. I searched his face for any sign of happiness, but there was none. Oh, no. I had moved to fast with the L word. I was scaring him off.

I reached for his hand, taking it in mine. "You don't have to say anything," I explained. "I don't want you to feel forced into saying something you don't feel. And it's okay. I just wanted you to know how I felt."

He dropped his eyes from me, rubbing his thumb over the back of my hand. My heart was slamming against my chest while I fought back a different type of tears.

He shook his head. "I don't deserve you, Seren. I'm not... I'm not what's best for you. I've been selfish."

I forced his face back up to mine. "What are you talking about? Of course, you deserve me. We both deserve this," I said, motioning between us. "We both deserve what we've built with one another. And you have never been selfish with me. Not for a single moment. That's one of the things I love most about you. How understanding you are, and how patient."

"I—" he said but stopped.

"I'm sorry," I finally said. "I ruined the moment."

"No," he said, pulling my head to his. "You haven't ruined a damn thing. You are perfect as always, beautiful. Everything about you is absolutely perfect." He smiled down at me before kissing the top of my head softly.

I felt something sticky in between my legs as I shifted under the sheets. I looked down, seeing a small pool of blood underneath me. Embarrassment flashed across my face as he caught glimpse of it. I tried to hide it, but he had already seen.

"I'm sorry, I—" I began to say.

"You have nothing to be sorry about," he whispered, pulling me against him. "It's completely normal. Why don't you go take a shower and I'll change the sheets and then meet you in there when I'm done. Sound like a plan?"

I smiled and nodded, moving to the bathroom while he began

to strip the bed. I ran the hot water, unsure of where my head was. He hadn't said it back, and basically had a panic attack when I admitted my feelings, but as always, he was kind about it.

So, he didn't love me. Not yet at least. That was okay. I knew he cared for me, and he was so good to me. That's what mattered... right? I stepped in, feeling the weight of my heart crash into me. I pressed my head against the cold black tile as the hot water beat against my back.

I tried to hold my emotions in, but I lost. I felt myself begin to sob as I wrapped my arms around myself, trying to regain control. A moment later, I felt two hands on my hips turning me towards him. I quickly wiped my eyes, trying to clean myself up before he could see.

"Hey, hey. What's wrong? Are you hurting?" he asked, forcing my face up to his.

"No, I'm fine, really," I said, sniffing away the remainder of my emotions.

He looked at me as if he knew exactly what I was feeling. "Seren," he whispered, pressing my back against the wall of the tile. He pinned me there with his beautiful body, finding my eyes with his. "I am very much in love with you," he whispered.

"Tony, you don't have to—"

"Hey, look at me," he demanded. "I'm not saying this because I feel obligated or forced. I am saying this because it's real for me and it scares the shit out of me. But if I'm being honest, I've been in love with you since that first day we had lunch in that little café. I've been with a lot of women before, but I've never loved one. Not like this."

I smiled, laughing a little with relief. "How many are we talking?" I asked.

"Not as many as our horned god, but enough," he said, matching my smile. "Beautiful, you have me completely wrapped around your finger. I love you more than I've ever loved anything in my life."

I pulled his face to mine, reaching between us until I found his hardness, throbbing and ready for me. He picked me up, holding me against the wall, entering me again. This time, there was no hesitation. He still took it slow at first, but the passion and the intensity was instant. I cried out as the steam from the water encased us.

"Fuck," he whispered, holding me up by my ass. "You are so damn beautiful." I took his mouth with mine, wanting more of him.

"I need you, Antonio. I need all of you." He slammed harder into me causing my body to erupt with the most pleasurable sensation I had ever experienced. I gasped, closing my eyes tightly, feeling as if I was going to explode.

His motions slowed followed by a deep laugh. "Beautiful, open your eyes," he whispered against my ear.

When I did, I was greeted with stagnant water droplets, suspended in the air around us. I smiled, realizing I had frozen them in place. "Did you enjoy yourself?" he asked.

"Very much," I whispered against his lips, while the water droplets began to fall. "Now, let's do it again."

Chapter Twenty-Five

The next morning, I woke up later than usual. I looked over at the man that I loved, still sound asleep next to me. My body was a little sore, but I didn't care. All I wanted was more of him. I trailed my hand beneath the sheets, finding my new favorite part of him long and hard.

I felt his fingers trace down the back of my spine, his eyes slowly opening, still sated from sleep. "Can I help you with something?" he whispered.

"Mm, I have a few things you can help me with," I replied, positioning myself on top of him.

"Don't you have training you need to get to?" he asked, skimming his fingers across my breasts.

"I do, but it can wait."

He swung me around, placing my body underneath his in a quick motion. I began laughing from the unexpected action. "Yes, it fucking can," he said before sliding into me. I gripped the sides of the pillow as a cry of pleasure escaped me.

I hurried through the shower, rushing to the front entrance of the castle to meet Orion. My legs were tender, and my insides were swollen, but I felt like a goddess. Last night, and this morning for that matter, had been magical.

I pushed open the front door, looking around for Orion, but didn't see him. I walked towards where his truck was usually parked and stopped as I heard the sounds of someone throwing up nearby.

"Just take the day off," I heard Adrianna's voice say.

I peaked around the back of the truck and saw Orion hunched over, vomiting into the grass near the front.

"I can't," he said, swaying before forcing himself upright. "She needs to be prepared."

"Orion, you are in no condition to go anywhere today, let alone be around her. You need to take care of yourself," said Adrianna. I didn't know what was going on or what they were talking about, but somehow it involved me. I slid my foot forward, knocking the gravel in the process. Their eyes snapped up.

I walked towards them. Orion looked a mess. He obviously was sick or had come down with something. The color was leached from his face and his eyes were hallow.

"Is everything okay?" I asked.

Adrianna crossed her arms, not daring to look at me. I didn't know what I had done to her, but she was obviously pissed about something.

"Everything is fine," said Orion, heading for the car door. "Let's go."

"I'm coming with you," insisted Adrianna.

"No," Orion stopped her, pointing a finger in her face. "You go back inside and wait till I return."

"Orion, this is—"

"I mean it," he interrupted her. "We will talk when I return."

I looked between them, feeling uncomfortable by the tension. He opened his door and got inside. I followed suit. The entire car ride he didn't say a word to me. No flirty comments. No questions. No sharing of ideas or theories.

Once we got to our normal parking spot before shifting to Ligurian I couldn't take it anymore. Orion came around to my side of the car, still looking completely dreadful. "Orion," I said softly. "What is wrong with you? Are you feeling, okay?"

"I'll be fine," he answered shortly.

"You're obviously not okay. You can talk to me. What is happening?" I asked, walking over to face him. He hesitated before finally looking at me. I could see pain and suffering there. His face was wrecked as if he didn't get a moment of sleep.

"I said I'm fine. Now, are you ready to go?"

I nodded, feeling like a fool for even asking. I walked towards him, but he stopped me from coming too close. He held out his hands instead. I took them. He closed his eyes as the wind whipped up around us. In a flash we were transported to our destination. I felt Orion's weight pull me forward as soon as we landed in the field. He let go, stumbling and falling to the ground.

I rushed to his side, not knowing how to help. I reached for him, touching his shoulder. "Orion, please," I begged. "Please tell me how I can help you. Please tell me what is going on!"

He shrugged off my hand, forcing himself to stand. "Get into position. We're working on your shadow power today," he insisted. I stood, doing as I was told.

The rest of the day dragged on. Usually, I enjoyed my lessons with Orion. He was also very informative and helpful when it came to parts of magic I was struggling with. Today, he was quiet. He watched, observed, and then told me what I had done wrong and insisted I try again.

We barely made it back to the car. He was stumbling around like a drunk. I insisted on driving back. When we arrived, he exited the vehicle without a word. That was the last I saw of him that night.

I returned to my room to find nonna, waiting patiently for me. "Hello bambina, how was your lesson?" she asked, standing to meet me with a grin.

"It was... fine. I think Orion is sick," I admitted.

Nonna's face slacked. "What do you mean 'sick'? The god's vessels do not get sick like the rest of us."

"Well, then there is something seriously wrong with him. Can you please send someone to check in on him? He won't talk to me and I'm worried."

"Of course," she said with a small grin.

My door opened. Antonio came in with a bouquet of roses. His smile was beaming, then faded as his eyes set on nonna. She straightened, looking at him as if he was nothing more than a servant.

"Mr. Simonelli," said nonna.

"Elder Salvo," he replied shortly. He reached my side, handing me the flowers before kissing me on the side of the head. I couldn't help but beam with happiness. "Didn't realize you had guests."

"You would have if you knocked," I replied.

"I thought we were past the whole knocking thing," he said, winking at me.

"Bambina, I need you to come with me. It is important," said nonna.

Tony stepped in front of me, standing straight and tall. "If your field trip involves more demons, she won't be going anywhere," he said flatly.

Nonna looked at him in shock and with something like disgust. "How dare you tell me where and what I will do with *my grand-daughter*, boy. Do you forget who you are speaking to?"

"I know exactly who I am speaking to. Someone who left *her granddaughter* locked in a room with four demons."

My grandmother's mouth gapped open. I placed a hand on Tony's arms, stepping in between the two of them. "Tony," I said, pulling him to look at me. "I'll be okay. We've already talked about this."

"I don't like it," he said, looking down at me.

"Your feelings on the matter mean nothing," nonna interrupted. "She is not yours."

"The hell she isn't," he said, taking a step towards her. I pulled him back.

"Tony, that is enough," I said. "I will be fine."

He looked down at me, grabbing my arms. "You better be," he whispered, kissing me softly. "I need you."

I smiled at those three little words. "I promise," I replied.

"I love you," he said.

"And I love you." I placed the flowers on my bed and headed for the door. After the door shut, I studied her, waiting for her to say something, but she never did. "I'm sorry about all that."

"And I am sorry as well. I should have never left you in that room alone," she said, guilt flickered over her expression.

"Thank you. I understand why you had too though. You were right. I never would have been prepared otherwise."

"That doesn't make my decision to do so any easier. If something would have happened, I—"

"But it didn't. I survived, just like you knew I would." Nonna smiled at me, nodding her thanks. "Now," I said. "Where are we headed?"

"A seer."

"What for?"

"I believe something is... lost or locked. I need your help to find out how to unlock it."

"What are we trying to unlock?"

"I... I can't say it but once you find it you will understand."

"Always with the riddles," I said, rolling my eyes.

"Did you read the book I gave you?"

"No. I've been a bit distracted."

"With young Simonelli I see. Your relationship with him has... has progressed? You are now in love?"

I blushed. "Yes," I replied. She scoffed. "Why don't you like him?" I asked.

"It's not that I don't like him. I just... we don't have time for this right now, bambina. Clear your mind so the seer will have an easier time reading you."

We entered one of the rooms at the bottom of the mountain. There were no windows in sight. The room was draped with fabric while a single ball of yellow and blue light illuminated the small space. A woman with long gray hair sat in a chair in front of a crystal ball. She was an ageless beauty. Her face showed her graceful journey in this life. Her soft blue eyes were peaceful and calming.

"Welcome Salvos," she said, gesturing to the two seats set out on the other side of her round table. "Please, take a seat so we may begin."

We did as we were instructed. Nonna sat, looking anxious. "Now," the seer said. "What can I do for you?"

"I believe a mistake has occurred. Something is lost or trapped, and I wish to release it."

"Is it a physical object?" asked the seer.

"Possibly," replied nonna. "I am unsure. I believe it is a secret." I was so confused. I couldn't follow what she was saying.

"And it has something to do with your granddaughter?" the seer asked, nodding to me.

"Yes... maybe... I am unsure," explained nonna.

"I see," said the seer. "Let's begin. Please, join hands." We all held hands, creating a circle between us. The seer began to chant as we closed our eyes and followed suit. I felt the heaviness of the magic as it entered the room. A small gust of wind fluttered throughout the enclosed space.

The seer continued to chant. I could feel her skin beginning to change in temperature. Within moments, it was as if I was holding onto a hand made of ice. She began to shake, as did the table and the objects on it. The wind around the room began to pick up. I opened my eyes, seeing nonna's eyes already fixated on her.

The seer struggled to speak, appearing to be in the middle of a mental battle that was physically daunting. "I—" she began to say, the wind whipping and lashing around her. "It's a... a curse," she blurted before she started screaming in agony. I went to pull my hand away from hers, but I was trapped, unable to break free.

Her voice was high and unhuman while she screamed and thrashed her head from side to side. Her grip tightened on my hand. The glowing ball erupted with a red and black flame.

"What is happening?" I yelled at nonna.

"I don't know," she yelled back. Wind and air violently swept through the small space, causing a tornado effect. The pictures and items on the walls fell, breaking into pieces as the remains flew around the room. Nonna was hit with a piece of broken glass, slashing the side of her face open. The crystal ball exploded in front of us, sending small shards of glass slicing through the air. I closed my eyes, feeling the morsels of sand scrap across my skin, making small tears along my face and neck.

Finally, the room silenced. I took a deep breath, opening my eyes to see the seer's gaze now locked on mine. She adorned a wicked grin that stretched across her lips before she tilted her head. Her blue eyes were replaced with red ones, no sign of white.

"Well, hello, hello, little bean," a voice deep yet still feminine came from the seer mouth. "I have waited so long to meet you." Nonna and my hands remained shackled to her.

"Do not speak to her you foul monster," yelled nonna. The thing turned its attention to her, yanking nonna's arm, forcing her to come face to face with it.

The thing clicked its tongue in annoyance. "Foolish of you to bring her here," the seer rasped. "Have you learned nothing over the years, Lucia? You are still the same power-hungry witch who would sacrifice anything for your own elevation and gain. First, your daughter, now her daughter."

Nonna's eyes widened with what I swore was fear. "Who are you?"

The seer turned her attention back to me in an assessing manner, smiling again. "Beautiful, aren't you," she said. "Just as I imagined."

The sound of sentiment took me by surprise. "Who are you?" I whispered.

"Don't worry. We will meet soon enough," it said, letting go of both of our hands as its red eyes trailed between nonna and I.

"You will not come near her," sneered nonna.

The creature laughed. "Not even you can stop me, *Elder* Salvo. Now, unless you want your entire coven butchered thanks to your intolerable need to snoop where you shouldn't, I suggest you stop looking for answers to questions you know nothing about," the creature said before it reached into the seer's eye sockets, plucking her eyes balls free, releasing them onto the table as they rolled towards us. The creature took its long, razor-sharp nails and sliced four fatal gashes into the sears neck. Blood sprayed everywhere as the body began to convulse and shake until it finally fell flat against the shards of glass left on the table.

Nonna and I both stood instantly, rushing for the door to escape. Once we were in the hall, we stared at each other, breathing heavily, both covered in the seer's blood.

Nonna took out her phone and began to dial. "Yes, Elder Salvo here. We need the medical team to Seer Avaltra's room along with a psych team. She is dead." She paused, listening to the person on the other phone. "Obsidian," she continued. "Now... contain it." She pulled the phone away from her ear.

"What in the hell was that? And what are you looking for?" I asked.

Nonna took my hands, desperation flashed across her face. "Seren, listen to me – read that damn book. Do you hear me?" She demanded. I nodded, still shaken up by what had just happened. "Good, now go clean yourself. I will let you know if we find anything."

I rushed to my room, going for the nightstand where I had last seen the book, but it was gone. I rummaged through the dresser, searching under the bed, but it was nowhere to be found. I heard the door click behind me. With my adrenaline still high, I swirled instantly, ready to kill whoever it was. Tony stood there, examining my current state.

"What in the hell happened this time?" he said rushing towards me.

I shook my head. "Don't worry, it isn't mine. Have you seen that book my nonna gave me a few days ago. I thought I put it on my nightstand, but it's just gone."

Tony stopped me, taking my face into his hands. His very touch calmed me. "What happened, beautiful? Why are you covered in blood?"

I took a deep breath and told him what had happened with the seer. When I finished, I was shaking from the shock of it. He held me as I steadied myself enough, beginning to breath regularly again.

"That's it," he said. "No more outings with nonna."

I laughed. "It wasn't her fault. Obsidian highjacked her seer. I feel so bad for her," I whispered, looking down at myself, still covered in her blood.

"Go get cleaned up. I think you deserve a night in," he said, ushering me towards the bathroom.

Chapter Twenty-Six

The next few weeks were calmer. I continued to train, both physically and with magic. Orion remained sick. He began to miss practices and when he did show up, he was too unwell to shift us to the Ligurian Alps, so we practiced in the empty fields instead.

He barely spoke to me unless it was about our lesson. I continued to try and make conversation outside of magic, but it was no use. After week four of trying, I had given up.

Nonna didn't mention anything else about the seer or what she was looking for. I believed Obsidian's warning about the coven being in danger had gotten the best of her. I had never seen nonna scared until that moment.

There were still no other signs of Obsidian on our continent. I eagerly waited to be sent out into the field, but the call never came. On a positive note, that left plenty of time for Tony and I to spend in bed. I had never been this happy before.

November was coming to an end, and it began to snow in the hills and mountains around us. Though the dusting was light, it was breathtaking. Our team received the weekend off from any training. Frankie was overjoyed and extra delightful for some reason.

The closer the new year got, the more distraught she was feeling about the upcoming ceremony. Whatever had gotten into her, was a breath of fresh air. She had shown up at my door early that morning, insisting we spend the whole day together in order to welcome December and the upcoming holiday festivities.

"Did Joe give it to you good or something last night?" I asked, teasing her.

"Well, yes, there's that, but why can't a girl just be happy?" she asked, twirling around me with a large grin.

"I like this Frankie a lot more than the doom and gloom one who has been haunting these halls for the past six weeks."

"Let's not talk about her. Today, is about me and you. That is, if you can pull yourself away from Simonelli for longer than five minutes."

I laughed. "I think I can make do."

The day was spent in a spa, shopping, and wine tasting. Frankie sent me off to my room instructed me to dress fancy for our dinner reservation that she had made. I was still tipsy from all the wine as I tumbled through the shower and my closet. I looked for Tony before I left, but he was nowhere to be found.

I met Frankie down at the front doors. She stopped, her mouth dropping to the floor as I approached. I was wearing a dress she insisted I buy a few weeks ago. It was a beautiful shade of deep purple. It plunged low in the front and back. It was made of velvet. The sleeves were off the shoulder and trailed down to my hands.

"Oh, Seren," she said as I approached. "You look absolutely stunning."

"As do you, sweet cousin," I said, kissing her on the cheek. I took my coat from the doorman and headed outside to the limo she had waiting for us.

We pulled up to an abandoned building that was on the edge of the town. I stepped out of the car just before Frankie latched her hand around mine, pulling me forward. "Uh, Frankie... are you sure we're in the right place? Because if so, I am afraid we're overdressed."

"Yes, yes, we're where we're supposed to be. Now, come on," she said pulling me along.

I followed close behind her as we ascended the staircase of the rundown building. The stairs were creaky and broken in some places. I picked up my dress, making sure the loose nails didn't snag the delicate fabric. I was afraid my cousin had lost her mind.

Once we reach the rooftop door, she turned towards me, beaming with joy. She took my hands in hers and kissed me on my cheek. "I love you, cousin," she said, her eyes welling with tears.

"I love you too," I laughed. "What is going on?"

"Just take a deep breath," she instructed, before opening the door to the roof. I stepped across the threshold into a beautiful wonderland escape. The floor was littered with mounds of snow while the small flakes continued to flutter around us. Balls of starlight floated in the air freely. Abstracted figures of ice created the most beautiful scenery. Candles were lit and placed on every surfaces. They lined a path along with red rose petals that led to a crescent shaped alter, full of candles.

I saw nonna and Aunt Thora standing off to the side. Aunt Nora was smiling with joy while tears escaped her eyes. Nonna gave me a small smile, the rest of her face, expressionless. I turned back to the center of the alter where Tony stood in a deep black suit. He had never looked more handsome.

I turned back to Frankie, unsure of what was happening. She nodded, now crying before ushering me forward. I walked towards Tony. He was beaming from ear to ear. He extended his hand towards me. I took his hand, stepping up towards him.

He took a deep breath, holding back tears. "You look so beautiful," he said tenderly.

"What is going on?" I whispered.

He laughed a little, looking down at our hands. His head slowly rose to mine. "Seren Lucia Da Salvo," he began. "From the moment I met you, I have been captivated. By your beauty, your strength, your selflessness, and your heart. I have truly never met another person so perfectly created. You are more than I could have ever imagined. You are better than me in every way, and I still can't seem to understand why you chose me, but I am so grateful for that choice every day.

"You have changed my life in so many ways and continue to amaze me and astonish me each and every day. The happiness I have experienced with you. The joy we have shared... there is nothing that compares to it, nor ever will.

"You are my guiding light in this life. The reason I get up every morning and try to be better. You have completely and utterly captivated me, putting me under your spell. I am hopelessly, truly, in love with you.

"You are a prize worth fighting for, which I plan to do for the rest of my life. Seren, I promise to never let a day go by without showing you how much you are loved. I promise to cherish you in the good and the bad times. I will protect you, laying down my life if I must, to make sure you are safe and cared for. I will stop at nothing until every aspiration, every dream, and every fantasy that you have comes to fruition.

"I will support you. I will care for you, and I will trust you in all things. I will build a life worth living. I will provide for you and our family when that time comes. I will devote every moment of my life to loving you because you deserve nothing less."

He stopped, taking a deep breath before he knelt to one knee. He pulled a box out from his jacket pocket. My breath caught as the realization of what this was took hold. He cracked the lid open, revealing a beautiful, large marquise shaped diamond in a gold setting.

"Seren Lucia De Salvo, would you make me the happiest man in the world and honor me by becoming my wife?"

Tears fell from my eyes. I nodded, unable to find my voice. "Yes," I gasped.

He rose instantly, taking me into his arms. "Yes?" he asked.

"Yes, yes, of course, yes!" I said, kissing him, feeling a sense of joy I didn't know possible. My family clapped behind us as he swept me up, twirling me around. We laughed and kissed some more before he finally took my hand and slid the massive diamond onto my left ring finger.

"Do you like it?" he asked.

"It's perfect... just like you." I kissed him again.

Frankie rushed me, squeezing the life out of me. "Ah, I am so happy for you!" she screamed, jumping up and down.

"You knew, didn't you?" I asked.

"Well duh. Who do you think helped him come up with this amazing proposal?" she replied.

Aunt Thora wrapped her arms around me. "I am so happy for you, sweetheart. And what a catch," she whispered.

"I know, right?" I said back to her.

Nonna walked over slowly towards me, giving me a light embrace. She pulled away, cupping my cheeks in her cold hands. "Be happy, bambina. Listen and follow your heart, always."

I smiled at her. "Thank you, nonna." Her face fell before she nodded at Tony.

That night we went to an actual restaurant to celebrate. After, we returned to his room. He worshiped my body until the sun rose. It was truly the perfect ending to the perfect day.

The next morning, I woke before him and snuck out of bed. I wanted to do something special for him. I figured I would personally cook him a spread so when he woke, we wouldn't have to leave his room. I turned the corner, texting Frankie on my phone about the explorative night we had embarked on when something hard and fast came slamming into me.

I looked up, seeing Orion's sickly eyes look down at me. He was panting, his fingers digging into my shoulder. He was in a pair of black pajama pants and a white shirt that was soaked through with sweat. His breathing was strained as his eyes burrowed into mine.

"Orion, what is—" I began to say.

"Please," he gasped. His voice was horse. "Please, wake up. You can't... you can't do this," he said. His body trembled as he buried his head in the nook of my neck. "Please, wake up... please listen," he begged. I could feel him gently kiss my skin before he collapsed to the floor.

I tried to catch him, but my strength was no match for his weight. I began screaming for help, cradling his head in my lap. "Orion, wake up," I demanded, smacking him in the face. "Orion don't do this. Wake up now! Help! Someone, please! Help!"

Roric came around the corner along with Tyler. Adrianna was next. "Get a healer, now," instructed Roric. Adrianna took off down the hallway.

I felt myself begin to sob as I looked down at his unresponsive face. His chest still rose and fell at least, indicating he was alive. The boys took him from me while I followed them to his bedchamber.

"Go get your nonna," demanded Roric. I took off down the hall, racing towards her chambers. I knocked franticly until she opened the door.

"What is it, bambina? What's wrong?" she said, wrapping her robe around herself.

"Orion... he... he fainted. He is sick nonna. Something isn't right," I explained.

"You don't say," she said, brushing past me, heading for his room. I followed closely until she entered. I waited in the doorway while the healers came in. "Tyler, call his mother. She needs to get here immediately," instructed nonna.

The healers began to work, chanting and waving their hands over his body, trying to find what ailed him. Nonna whispered something to Roric and he nodded, leaving the room. Nonna came over to me, running her hand down my arm. "Go back to your fiancé, bambina. We've got it from here."

"What? No, I am staying," I insisted.

"No, you are not. Now leave," she said. Frankie showed up at the door, out of breath with Roric trailing her. Her eyes locked onto Orion. She rushed to his side. I took a few steps back before the door shut in my face.

I slowly walked back towards Antonio's room, gathering myself before I returned to him. So much for a romantic breakfast. I opened the door softly, trying not to wake him. He was no longer in bed. He sat in front of the fire on his black velvet couch, holding a piece of paper. I walked cautiously towards him, noticing his hands trembling while he read the letter.

"Tony," I said softly. He jumped, shoving the piece of paper in a stack of others that sat in front of him on the coffee table.

"Good morning," he said, running his hands through his hair without looking at me.

I joined him on the couch. Something was wrong. He was more fidgety than I had ever seen him. There was no sense of joy or happiness on his face.-"Is everything okay?" I asked.

"Perfect. Why wouldn't it be?" he replied.

"You just... you just seem a little off."

He didn't respond. He just sat, fidgeting with his hands, looking into the fire. I had never seen him like this before. I didn't know what that piece of paper said, but whatever it was, it had ruined our morning, along with Orion passing out on me.

I reached for his hand. He took it, still not daring to look at me. "Are you—" I started to say but choked on the words. "Are you regretting asking me to marry you last night? Is that it?" I guessed.

His eyes snapped to mine. His eyebrows furrowed. "Absolutely not. No matter what happens, I will never regret loving you."

I smiled hesitantly. "What do you mean by, 'no matter what

happens'? What is going to happen, Tony?"

He paused for a moment allowing his mask to fall. He was hiding something. In an instant, he put it back on, shaking his head and smiling at me. He kissed the back of my hand. "Nothing is going to happen, beautiful. Everything is okay. I promise."

I inhaled. "Actually, something is very wrong."

"What is it?"

"Well, I was headed to the kitchen to make you breakfast this morning when…" I paused, adjusting the story a bit. "When I found Orion unconscious in the hallway. I got my nonna and the healers, but he is sick, Tony. No one knows what's wrong with him and I'm beginning to worry. The vessels aren't supposed to be able to get sick."

"Hey, hey," he said, taking my face in his hands. "Let your nonna and the elders worry about that. There's nothing we can do to help him right now, okay? Why don't we just try to focus on us and our engagement?"

I nodded, still feeling that pit in my stomach. "I'm going to go back to my room for a bit to get some clean clothes and take a shower," I said, standing from the couch.

"Do you want me to come?" he asked.

"I'll be okay. I'll catch up with you after," I said, pressing a kiss to his lips.

"I love you, beautiful."

"I love you too, fiancé."

He brushed the hair back from my face, taking me in. "You are truly the best thing that has ever happened to me," he whispered.

"Well, it's a good thing I agreed to marry you then, isn't it?"

He laughed. "A very good thing." He kissed me again before I left.

CHAPTER TWENTY-SEVEN

I found things to busy myself with for the remainder of the day. Orion's dragon of a mother had arrived, so I made sure to stay clear of that one for as long as possible. Frankie informed me they still couldn't figure out what was wrong with Orion. Healer after healer came up empty handed.

That night, I spent with Tony. After we had made love, I was unable to sleep, worrying about Orion. There had to be something that we were missing. Maybe the book about the gods nonna had given me contained some hidden secret. I slipped out of bed just as the sun rose and headed for my room. After I cleaned up and changed, I searched for the book, but it was gone.

Frustrated, I headed to the kitchen to try and bake out some of my anxiety. I saw my Aunt Thora in the hall a few paces ahead of me. "Aunt Thora," I yelled, but she continued walking like she didn't hear me. "Aunt Thora," I called out again, running to catch up with her.

She turned, seeming startled. "Morning," I said, smiling up at here.

"Oh," she said, taking a step back like I had startled her.

"Didn't you hear me calling?" I asked.

"No, sorry little bean, my mind was elsewhere," she said, trying not to make eye contact with me. She seemed off, but everyone was right now.

"Has there been any update on Orion?" I asked.

"No, unfortunately not," she replied shortly.

"Has his mother been any help?"

"What?" she asked, confused.

"His mother. She arrived yesterday. Has she found anything?"

"I'm not sure. Listen, I have a million things to do today so let's catch up a little later, okay?" she said, rushing off.

I stood in front of the fridge for what seemed like forever. The door alarm was now beeping, signaling for me to close it. My eyes snagged on a fresh bowl of lemons. I smiled, gathering what I needed and began to bake.

An hour later I was headed to Orion's room with a batch of

lemon tarts in my hands. I stopped at his door and hesitantly knocked. I took a deep breath, readying myself to come face to face with the she-dragon. Sure enough, her little figure and grim face answered the door.

Her eyes narrowed on me like she was debating if she would rip my throat out. "What do you want?" she snapped.

I took a deep breath and smiled at her. "I came to see how Orion was feeling," I said softly.

"He's no better than he was yesterday. You have your update, now leave," she spat, making to shut the door on me. I slammed my hand forward.

"Mrs. Camerino, I want to apologize for my behavior the last time we met. I was out of line. I am very protective over my family, but I still shouldn't have acted out in that way. I let my emotions get the best of me and for that, I am sorry. But please, do not kick me out because of a rivalry that has nothing to do with Orion or myself."

"This has nothing to do with some stupid rivalry girl."

"Orion is my friend, and I would like to visit him. Please allow me to do so," I pleaded.

"You have done enough, don't you think?" she snarled.

"Mother," I heard Orion's weak voice in the background. "Let her in."

His mother huffed, moving aside hesitantly, still tracking my every move. I walked to the side of the bed where he was lying. The sheets and pillows around him were drenched in sweat, his face looked clammy and pale. His mother returned to his other side, tucking in the sheets. He turned towards her and smiled softly.

"Can you please give us a few minutes?" he said to her.

She stiffened, looking from him to me. "But son, I don't think—"

"I will be fine, mother. Thank you," he said, turning back to me as she walked cautiously out of the room. I sat on the edge of the bed, placing the dessert on his side table.

"I... I didn't know what to do," I admitted, "so I made you lemon tarts. I remember you saying they were your favorite."

He chucked, before coughing. "Going to cure me with lemon tarts, are you?"

I shrugged. "Who knows? The healers haven't found an answer yet. Maybe some sweets will do the job." We both smiled as I dropped my eyes to my hands. I covered my left hand with my right, having forgotten to take the ring off before I came in. He picked up my left hand, pulling it closer to his face.

"Congratulations," he whispered.

"Thank you," I smiled, pulling it back.

"Are you happy?" he asked, with a heavy tone.

I nodded. "I am. Really."

"Then that is all that matters. No matter what, I want you to be happy, little dove. I hope you believe me."

"Thank you, Orion. I want the same for you. Truly." He smiled back at me, pushing himself up against the headboard. "How are you feeling?" I asked.

"Weak. I can't control my powers and my body is failing. On paper, I am completely healthy, but I can barely make it to the bathroom on my own."

"It has to be Obsidian," I said, thinking to myself. "Maybe they poisoned you somehow."

He smiled. "Maybe."

I looked at his long face. His cheeks were hollow, and he had black bags around his eyes. His hair was slicked back and unkept. For the first time ever, he didn't look like a god. He looked... human.

"Is there anything I can get or do for you?" I asked.

"I think my mother has all my basic needs covered, but thank you."

I nodded, leaning towards him. I kissed his cheek softly. His eyes remained shut. I went to leave but I felt his weak grip latch onto my wrist. I looked back down at him. His deep brown eyes filled with pain, and tears.

"I want you to know," he said softly, "that no matter what happens, I tried."

"Tried what?"

"Just listen," he said, fighting to speak. "I tried and I don't regret one moment spent with you... not one. You are everything I imagined you'd be... and more. I'll find you again... I promise." He let his hand drop from me as I backed away slowly. I didn't know what he was talking about, but it made me uncomfortable.

I left his room, heading back for Antonio's, thinking about what Orion had said. Maybe it was his fever. Maybe he was delusional from the sickness. Whatever it was, it didn't make sense.

I pushed Tony's door open greeted by an empty room. My head couldn't stop thinking about what Orion said. *I'll find you again.* He was talking like he knew he was going to die. No. He couldn't die. He couldn't. I felt sick.

I opened the balcony doors and stood on the terrace, overlooking the mountains. The cool winter breeze helped calm my nerves as I worked to clear my head. There had to be a way to save him. He was supposed to become the horned god. He couldn't die. What happened if he did though? Would the ritual skip our generation? And how would that affect our magic? Our offspring?

The door to Tony's room opened and shut quickly. I turned to go back inside to greet him when I noticed he wasn't alone. On instinct, I moved to the side of the wall just behind the door so I wouldn't be seen.

"What in the fuck are you doing here?" I heard Tony say.

"You stopped responding to my letters, so I figured a little checkup was in order," said a voice I recognize. "And what do I find? You *engaged*. How lovely. Does complicate things a bit more for you, though, doesn't it?"

I peeked around the edge of the glass door frame to see Aunt

Thora standing in front of Tony. My heart dropped. What in the hell was going on?

"I've already told you," Tony snapped, "in order for me to continue to help you, you need to come up with another plan that doesn't involve killing her. If that's the only plan, then I am out."

"Oh, poor little Antonio caught feelings and now he thinks he has a right to bargain. How sweet. Tell me, have you forgotten the little thing I've been keeping alive for you all these years?" Aunt Thora walked over to him with swagger in her step. "Should I just... stop keeping her alive so you can go run off into the sunset with your new little wifey?"

"You are impossible," he said, shaking his head in frustration.

"I am impossible?" she laughed. "You were the one that went and fell in love with your target. If you would have just brought her to me in the first place like you were supposed to, she would have been dead by now. Instead, you brought her here. Allowing her to grow in power and allies, complicating the whole damn plan," she yelled. The walls around us shook from a release of power.

My heart dropped. They were talking about me. About the night he saved me from the demons in the abbey. He wasn't there to save me at all. He was just supposed to bring me somewhere else to be murdered. No, no. This couldn't be right.

"I had no choice," Tony said. "You know that."

"Yes, yes, so you've told me. And what is your plan now that you've asked her to marry you? Do you really think she is going to forgive you after learning the truth? Do you think she is just going to give up her powers willingly, knowing she will be the downfall of the seven covens?"

"I can make her understand," said Tony.

"And why would she believe a word that comes out of your mouth?"

"She..." he hesitated for a moment. "She loves me."

Aunt Thora stood stoically still for a moment before she erupted into laughter, placing a hand on his shoulder as the other curled into a fist.

Tony began to panic, placing a hand over his heart, gasping for air. His face turned shades of blue, his eyes, now bloodshot red. He hovered above the floor while his body shook from affixation. Thora released her fist, slamming her arm down with force. Tony plummeted to his floor, gasping for breath.

She bent down next to him, smiling from ear to ear. "You're cute, Antonio. I'll give you that, but you will lose her. You need to prepare yourself for the inevitable. There is no happy ending for the two of you at the end of this. She will die and you will become the horned god as planned so you can save your dear little sister. Now, enough with the side quests. Do as you are told, or little sis dies. Are we clear?"

He nodded, still unable to speak.

"Good boy. I need you to travel to Paris tonight. There is something you will be taking care of for me. Call it... an apology gift.

Then, after, when you return, you will bring her to me. Any questions?"

He shook his head.

"Perfect. I'll see you in a few days," she said before leaving his room.

I was sobbing. My brain tried to process what I had just learned but my emotions were sending me into a fit of panic. The man I had fallen in love with, who I had trusted, had given myself to, had agreed to marry, planned to kill me. And his sister was alive? He was planning on becoming the horned god? How? This didn't make sense.

I watched Antonio on the floor of his room. He sat back and began to cry. He held his face while he sobbed and pulled at his hair. I pressed my back against the wall trying to come up with some type of plan.

My aunt wanted me dead. Did Frankie know about this? Did nonna? I had no one. No one I could trust. *Orion*. I covered my mouth. Oh, my God. Orion. Tony must have been the one who was poisoning him so he would be weak enough to kill.

I had to find more evidence. I had to get a clear answer before coming up with a plan. For now, I would act like I knew nothing. I had to remain strong. I was the only one I could trust.

After an hour, Tony finally gathered himself enough to leave the room. I waited a few moments and snuck out, doing my best to avoid him. I didn't know what I was going to do, but I did know

Tony would be gone tonight in Paris. I would use the time to go through his things in order to hunt down the answers I was so desperate to uncover.

I flung my door open, locking myself inside. I felt like I was going to burst.

"There you are, beautiful," I heard Tony say from across the room. I all but jumped out of my skin. I gathered myself as quickly as possible, remembering the role I had to play to survive. I held the tears back.

"Hi there," I said, forcing a smile across my face. God he was so beautiful. All the plans I had imagined for our future flashed across my mind in that moment hitting my heart like a ton of bricks. It was all a lie. He was a lie. He didn't love me. He wanted me dead.

He walked over, pulling me into him, kissing me. I played along, trying to remain clam. "I missed you," he whispered against my lips. "You know, I would like to wake up at least one morning to my beautiful fiancée lying next to me in bed. Would be nice."

I smiled. "Tomorrow, I promise," I said, knowing damn well he wouldn't be sleeping in my bed tonight.

His face fell. "I have to leave today, on some business. Nothing serious, but I should be back tomorrow morning."

I forced my face to fall in disappointed. "Now?" I said, wrapping my arms around him.

He smiled, nuzzling his head into mine. "Unfortunately."

I pulled away. "I was thinking," I began, setting my trap. "Maybe when you get back, we can leave a few weeks early for our New York trip. It could be an early engagement get away where all we do is stay in bed and make love. What do you say?"

His masked faltered. I saw it all in that moment. The pain, the lies, the betrayal, the conflict. It was all there. How had I been blind to it for all these months? He had been playing me this entire time.

He bent down, taking my lips with his. "I love it," he whispered, kissing me again. "And I love you. I want you to know that. No matter what, I love you."

I smiled up at him. "And I love you," I forced the words out of my mouth. "Please hurry back," I wrapped my arms around him, knowing this would be the last time I would ever let him touch me again.

"I will," he said, kissing me on the head before leaving. Once the door was shut, I locked it behind him. I slid against the door allowing every emotion free. I plunged the room into darkness as I sobbed and sobbed. I lost track of time, but I didn't care. I had to get it all out so I would have a clear mind for what came next. The truth.

Chapter Twenty-Eight

Once I was certain Antonio had boarded his plan, I locked myself in his room and began my search. I tore through every book, every drawer, every cabinet. Nothing. I found family business plans but there was nothing that detailed his betrayal. There had to be something.

I thought back to the other morning when I had come in and he was holding a letter. He was unnerved by it and hid it from me. Yes, the evidence was here, I just had to find it. I casted a finder's spell, but the magic slammed back into me with force, indicating that whatever he was hiding wasn't going to be found by using my powers.

I took my knife and tore apart every cushion, his mattress, his pillows. Still nothing. I was sweating after hours of searching. I sat on the edge of the mattress, enraged.

I calmed myself trying to think back to any memory or clue that could help. I looked around the room slowly. My attention snagged on the golden framed mirror hanging on the wall across from his door. A few months back, I had come in and found him closing it.

I jumped from the bed, pulling the mirror away from the wall. It was on hinges and opened like a door. He was hiding something. I scanned my fingers over the surface, noting that one brick was missing the mortar around it. I took my knife, pulling the rectangle free. Inside, was a compartment full of papers, vials, and a book. The book nonna had given me.

I pulled everything free, setting it on the floor in front of me. I didn't know where to begin so I picked up the letter on top and read. It was correspondence between Tony and another person who I assumed was my aunt.

Times, dates, and people's names were listed with instructions of where to be and who to kill. A letter, detailing the murders of all those children a few months back was in the pile. Questions in regard to my progress with my magic. The person wanted details of my relationships with my cousin and nonna. Also, Orion.

The next letter I picked up was title, *Subject Camerino*. The letter outlined the poison Tony had been using to kill Orion. It had to be administered orally. Tony must have been sneaking it in his food or water somehow. I picked up the vial of dark blue liquid, assessing the deadly substance. Tears fell from my eyes. This was it. This was what I hoped I wouldn't find.

I picked up the book next and cracked it open, reading the first line:

This Journal Belongs to: Josephina Ortero, vessel of the moon god-

dess.

Date: 7th of March, 1421

I began to read the accounts of the moon goddess, 600 years ago.

7th of March, 1421:

My powers have awakened. With the horned god by my side, the possibilities are endless. I control the moon and stars. The night bends to my will. The fire of the moon is within me, my greatest weapon. The sea and oceans bow to me. There is nothing I cannot conquer. Now that we have joined in spirit and body, our covens have grown in numbers and power. The legends are true. We are the conduits for our power here on earth.

21ˢᵗ of March 1421:

I cannot keep myself from him. The desire is beyond our control. My powers call to him, as his does to mine. With a single touch from me, he lights the world on fire, and I plunge it back into darkness.

I paused, thinking back to the festival in July when I touched Orion. He glowed like the sun... and then anytime we got too close I... *no*. My heart sank. No, this couldn't be right.... I couldn't be the moon goddess. This wasn't possible. Nonna would have... Oh, my God. That was it. That was what she and Orion have been trying to tell me for months but couldn't because of the curse the seer spoke of. Tears ran down my face but I forced myself to continue reading.

My soul recognized his immediately. Though he was engaged, we still found our way to each other. Our union was destined by centuries of fate. There was nothing and no one that was going to stand in our way. He infuriates me, but in the most exciting and pleasant ways.

I continued reading for the next hour.

December 21, 1422:

I feel weak. My power feels as if it has been leeched from me. My body will not listen to my commands nor heed my will. Alister has taken another lover. Our fighting has turned him away from my bed and led him into another's.

The battle with Obsidian has drained me. I have tapped into my power's reserve and reached too far. My life force is slipping. This self-inflicted sickness grows inside of me by the day. I should have listened to the Elders. I shouldn't have used that spell, but our covens were in danger. I had no choice.

I must speak to him. I must make this right. If we remain apart, I'm as good as dead. But if I can make this right. If we can find our way back to each other... we can heal. I can heal... and live. I must try. Before there is nothing left to make right.

I continued to read, finding that once Alister and Josephina had been reunited and conducted the ceremonial rite, their united magic healed the bond between them, restoring their power and health.

I slammed the leather binding shut, gathering the papers and documents into a pile. I had spent all night reading the letters and the journal. The sun had already risen, and I was running out of time. Tony said he would be back in the morning.

I held the papers close to my chest and rushed towards Orion's room. Nonna had given me the journal. She was trying to break the curse. I could trust her. That I was sure of. Thank God.

I pushed the door open to Orion's room in haste, now out of breath. His mother jumped from the chair she was sleeping in, looking like she was going to strangle me. Orion's eyes fluttered open, peering lazily at me behind his long dark lashes.

"What in Aradia's name do you think you're doing?" Evaline said, storming towards me.

"Get out," I demanded, still trying to catch my breath.

"Excuse me?"

I pushed the papers and journal into her arms and nodded. "Take this to my nonna. Do not give it to anyone else. It is important. It has to do with Obsidian."

Her mouth fell open as she looked at the pile of paperwork. "What are you playing at?" she asked.

"I'm not playing at anything. Tell nonna I found these in Antonio Simonelli's room, hidden behind a wall. Now, please, can I trust you with this?"

She nodded, looking back at her son one last time with a soft smile before she brushed passed me. I shut the door, locking it behind her.

I looked at his frail and dying body. I was the cause of this. I covered my face in shame while tears fell down my cheeks.

He smiled at me softly. "Say it," he whispered. "Say it out loud, little dove."

I took a few steady breaths, gathering the strength. "I'm the moon goddess," I whispered for the first time.

A blast of dark magic unleashed, shaking the castle to its core. It felt like a weight had been lifted from me. Orion took a deep breath in, smiling and laughing while his weak body shook from coughing.

"Thank the gods," he said.

I rushed to his side, taking his hand in mine. "I am so sorry," I cried. "This is all my fault. This is all because of me." Then, everything began to click into place. "My 'to look into' list you made me. You were trying to lead me to the answer."

He nodded, still smiling. "I knew you were smart, and that you'd figure it out."

"Why not just tell me?"

"I couldn't. No one could. It was the curse. We couldn't talk about it with anyone or say a word of it to you. Believe me, I tried."

"So did nonna. Multiple times."

"Do you think Obsidian is behind the curse?"

"Most likely," he replied. "How did you figure it out?"

"Josephina's journal. Nonna gave it to me months ago, but... it was stolen."

"By whom?" he asked.

I bit my lip. "Antonio. He's been working with my aunt. They plan to kill me and make him the horned god's vessel."

"What?" Orion said in shock, trying to sit up.

I told him everything, not leaving out a single detail. I shared the documents I had found. The detailed accounts about each of us. The poison. All of it. I cried during some of the parts. He just sat there, holding my hand through the entire thing. I got to the end, still trying to come up with a plan. I was confident that nonna would know what to do once she received the information I had found.

"I'm going to kill him," Orion growled, now sitting against the headboard.

"That honor is mine," I said, feeling a twinge of pain at the thought. "Orion... I—"

"Stop," he interrupted, still holding onto my hand. "You didn't know. How could you? What matters now is that you know the truth and we are here, together."

I smiled at him, not sure how I felt about everything. "I'm... this is a lot," I admitted.

"I know. You will need time. I am fully aware of that," he said in a soft and understanding manner.

"When did you know?" I asked him.

"The very first time we met. My power flared inside like I had never experienced. Then, when you brought the moon and stars down to us, I knew," he said with a cocked smile.

"You knew this whole time and stood back and watched me fall in love with someone else?"

"It wasn't easy, believe me. But the curse made it impossible to interfere. You had to find out on your own."

"And you were just going to let me marry him while you laid here and died?"

He shrugged. "I love you enough not to be selfish with you. At the end of the day, if you were happy, that was all that mattered to me, little dove. I have no care for myself. You as the moon goddess or just as Seren, will always come first."

I felt another sting of pain hit my heart as tears fell from my eyes. "Why do you call me little dove?" I asked.

"In your Bible, what symbolism does a dove hold?"

"Peace, hope, purity, a promise," I replied.

He nodded, smiling at me. "From the moment I laid eyes on you, you were all those things to me. You were a peace I had search my entire life for. You were my hope of a love and life worth living. You were the purity that lit the way in our dark and unforgiving world. And you were a promise that I would never have to walk through this life alone again. With or without the prophecy, I loved you from the first moment and I will love you till the last."

I sobbed, falling into his arms. He held me, kissing me on top of my head. His entire bare chest lit as my darkness sent the room spinning. We laid in bed together for what seemed like forever.

Finally, I pulled myself from his embrace, knowing work still needed to be done. I pressed a kiss to his cheek, as he brushed the hair from my face. "I'm going to fix this," I whispered.

"I don't want you doing anything alone," he said, looking into my eyes. "Let me come with you."

"No, this is my fault. I am going to fix this and then fix you. We're going to get that life you want so badly, I promise," I said, sliding off the bed.

"Seren, please," he begged. "Don't do anything alone. Promise me."

"Nonna already knows everything. I'm not alone. Don't worry, I'll be back later," I said, before heading to my room.

Then... the waiting began.

Chapter Twenty-Nine

I sat in a chair by the table. I had poured myself a glass of whisky and waited, calmer than I had been the past 24 hours since my discovery. He would seek my out. His arrogance and hope for a life with me would get the best of him. But my aunt was right. Now that I knew the truth, there was no hope for a future for us. There was no hope for him.

The door swung open thirty minutes into my solitary. Antonio stepped into the room breathing deeply. He locked the door behind him, eyes landing on me with heaviness. I knocked back the rest of the whisky, keeping my face calm and unfeeling.

He took a step towards me. "Please, let me explain," he said.

I slammed my hand forward, freezing him in place. I stood from the chair with more power and control than I had ever felt. I walked straight towards him, fighting the desire to completely shred him to pieces.

"There is nothing to explain," I stated. "I found your secrets. I heard your conversation with my aunt, and I've read the journal. I know who I truly am." I dropped my hand allowing him to move freely.

"Seren, please. This isn't that simple."

"How long did you know?" I asked, feeling myself coming undone. "How long did you know I was the moon goddess?"

He froze, dropping his eyes. "Since before I found you in the abbey."

"How?"

"Obsidian has always known," he admitted. "They placed you in that abbey when you were born, hoping to keep you away from your family until you came of age. The nuns knew what you were. That was why they drugged you. They were hoping for a miracle."

"And how long have you been working for them?"

"Two years. One of them is keeping my sister alive. Once I become the horned god, I will be able to heal her completely from her sickness."

"So that was the plan. You hand me over to them and you get a chance at healing your sister?"

"Yes, but—" he paused. "But I fell in love with you. I couldn't let them kill you."

"Oh, give me a break, Antonio. This whole thing has been a joke."

He rushed towards me, trying to touch me but I moved out of reach. "No, Seren, no. I truly love you. I want to marry you. Everything I told you the night I asked you to marry me is true. I have never lied about my feelings for you. Please, if you believe anything, believe that."

I couldn't help it. Tears fell from my eyes. "Liar," I growled between my clinched teeth, trying to regain control of myself. "You knew I couldn't be with you. That I was meant for Orion. Yet you've been pumping him for weeks poison in order to weaken and kill him, all while keeping me from him. Keeping the one thing that you knew would heal him."

"You fell in love with me for me," he said adamantly. "I never forced a thing on you. Not that day in the pool, not our first kiss at the ball, and not the first night we shared together. These have been your decisions. You chose me because you truly love me as I do you. Fuck Orion. Fuck the rest of them." He rushed towards me, grabbing my hands. "Don't you see? Once I become the vessel for the horned god, we can truly be together. We can take down Obsidian, I can save my sister, and we can give back to the coven's as it should be."

"But you weren't chosen as the vessel, Antonio…. Orion was."

"It doesn't matter. Obsidian has found a spell, a ritual to transfer the mark of the vessel. We can have it all, beautiful. Everything we've ever wanted."

"And what, Orion is the one we have to sacrifice so we can ride off into the sunset together?"

"It's one sacrifice for the future we've dreamt of."

I took a step back. "You can't be serious," I whispered, looking at the monster I had allowed myself to love.

"Please, Seren, please stop and think. We love each other. We want the covens to survive. We want to take down Obsidian. We can do this – together."

I shook my head in disbelief. "I won't murder Orion, and it's too late, Antonio. Nonna knows everything. I gave her everything I found in your little hiding space."

His face fell. His jaw tenses as I watched the rage inside of him grow. He slammed his arms across my dresser, knocking everything to the floor. He yelled in a fit of anger, holding his head in his hands. He took a deep breath, calming himself as he paced back and forth.

"Not the end of the world. We can explain this to her," he said, seeming to try and rationalize what was happening.

"Antonio, it's over," I whispered. "And we are never going to be together. You made your decisions, now, so have I."

He froze, his eyes were glued to the floor. "You don't mean that," he said, shaking his head.

"Yes, I do."

"So, what," he said sarcastically. "You're going to skip a couple doors down to Orion's room, spread your legs for him and make all his booboos go away?"

I froze, not knowing how to respond.

"Oh, I read the journal too, beautiful. I know that's how Alister healed Josephina. Completing the rite. Joining the two gods together as one."

"I've already seen Orion this morning," I said, knowing I was playing with fire. "He knows everything."

Tony's mouth fell open as he stood in front me in shock. I knew what he was thinking, and I allowed him to believe whatever his mind was telling him. "You... and Camerino were—" he stopped, unable to finish his sentence.

"Like I said, it's over, Antonio." A massive force of power unleashed from him. My entire room trembled. I went flying back, trapped against the wall. My table exploded, along with my nightstands and dressers. He walked towards me holding his hand steady while I fought against his power.

He lifted me off the ground sliding my back up against the wall as he levitated in front of me. He wasn't hurting me, but I was trapped. We were now eye to eye.

He slammed his hand against the wall near my face. "You let Orion, put his hands on your body?" he sneered. "While you were still wearing my ring?" He pinned my left arm against the wall.

"Who touches me is no longer any of your concern!" I yelled.

"You are mine. Mine!" he screamed.

I felt the burning erupt deep inside of me. I allowed it to well, before it finally unleashed. My power ricocheted him across the room, slamming him into the opposite wall. I fell to the ground, catching myself on my feet before standing, readying for battle.

I wrapped my shadows around a broken dresser drawer and launched it at him, lighting it on fire as it flew across the room. He avoided it, causing the floor beneath me to warp, sending me to the ground.

I gathered the moisture in the room, creating a solid surface for myself to stand on before picking up shards of my broken glass. I launched them in his direction. He dodged, missing most of them, but I saw one sliver make contact with his left shoulder. He winced, pulling it free. Blood streamed from the wound.

Fire erupted from my hands as I steadied my breathing, feeling my life force fueling the chaotic magic.

"What are you going to do, beautiful?" he said, walking on air towards me. "Kill me?"

"Yes," I said, before launching the flames towards him in a cylinder of pure rage. I screamed, allowing it to take as much life as it wanted. I needed this to be over. I needed to erase him. I needed to be free.

I let my hands fall to my sides, feeling drained from the amount of energy it had taken from me. The floor had stopped moving. I lowered my liquid platform to the ground, dropping to my knees. I began sobbing unable to look away from the mound of fire that now consumed Antonio's body. The man I had loved.

I gripped my head, trying to force the pain to stop when a scream of pure pain erupted from within me. I covered my face, wishing there had been another way. When I removed my hands, I looked up to see Antonio standing in front of me completely unphased. His face was racked with worry and fear.

"Run," he whispered, but before I could, my aunt materialized in front of me next to him. Her arm patting the side of his shoulder.

"Oh, now. I couldn't have you barbecuing my favorite little spy now, could I?" she said, looking down at me. I stood with shaking legs to face the two of them.

"There is still time," Antonio said to her. "There is another way, I promise."

She snapped her fingers, and he became mute. "That is enough from you. You've had time to play with the little goddess.... My turn," she said, grinning from ear to ear. "Two other figures appeared behind me, shoving needles into my neck. I winced, feeling the instant paralytic swimming through my bloodstream.

My aunt leaned down next to me, clicking her tongue as she frowned. "Should feel familiar right?" she said. "It's the same little concoction Sister Odette pumped you full of all those years. Little did she know she was administering a potion made by witches." My aunt laughed at herself. "No need to worry. Everything will soon be over. Night, night, little bean.'

The darkness took hold, pulling me into the deepest sleep I had ever experienced. I remember falling, but nothing else. The sounds around me muffled and all I could do was pray. Pray that nonna would find me. Pray that there would be time to save Orion. Pray the covens would survive.

Chapter Thirty

"Keep her drugged," I heard a female voice say as I began to come to. "We're not taking any chances."

I was strapped to a St. Andrew's cross with needles in each arm. I felt weak and lethargic. They were siphoning my blood with some type of machine I could hear pumping off to the side. My head began to spin as more of the drug took hold, pulling me back under.

"Sweetheart," I heard a voice whisper. "Sweetheart... Seren. Wake up, baby. You need to wake up."

I opened my eyes, willing the haze to dissipate. I could hear chains rattling in the distance. I was barely able to move my body as I lay on the cold stone floor of a cell. I tried to force myself up, but

I was too weak. Shackles were locked around my wrists and ankles, feeling as if they each weight a hundred pounds.

"Seren, look at me," said the voice. "You need to wake up. You need to fight the drug."

I turned towards the voice to see my aunt, shackled alongside me, just out of reach. My body jolted farther away in response. I forced mind to clear, trying to focus. She was the reason I was here. She was the reason for all of this.

She put her hands up in a defensive gesture. "I'm not going to hurt you, honey. You need to listen to me," she whispered, looking back towards the door to make sure we were still alone. "You have more power than you know. You need to reach deep and tap into that power. You can get yourself out of here before it's too late."

"Stay away," I whimpered.

Tears began to fall from her eyes. "Honey, I—" the door unlocked, as two Obsidian warlocks strolled through. My aunt looked to me and then back to them. "She needs rest. If you take anymore before her body recovers you are going to kill her."

"Shut up, elder," one of them snapped.

"We aren't here for her," the other said, laughing wickedly.

My aunt looked at me with heavy eyes and smiled. I could see her face was bruised and cuts adorned her temples and cheeks. "Dig deep," she whispered as they took her by the chains and dragged her across the ground out of the cell.

She fought and yelled, but in her condition, she was no match for them. I watched while they hit her a few times, until her body went still. Not bothering to care, they continued to drag her unconscious form out of the room.

"Seren, wake up," whispered a male's voice. *Tap, tap, tap.* I heard something banging on the ground near me. "Wake up, beautiful," the voice said again. Something in my heart tugged at the nickname.

I forced my eyes open and saw Antonio sitting next to me with a cup of water and a plate of food. He gave me a tender smile. I had enough energy to push myself from the floor, scooting as far away from him as I could manage. His face fell.

"Please," I whispered. "Just leave me alone. You've done enough."

"I'm going to get you out of here," he said softly.

"How?" I asked, desperate.

"I'm working on it. You just need to trust me."

I laughed. "I did. That didn't work out too well for me last time."

He dropped his eyes to the floor, pushing the cup of water

towards me. "You need to hydrate."

"How do I know it's not more poison?"

"Seren, please. I know we are in a bad place, but… just drink."

I took the glass and slowly tried bringing it to my lips, but I was too weak. The water sloshed and spilled out of the cup. Tony reached out steadying the glass and gently tipped the cup to my lips. The water felt like nails scraping against my throat. When I was finished, he set the glass aside, staring at me.

"I am so sorry," he said, his eyes welling with tears. "I am so sorry, for all of this."

"Was… was it all a lie?" I asked, my emotions raw and exposed for the world to see. "Was any of it real?"

I felt his hand grab mine. I was too weak to pull away. "Every moment between us was real. Please do not question that. Please, Seren."

"I… I really loved you, Antonio. I wanted to build a life with you. A family," I cried.

"And we can have all of that. You just… you just have to forgive me and let me make this right. I love you, beautiful. I am going to get you out of here." He kissed me gently on the head before going to get up. I grabbed his arm. Something like desperation took hold of me.

"Please don't leave me here. Please," I cried. "Take me with you."

He cupped my cheeks with his hands. "I will come back for you. I promise," he said, kissing my head again before leaving the cell.

The lights went out and I was left in the dark; cold and broken.

"Get her up," said a deep and raspy voice. "She's ready to go another round."

"Should we drug her again?" asked another. I didn't move, allowing them to believe I was still passed out.

The other one kicked me in the stomach. I held my breath, willing myself to reman still. "She looks pretty out of it to me. Get her up," he said just before the other flung me over his shoulder with ease.

I opened my eyelids slightly, catching glimpses of my prison. The halls looked new and clean. It resembled the layout of a hotel. The carpet was black with gray speckles woven into the design. The walls were painted white with black doors and golden knobs. Artwork hung every few feet along with wall sconces.

We passed through a doorway, and I could physically feel the magical energy rippling through me. The entire ambiance changed. The bright hallway faded away. A dark and damp room appeared revealing a medieval dungeon. The floor was made of gray stone that extended to the walls. There were no openings...

no windows.

I closed my eyes while the two guards strapped me to the St. Andrew's cross. The raw wood of the cross scraped my exposed skin as splinters burrowed underneath. Once I was strapped onto the structure, I heard cranking of gears. The cross slowly rose into a vertical position.

The shaking of shackles caught my attention. I wearily opened my eyes and saw Aunt Thora, bloodied, and bruised, laying a few feet from me. She forced herself up on her arm and looked up. Her left eye was so swollen I couldn't see her eyeball. Her lip was split, and her right leg appeared broken.

The back door opened. Aunt Thora walked in followed by Antonio. My eyes widened. I looked from the Thora shackled to the ground to the Thora walking freely into the room. The healthy Thora stepped up to the table where the needles and blades were displayed.

"Oh, good. You're awake, little bean. Now, we can finally have a proper conversation," said the healthy Thora.

My mind was spinning as I tried to figure out what in the hell was going on. I look to Antonio, but he refused to make eye contact.

"Annalise, please," begged the Thora on the ground. "She is your daughter."

My heart dropped to my stomach. My mother... she was alive... and she was... she was working with Obsidian.

My mother walked over to my aunt, taking her face violently in her hand. "We've already had this conversation, sister. Shut up or I will have your tongue removed. You've been little help thus far. I'm about to dispose of you completely unless you give me what I want." Annalise returned in front of me, taking a long hard look at my face.

"You are beautiful," she said, drawing the back of her knuckles down my face. "Too bad the universe chose you to be the goddess's vessel. We could have ruled this world, side by side. Mother and daughter."

I didn't reply. I was still too stunned by the fact that my mother was alive… and trying to kill me. And Antonio knew. He had been working with her this entire time. I heard the chains that contained my aunt rattle. Thora sat back on her knees, her eyes focused on her sister with pure hate and rage.

"Something to say, little sister?" Annalise asked.

"Like Seren would ever join you," replied Thora. "She is the definition of purity. There is no world where she would work with you. You're delusional."

"You never know," said my mother. "If I would have been the one to raise her, all of this could have been different. Instead, I gave her to the nuns to raise because I knew this day would come. Still, what a waste."

"You knew?" I whispered. "You knew I was the vessel from birth?"

"Long before that, little bean. I knew as soon as I conceived you. I hadn't been with a man and yet, there you were, growing inside of me. The timelines matched up to when the gods were supposed to return so it wasn't too hard to put the pieces together. I just told everyone you were a result of my bad choices when it came to men. My mother and sister believed it without question." She leaned in, pretending to whisper. "I was the black sheep of the family. Surprise, surprise," she laughed, walking back to the table.

"This isn't you," cried, Thora. "This isn't you Annalise. Think about what you are about to do. You are good, I know you are."

Annalise touched the side of Tony's arm, flinging her hand towards her sister. "Shut up!" she yelled. Thora grabbed her head in pain as she began to scream. "You do not know me. You never did. We may have shared a womb but that is where the similarities end. I am more powerful than you will be or have ever been. You do not hold a torch to what I am capable of. You never have and never will!"

Thora dropped to the floor as Annalise released her. Thora curled her legs into her chest, muffled cries of pain followed.

My mother moved back over to me, tapping her finger on her bottom lip. "I think we're ready for phase two," she said. "Go get the doctor," she ordered one of her guards.

Antonio's eyes widened. I saw panic streak his face. "You can't rush this," he said, moving to her side. "You don't have enough plasma or blood. If you complete the process now and you need more to withstand the transfusion, there is no bringing her back from the dead."

My mind began to race. What were they talking about?

My mother smiled at Antonio. "Oh, honey, would you like me to leave so you can have one more roll in the hay with my daughter before she is dead. Is that it?"

"No," he snapped. "I am serious. You are letting your emotions get the best of you." My mother walked over to my aunt and slid her foot towards her, making contact with her arm. "You get one chance at this and if it fails we—"

Annalise threw her hand up towards Antonio causing him to choke and gasp for air. His body began to shake and convulse.

She walked over to him, smiling. "Now, now, sweet spy. Everything is on track, and it is time to test our theory. The faster she dies, the faster your sister lives, remember? We have our orders. He grows impatient. Now, do as I say." She dropped her hands, releasing the hold on Antonio.

"What are you going to do with me?" I asked.

"Nothing you'll remember," she said, giggling to herself.

Thora began laughing as she pushed herself back up from the floor. My mother rolled her eyes, making an exasperated motion. "What is it now, Thora? For the love of hell, am I going to have to dose you to get you to shut up?"

My aunt began to laugh hysterically. She had cracked. She had lost her mind. She swayed back and forth.

"Out with it, dammit," my mother yelled, taking a step towards her.

My aunt paused, looking at my sister with a wicked smile. "You've forgotten who her mate is, haven't you?" asked Thora.

"Of course not. What are you getting at?"

"Her mate is the god of the hunt. By now, he has been able to track her to this very location."

My mother chuckled, "There is no way he can track us here. Believe me, I've made sure of that."

"You also forget who our mother is," Thora said just before the door blasted open, sending shards of stone and wood soaring through the air.

Annalise went flying back, slamming into the table of knives. Her two guards began to conjure chant, conjuring their magic, aiming for the intruders. Tony got up and rushed over to me, working to undo the latches on the straps.

My mother flung him across the room, rising to meet whoever had interrupted her. Nonna stepped through the door, sending bolts of electricity into the two guards that tried to attack. Elder Mystic and Elder Strange, along with Mrs. Camerino stepped out from behind her, casting a magical net, trapping my mother, Antonio, and her guards inside.

Orion appeared, still looking sickly and frail. He scanned the room until his attention locked onto me. He marched down the stairs, appearing to be stronger than the last time I had seen him.

Frankie appeared next, along with Gabby and Bella. She rushed to her mother's side, working to remove the shackles.

Orion appeared in front of me. His warm scent was like life itself. His large hands unfastened the latches. "You came," I whispered with relief.

"Of course, I did. I will always find you," he whispered with a soft smile. My weak body fell into his arms. I was unable to stand let alone walk. He propped me up against him while the girls helped Aunt Thora make her way towards the elders.

I watched nonna walk with her head high towards the magical prison that encased my mother. Her daughter. Nonna's face was mixed with something akin to shock, disbelief, and disappointment.

"*Mother*," Annalise said, mockingly.

"Annalise," nonna hissed. "What has happened to you?"

"Evolution happened to me. Power happened to me. Control. Everything I have ever wanted, I now possess. No thanks to you."

"Why?" nonna whispered. I saw the despair on her face. "You are our family. We loved you. Why do this? Why help them?"

Annalise began laughing. "Love is a weakness mother, not a strength. I don't want your love and I don't want this family. I have come into my true power, and it is delicious. Worth any sacrifice, including that of my only child. They power he has gifted me, in return for her sacrifice has no comparison. And I am not helping them... I am them. I am Obsidian."

My mother slammed her hands down causing the building to rumble. The stone in the walls cracked and broke apart. An earth-shattering scream erupted from Annalise. Her eyes went black. All color leeched from her skin as black veins appeared, crawling along her veins.

With one powerful movement, the magical cage around her shatter. Obsidian demons busted through the door across from us by the dozens. My mother opened her mouth, consuming the magic that the elders had used to create the cage, eliminating it complete. Nothing stood between us and them.

"Get them out of here, now!" nonna ordered as the elders prepared for battle. "We will hold them off as long as we can. Now go." Without another word, Orion picked me up and bolted down the hall. Frankie and the others followed, carrying Thora with them. We passed room after room. The walls around us shook and the lights flickered. One by one the black doors of the hotel hall blew apart in a fit of rage.

They ducked and dodged, trying to stay upright until we reached an exit. A door in front of us blew apart just before we crossed it sending all six of us slamming back into the wall. Orion held me tightly, shielding my body from the blast with his own.

I looked up, peering across the hall inside of a dimly lit room. The dust and debris settled around us. A young woman laid in a bed. Her hair was jet black. Her skin was pale, and her body frail. She was hooked up to tubes and machines as the beeping echoed throughout the hall. I knew instantly who it was.

"We need to get her out," I said, looking to Aunt Thora. "Can you walk with just Frankie helping?"

"I can," she answered.

"Gabby and Bella, can you carry that girl out?"

Both nodded.

"Who is she," asked Frankie.

"It doesn't matter. She's innocent and she's coming with us," I said, trying to move my legs but it was pointless.

"Hurry, up," ordered Orion. Gabby and Bella went in, detaching the girl from the machines. They each took a side, dragging her from the bed and out the door.

"What about nonna and the others?" I asked Orion.

"They will be fine," he assured me, hoisting my body up and into his arms. Frankie and the others rushed ahead. Parts of the ceiling caved in right in front of Orion and I, dividing us from the group. They turned back, hesitant to continue without us.

"Go," yelled Orion, searching for another way out.

"What do we do now?" I asked.

"Don't worry, little dove. I'll find a way out." Orion was burning up. The sickness the poison had caused was still affecting him. I wrapped my arms around his neck, holding tightly.

Two doors on either side of us opened. Four Obsidian witches and warlocks stepped through, strung out on demon possession. Their bodies cracked and moved just like the ones I had killed in the dungeon back home. Orion backed up, placing me gently against the wall.

I was able to sit up on my own. I focused, trying to summon any ounce of magic I could. Orion stood, blocking them from getting to me.

"How noble," one laughed as they surrounded us.

"The god protecting his goddess."

"You know, horned god, the two of you always repeat the same pattern," another said.

"The two of you are good for a couple of decades."

"And then," interrupted another, "one falls in love with another, killing the other god."

"Or the mating bond never clicks into place."

"That one is always fun to watch."

"We thought it was happening ahead of schedule this time," laughed one of them.

"It would have been so easy then."

"But you two had to ruin it," one snapped.

"History always repeats itself."

"It's just a matter of time."

"She isn't yours, little god."

"She never will be."

"She is his. Always his."

Orion was apparently done listening to their side chatter. He took a dagger from his belt and slammed it into one their heads without hesitation. He took out his gun, slamming bullets into the second's chest and then skull. The remaining two demons lunged at him, jumping and slashing, beginning to chant. Orion was able to throw them off, emptying the rest of his clip into their heads and hearts.

Orion reloaded his gun before bending down to pick me up. He took off through another door which led to a series of new doorways. I could hear his lungs rattling as he fought to breath. His energy was depleting.

The sound of growling and scratching nails trailed behind, closing in all around us. I looked over his shoulder, seeing six demons and counting who were running on all fours.

"Orion," I whispered.

"I know," he said in between breaths. We opened the door into a circular outdoor courtyard that was completely bricked off without a visible exit. The walls were smooth and too high to climb. There was nowhere to run.

Orion backed away from the demons as they guarded the only way in or out. "Do you have enough energy to shift?" I asked.

He shook his head, looking down at me. "No, I'm sorry," he whispered.

"How many clips do you have?" I asked.

"This is my last one. I used the rest getting into this place," he answered. I felt the terror and dread fill me. He placed me against the far back wall before getting into a defensive stance, pointing the gun towards them.

"No where to run, little gods," one said with a snicker. Orion opened fire, putting two pullets in his head. The other five attacked, crawling on the rounded edges of the courtyard like wild animals.

Orion aimed, firing off a few bullets at a time. He nailed two of them, but they weren't lethal hits. Orion continued to fire until his chamber clicked, indicating the clip was empty. He dropped his gun pulling out a knife. A small flickering flames swirled around his hands. It was nothing in comparison to the power he had before the sickness.

I focused on my own magic, trying to conjure my shadows, but the poison still swam through my system. Nothing but flickering fog formed at my fingertips. Orion unleashed his small funnel of fire, missing them completely. He hunched over in pain. He stumbled back. He was approaching burnout.

The demons laughed. "Oh," one said, now walking on their hind legs towards us. "You want to play with fire, do you?" The demon began chanting conjuring a pool of blistering hot flames between his hands. Orion turned around, dashing for me just in time to throw his body over mine as the demon unleashed the tunnel of flames, heading straight for us.

Orion scooped me underneath him, cocooning me from the heat. With every last ounce of strength I had, I threw out my arms, allowing my icy shadows to act as a barrier. The flames slammed against my magic. I cried out in pain, but I held my hands steady, taking as much of the heat and energy that I could manage.

Orion cried out. Even with my weak shield, the flames still ate away at his back. I could smell his flesh burning. I pushed harder, fighting to stay firm for as long as I could. Orion's head pressed against mine. My arms began to shake along with my body.

"You're... burning... out," he grunted, between his clenched teeth.

"I know," I cried, tears falling from my face. Some were because of fear, but most were because of the pain. "Thank you... for coming for me."

"Always. I'll find you again. I'll find you, no matter how long it takes," he said, right before he screamed in agonizing pain. My shield was failing. I pushed hard, now forcing myself to my knees as I extended my arms towards the heat above Orion's shoulders.

I screamed and screamed with every ounce of passion, anger, and hate I had. I watched the flames crawl closer. This was it. This was the end.

A sharp snap sounded above me accompanied by a blinding white light that slammed into the courtyard, sending the demons flying backwards, smashing into the stone walls. I wrapped my body trembling body around Orion's. I was burning out. I closed my eyes, holding onto him while I shivered from the excess of energy I had exerted.

I felt the ice crawling up my extremities, making its way to my heart. I continued to hold onto him like a lifeline. My vision blurred and the ringing in my ears grew. Another snap of white light appeared, knocking the dirt into the air around us.

My fingers were now completely black. My muscles involuntarily spasmed and my teeth rattled together. My lungs became cold, making it impossible to breath. I gasped short, little breaths, looking down at Orion lying unconscious against my body.

My throat constricted.

My head spun.

And then... my heart stopped.

CHAPTER THIRTY-ONE

*B*eep. *Beep. Beep.* My head felt as if I was stuck in a fog. I tried to open my eyes, but all they seemed to do was roll into the back of my head. My limbs felt glued to the bed. I started small. Moving a single finger at a time until I could lift my hand and then my arm.

I groaned, feeling the tubes sticking up my nose. I pulled them out, forcing myself to sit up. My head was pounding. I was going to be sick. I fell out of the bed onto the cold floor, grabbing a bucket and puking my guts out. Tubes pulled at my skin from the IV stuck in my arm. I ripped everything I was attached to out and stumbled towards the door.

Frankie appeared on the other side, looking like she had just finished running a marathon. Her lips stretched into a smile. "Nonna, come quick!" she yelled.

Thank God, I thought to myself. They both were alive. Frankie rushed to my side, helping brace my weight against her.

"Orion," I said softly with a raspy and dry voice.

"He's okay," she said. "Still unconscious, but alive."

I began to cry with relief. "Did we lose anyone?" I asked. She set me back on the edge of the bed, bringing a class of water to my lips.

"Elder Strange didn't make it. Neither did a few younger witches and warlocks that volunteered to help with the rescue mission. We lost seven total."

I felt the weight of their losses deep inside of me. This was my fault. All because I trusted the wrong person. Because I let someone in. I let someone too close.

"How's your mom?" I whispered. At the same moment, Aunt Thora appeared in my doorway alongside nonna. Tears began to run down Thora's face. She rushed forward, pulling me into a violent embrace.

"Oh, thank you gods, thank you," she cried, sobbing as she kissed my head over and over again. She pulled back, brushing the sides of my face with her hands.

"I am so sorry," I cried, knowing she had experienced torture because of me.

"Oh, sweetheart, it wasn't your fault. None of this was," she replied, kissing my cheeks.

"We survived," said nonna, her voice firm and strong as always.

I looked up at her and smiled. "Thank you for coming for me," I said.

"Always, bambina. Though, we had no choice," she laughed, looking at the other two.

Frankie smiled. "Orion was up in arms when he found out you

had been taken," she explained. "He didn't even give anyone a chance to form a plan. He was able to track you well enough thanks to your little birthday present he gave you and then as soon as he had a locked location, he shifted us all there without our consent."

"What?" I gasped.

"It's true," said nonna. "We were in the middle of a meeting in his room when he transported us to where you were without our permission. Little shit." We all started laughing.

"I need to see him," I said, forcing my weak body to move.

"Woah there," said Frankie, stabilizing me before I fell.

"You need to rest, bambina," said nonna.

"Take me to him. Please," I said in desperation.

Nonna looked me over and then signaled to the nurse behind her. She brought in a wheelchair. Nonna took me down the hall to where he was being monitored. The chair stopped at the edge of the bed. After locking the breaks, nonna bent down beside me.

"You were so brave, my darling," she said, brushing her hand against my arm. "I was worried sick."

"You knew who I was. How?" I asked.

"I always felt like something was off when Frankie was named as the moon goddess's vessel, but no other candidate showed any other gifts that could rival hers. But when I first met you...when I looked into your eyes... I knew."

I paused, looking down at my hands. "Did you... did you kill Annalise?"

Nonna sucked in air, like if I had physically struck her. "No... I... I couldn't," she admitted. "She got away. Elder Strange is dead and it is because I hesitated."

I took her hands, bringing them to my lips and kissed each one. "We will find a way to defeat them. Like you always say, we are stronger together."

She smiled at me with tears in her eyes. "Together," she whispered.

I turned my attention to Orion. His curly hair framed his face. His large muscular body laid deathly still. No signs of life besides the heart monitor beeping next to him. "Can I have some time with him?" I asked.

"Of course, bambina," she rose, kissing me on the head before shutting the door behind her.

I pushed myself up and out of the chair, painfully crawling in bed next to him. Making sure not to disturb any of his IV's, I nuzzled myself in between his side and arm, laying my head on his strong, high chest. I wrapped my arm around him, take in the comfort I felt of being this close. I closed my eyes, submitting to my body's need for sleep.

Chapter
Thirty-Two

"**A**re you good?" asked Frankie, hovering over me like I was a helpless child.

"How many times are you going to have to hear me say yes before you believe me?" I answered, pulling my shirt on over my head.

"A few more times wouldn't hurt," she shrugged.

"I have been cooped up in here for two weeks. The healers say I am fine. I feel great and I even ran a few miles yesterday on the treadmill. How much more proof do you need?"

"Well, shame on me for being so overbearing," she said, making a dramatic gesture with her hands. "When I found you in that mosh pit, you were twitching like a junky and frozen solid. It was the scariest shit I have ever seen."

I paused, thinking back to that memory. Back to the moment I thought I was dead. "Thank you," I said softly. "For saving us. If you hadn't gotten there when you did, we would have—"

She held up her hand. "Don't even say it. I don't want to hear it," she replied. "I may not be the moon goddess, but that doesn't mean I don't have some wicked star powers, thank you very much."

I laughed, wrapping my arms around her. "You were brilliant."

She shrugged. "I know."

"Any word on Orion this morning?" I asked.

He still hadn't woken up. His body seemed to be healing but his brain activity was minimal.

"Not yet," she said. We exited the room, heading down the medical wing towards the living quarters of the castle. "I bet you're excited to sleep in your own bed again."

Bile rose in my throat. My bed. The bed I had last shared with Antonio.

"How about we get a new one," I said plainly.

"Oh..." Frankie stopped, looking uncomfortable. "Right. We haven't talked about To—"

"And I don't want to. We have too much on our plates right now."

She grabbed my arm, pulling me back. "Seren, you need to talk to someone. What he did... what you two had... I can't begin to imagine—"

"It's over," I said firmly. "It was all a ploy. It meant nothing, and it's over."

Aunt Thora came rushing down the hall towards us.

"What is it?" I asked. "It is Orion?"

She shook her head. "No, but someone else is awake and asking a lot of questions."

We followed her to another medical room. I turned the corner to see a beautiful young girl with piercing green eyes and jet-black hair sitting up in her bed. She looked frightened and unsure as she scanned the room. Frankie and Aunt Thora stood on either side of me as we stared at her.

"You still haven't told us who we rescued," stated Frankie.

I took a single step towards the girl, noting her small, frail frame. Her soft, supple face. The resemblance was uncanny and, frankly, made me uncomfortable. Her bottom lip quivered as her eyes found mine. "Who are you and where am I?" she asked.

"Aunt Thora," I said, keeping my eyes on the girl. "Contact the Luna Coven. Inform them we have Giana Simonelli in our custody." I turned away from her, passing my family. Frankie followed me out.

"You've got to be shitting me," she said, running to catch up. "Did we just steal Antonio's presumably dead sister?"

"Sure did," I said, heading up the stairs towards the main hall.

"And what the hell are you going to do with her?"

"She's our bargaining chip. A way to control Antonio if need arises."

"And what happens when her parents arrive to take her home?"

"They won't be permitted to leave the castle," I said plainly.

Frankie stopped, pulling me to the side of the hall. "Seren," she said softly. "We aren't at war with the Luna Coven. You can't hold members of their coven here against their will."

"Says who?"

"Our treaty."

"I've read the treaty. Their son has been working against all seven covens for years. He attempted to murder and then successfully kidnap the moon goddess. He opened fire against three coven leaders and their members. As a result, one leader and seven members died. He has been sharing personal information with Obsidian and acting as their spy." I took a step towards her, feeling the rage burn underneath my skin.

"Once the other two arrive," I continued, "they will remain under our roof as our guests, our prisoners, whatever you want to call it. They will not be leaving until I say otherwise. Am I clear?"

Frankie looked at me as if she didn't recognize the person standing before her. She nodded.

"Good," I said, moving towards my room.

Once I was inside, I shut the door, locking it behind me. I had been surrounded by people since I had returned to the land of the living. I just needed a second to breathe by myself. I turned around and noted that my room had been cleaned from the fight Antonio and I had right before I was kidnapped. Everything was put back in its original places.

The pictures where my mother's face had once been where now replaced with those of me and my family. Frankie and I on my birthday. Nonna, Aunt Thora, Frankie, and I at the ball. Some of Gabby and Bella. These were my pictures. My life.

I sat on the bench in front of my vanity and looked into the mirror. I felt the tears fighting to be released. I covered my mouth, fighting them back. The diamond on my engagement ring shimmered in the light.

I pulled my hand back, looking at the beautifully cut stone. Everything this ring once meant to me was now dead. I pulled it from my finger and shoved it inside a drawer. I covered my face, allowing the emotions of the past few weeks to envelop me. I was tired of being strong. Tired of appearing emotionless. It was exhausting.

"Beautiful..." I heard a faint voice in the distance whisper. My head sprung up, searching the room in terror. There was no way he had made his way back into the castle. Nonna had made sure that he nor my mother would never be able to set foot in these walls again.

"Over here," he whispered in his normal deep tone.

I turned around, looking into the mirror. Black fog faded, revealing Antonio's face. I sprang to my feet, calling my shadows to me, preparing for an attack. He laughed, shaking his head with his sexy and devious smile. "I can't hurt you from here, nor would I."

"And why in the hell should I believe a word you say?"

"Because I love you."

"Shut up," I cried. "Shut up!"

"It's true... and it always will be. Now, put your shadows away and calm yourself so we can talk."

I reeled my magic back, standing in front of the mirror. "How are you here?" I asked.

"That's not important. You've taken something of mine," he said, leaning back in his chair.

"I presume you mean Giana?"

"Yes. Seren, she needs your mother. She has been syphoning the sickness from her body. Without her, she will die from her illness. Please. Let her go."

"Nonna is a syphon. She can keep your sister alive."

He shook his head. "No. Lucia doesn't possess the power it requires."

"She is the most powerful witch this coven has ever seen."

"Your mother possesses a different power. A power far greater than anything the covens have seen."

"How?"

"I don't know. But I do know it's of demonic origin."

"You mean to tell me there's a demon riding shot gun with my mother?"

"No, Seren. Her power comes from a far greater source. A pure source of evil. Something older and stronger than anything we've ever encountered. I don't know what it is, but I plan to find out."

I paused, chewing over his words, making mental notes of what to share with nonna and the others. "She's awake," I said, attempting to change the subject.

His face fell in shock. "What? How?"

"I'm not a healer, but she's awake. Your parents are on their way."

"Is she healed?" he asked calmly.

"No, but the illness is weakened. Once Orion comes into his power, I will ask him to heal her completely."

Antonio dropped his eyes from mine. I could see the pain. "Thank you," he whispered.

"Let me make myself clear," I said, leaning against the vanity. "I am not doing this for you. She is an innocent and doesn't deserve to die because of your lack in judgment. But make no mistake, once your parents arrive, they will be placed under arrest, unable to leave unless I say. So, I suggest that if you want your family to stay alive, you better stop playing games and feed me as much information as you can get your hands on."

He smirked. "How strong you've become," he said, with something like pride flickering behind his eyes.

"Am I clear?" I asked again.

"Perfectly," he answered, leaning forward. "Now, how are you feeling? I heard you almost burnt out."

"Why do you care? If I'm not mistaken, you had plotted with my mother behind my back for months to kill me."

He rubbed his hands down his face. "Alright, let's have it out. I'm an open book. Anything you want to know."

I thought to myself about how I could use his desperation to my advantage. I gave him a cocked smile, taking a seat in front of the mirror. "Fine," I said, "but first, I need you to repeat after me."

He laughed. "An honesty spell? Seriously, beautiful?"

"Do you want me to trust you or not?"

"Fine, have at it."

I placed my hand against the mirror, as did he. "*Veritas, asept delmito forgoious,*" I said softly, pulling from my power.

"*Veritas, asept delmito forgoious,*" we said together. "*Veritas, asept delmito forgoious. Veritas, asept delmito forgoious. "Veritas, asept delmito forgoious.*"

I could feel the spell click into place assuring me Antonio would never be able to lie to me again. I pulled my hand away.

"First question," he said with a smug smile on his face.

"How did you meet my mother?"

"She approached me when Giana was on her death bed back in Sicily. I thought she was Thora at first, but quickly realized she was Annalise. At first, she told me that she could heal my sister if I agreed to feed her information about the Étoile Coven. After a few months, when my sister still wasn't healed, she told me the real plan."

"Which was?"

He exhaled. "She had found a way to change the vessels that the gods had chosen for their reincarnation. She was planning on become the vessel for the moon goddess and I would be the vessel for the horned god, giving me the power to heal my sister completely."

My stomach dropped. He was... he was willing to become my mother's mate... my mother's lover. "You... and my mother?"

"It was never like that," he blurted. "I never even thought that far ahead. All I cared about was healing Giana."

"Why not just ask Orion when he came to power?"

"It was taking too long. By the time Frankie was announced as the moon goddess and the proper amount of time had passed in order to conduct the rite, my sister would have been dead. Your mother has been the only thing keeping her alive these past two years."

"And when did she tell you about me?"

"Last year when Frankie was announced as the vessel. That's when she assigned me to you. To watch... and study."

"You've been spying on me for the past year?"

"Yes. I had to make sure the nuns didn't kill you."

I paused, thinking back to the night he saved me. "And the demon dogs?"

He dropped his eyes. "Obsidian was controlling them. They wouldn't have attacked me. It was a plan to help you trust me."

I ran my hands through my hair. I didn't know if I wanted to cry, scream, or punch the mirror.

"Seren, please listen. Everything after that point was not controlled by your mother, Obsidian, or anyone for that matter. I wasn't planning on seducing you, or making you fall in love with me.... It just happened. And I don't regret it. I regret a lot. Betraying you. Putting you in danger. Making the deal with your mother in the first place, but not you... not loving you. You are the best thing that has ever happened to me. Those words have always been true."

I bit the side of my cheek, trying to keep myself together. "I'm done for today," I whispered.

"I understand," he said, leaning against the table. "When you want to talk again, all you have to do is touch the mirror and think of me. For what it's worth, I'm glad you're healthy and safe."

I looked up in the mirror at the man I loved, feeling like a part of myself was dying. How could I still love him, after everything he had done? After how he betrayed me? My heart was a curse. These feelings... love... it was all a curse.

"Goodbye, Antonio,' I said, waving my hand across the mirror. He vanished into a black haze of smoke.

After an hour of processing what direction my life was now taking, I headed back down to the medical wing to Orion's room. He was still unresponsive. His mother sat on the other side of the bed, holding his hand in silence.

I knocked on the doorframe, trying to be respectful. Her eyes snapped to mine, expressionless. "Hi Mrs. Camerino. My I come in?" She nodded, turning her attention back to her son.

I went to the other side of the bed, sitting in the chair next to him. There were still wrappings around him from the burns on his back. Other than that, he looked beautiful, like an angel. There was a pile of wadded up tissues on the table next to Evaline. She had been crying.

I dropped my head, feeling the weight of my guilt. "I am so sorry Mrs. Camerino. Can you ever forgive me?" I whispered, not brave enough to look at her.

I felt her eyes on me. "Tell me, what are your plans if he wakes up?" she insisted.

My head snapped up. I hadn't really gotten that far. I was still processing.

"Do you love my son?" she asked, straightforward.

"I... I care about him, very deeply," I replied, honestly.

"But there's still the Simonelli boy." God this woman was direct. If her fire wasn't aimed at me, I might even admire her.

"There's no chance of that now," I said.

"But your heart still belongs to him. I saw you two together. Your connection." She paused, looking back to her son. "The heart is a finicky thing, child. It wants what it wants even though the mind knows better."

"Orion and I belong together," I said softly. "It's destined and once the ceremony is complete—"

"Regardless of what you've been told, I don't believe the god and goddess's bond works that way. That, once you say a few small words and complete the rite, the two of you will instantly fall madly in love with one another. No. I believe it's much more."

She turned her eyes towards me. "My son was already very much in love with you long before you discovered you were the vessel. He's been in love before. Separating from Delphine after your cousin was announced as his mate about did him in, but you... you were different. He is a private man, but I have never seen him light up like he does when he's around you. When he speaks about you, or your name is mentioned in the same room as he.

"The moon and horned gods are mated, yes, but I believe the vessels must choose one another as well. After the ceremony is complete, you will still be you Seren, and Orion will still be him. Antonio Simonelli will still be in your heart and my son will be forced to live a life where the woman he loves, loves another. No mother wants that for her child."

I swallowed down my emotions, trying not to break. "I'm trying," I said.

"You must try harder," she said flatly. "My son has given enough. Sacrificed enough. And if you truly opened yourself up to him... to the possibility of allowing yourself to love him, and in return he you, you would quickly see there is no other man like him. God or not."

I wiped my nose with the back of my hand, looking at Orion. "I've been thinking," I said. "When he wakes, what if we complete the ceremony ahead of schedule. Do you think that will heal him?"

"It could. I'm not sure, but it would be worth a try."

"I want to do it. If there's a chance it can help quicken his recovery or heal him completely, I want to do it."

"The ceremony won't erase the Simonelli boy, Seren."

"I know. Regardless of my feelings for Antonio, I do care about Orion. And now, with Antonio out of the picture, maybe you're right. Maybe I can finally give us a shot. Your son is amazing. I've always seen that." I stood, making my way to the door.

"Salvo," said his mother. I turned to see her eyes well with tears as her bottom lip trembled. "If there is a way to heal him. Even marrying him, though you don't love him as he does you.... Please do it. Please save him. Save my baby... I beg you."

"I will do whatever it takes, Mrs. Camerino. You have my word," I said closing the door behind me. I pressed my back against the wall, feeling the weight of my promise.

After meeting with the leaders of our coven, discussing plans, and sharing the information we had gathered on my mother and Obsidian, I was exhausted. All I wanted to do was head back to my room and soak in a bubble bath. There was still so much I was keeping inside. So much I was afraid to let out. Rather it be because of my guilt or my desire I didn't know.

I entered my room, locking the door behind me and took in my empty, quiet space. I hadn't slept by myself in months. I took a bath as planned and then crawled into bed, shutting off the lights. After tossing and turning, I realized there was no hope for sleep.

I started a fire in my fireplace and then paced the length of the room, trying to work my way through the different plans and strategies we discussed in the meeting earlier that day. My head was spinning with different scenarios and information. I couldn't focus. I was useless in this condition.

After fighting it, I looked at the vanity mirror, knowing he was only a touch away. I chewed on my lip, resisting the urge to summon him. But this could be a good thing. I could gather more intel from him. I could learn more and maybe derive what they had planned next.

I sat down at the vanity, hating with myself. Finally, my desire overpowered my logic. I pressed my fingers to the mirror. I closed my eyes, thinking about Antonio. His tall and elegant frame. His beautiful black head of hair. His soft and loving eyes. The way he touched me. The way he held me. Kissed me.

A tear ran down my cheek. I began to tremble from my our memories. My heart was broken, but I couldn't let anyone see. What would they think of me? Still in love with a traitor who worked for monsters. I hated myself for the way I felt, but I couldn't stop it. No matter how hard I tried to fight it, I still loved him.

"Hello, beautiful," came his rich and sultry voice from the other side of the mirror. I opened my eyes and was greeted by his perfect smile. "Couldn't sleep either?"

My face betrayed me... and I smiled.

Chapter
Thirty-Three

*B*am. *Bam. Bam.* My back ached as I opened my eyes. I had fallen asleep on the vanity table. *Bam. Bam. Bam.* Came a knock at the door. "Seren!" yelled Frankie. *Bam. Bam. Bam.* "Wake the hell up!"

I rushed to the door, flinging it open. Frankie was out of breath and smiling.

"What?" I asked. "What is it?"

"Orion... he's awake," she said, smiling from ear to ear. My heart slammed into my chest with relief.

"Thank you, God," I cried, placing my hands on my face.

"Hurry up and get dressed. He's asking for you," she said before taking off down the hall.

I quickly dressed, brushing my teeth, and running a comb through my hair. I tripped and stumbled, sliding on my boots, trying to wrap my head around the good news. I looked at the vanity mirror, brushing aside my hair, checking my complexion and then froze.... Antonio.

No, no, not today. Orion is awake. The man who risked his life to save you. Who, without, you would be dead right now. I pulled my attention away from the mirror and bolted out of the room towards the medical wing.

By the time I arrived his room was full. His mother, his friends, and my family all stood around his bed with smiles as laughter sang through the air. He looked better. Not completely healed, but better. They all stopped as I stepped across the threshold. Their attention turned to me. I nervously walked forward, uncomfortable by the weight of their assessing glares.

"Will you all please give us the room," Orion said. Everyone nodded, heading for the exit. Evaline stopped at my side before leaving, placing a hand on my forearm.

"Remember your promise," she whispered, patting me softly. I swallowed, trying to keep myself from reacting.

Once we were alone, I walked over to the bed and sat on the side of the mattress. He smiled at me, diverting his eyes from mine. "How are you feeling?" I asked.

"Good. Better than I have felt in weeks. You?"

"Good. My power is a bit weaker than before, but nothing some practice shouldn't be able to fix."

"We should probably resume practice soon, now that we know what we're up against."

I laughed, trying to hold it back.

"What?" he asked.

"Orion, you can't even stand. How are you supposed to train

me? I'm quite confident I could take you in this position. Not that I would ever prey on your weakness and all."

"Oh, I'm weak now, am I?" he said, pinching me in the leg.

"Maybe a little," I said teasingly. I paused, realizing my joke had created an opening. "On that note," I continued, working up the courage to propose. "I want to move forward with the rite... immediately."

His eyes snapped to mine, his face, a mixture of shock and surprise. "What? Why?"

"We are both confident we are the vessels. Obsidian is at full strength and has plans to do who knows what with that power. My mother is working for some unknown man who possesses power we supposedly have never encountered before. We are both weakened from the last fight. Why not?"

"Why not? Are you kidding me, Seren?"

I paused, waiting for him to finish.

He made a scoffing noise as he shook his head.

"Orion," I said, taking his hand in mine. "Everyone needs this. We need this. The covens need this. Our magic needs this. Why wait?"

His eyes bore into me. "You are in love with another man," he said flatly.

I exhaled in aggravation. "No, I am not."

"Don't lie to me. I can feel it. I know you are trying to fight it, but I can still feel it."

"So what? Yes, am I going to need a little time to... to switch gears? Yes. But that doesn't mean that my commitment to you and to us won't be real. We need to start somewhere Orion. And this needs to happen, now."

"Seren, I can't—"

"Orion, look at me," I said, taking his face and turning it towards mine. "There has always been something between us. Since day one, we couldn't stay away from each other, regardless of if Antonio was in the picture or not. I have had to fight my feelings for you for months. The desire to run to you when things got hard or when I needed to be comforted. It has always been there, and I believe... no, I know it can grow into something beautiful and real. You just have to trust me and believe me when I say I am going to fight for this. Just like we fought for each other back in that courtyard, remember?"

He nodded his head as his eyes fell. "This isn't how I imagined this moment happening."

I laughed. "I'm fairly certain the universe has a very messed up since of humor." I leaned down, only a few inches from his face. "We can do this... together. We can do anything if we stay together."

He brushed the side of my face with his fingers, tracing my lips with his thumb. "Okay," he whispered with a hesitant smile.

"Okay?" I asked, trying to sound excited.

He nodded. I smiled, jumping from the bed. I stuck my head

out of the door and called everyone back into the room. "What are you doing?" Orion asked.

"Celebrating, of course," I replied. Once everyone had entered the room, I stood by Orion's side, taking his hand in mine.

"What's the meaning of this?" asked nonna.

"We have some news," I said, looking down at him. "Orion and I have decided to move up the rite and the wedding. We want to get married as soon as possible." As soon as the words left my lips, I felt like a fist had punched me in the gut.

"What?" exclaimed Frankie with excitement. "Oh, my Aradia, this is so romantic."

"You're sure?" asked nonna.

I looked down at Orion and smiled. "More than anything." Our friends and family laughed and celebrated alongside us. They each hugged me, congratulating us on the engagement.

Evaline held me firmly against her in an embrace. "Thank you," she whispered in my ear. I nodded, continuing to the next hug.

Aunt Thora looked at the two of us and smiled. "We can have everything ready by tomorrow evening, if that is okay with the two of you," she said.

I looked back at Orion. "You think you'll be able to get your lazy butt out of bed to attend your own wedding?"

He smiled up at me. "If you're the one at the end of that altar, I will crawl if I have to." I leaned down and kissed him on the cheek.

"Sounds like tomorrow it is," I said, forcing a smile.

After the celebrating had died down, I excused myself, claiming I was still recovering and needed rest. I closed the door and headed back to my room. I turned the corner and stopped, noticing two additional figures in Giana's room.

I opened the door without knocking and stepped inside. "Hello," I said flatly, placing the mask needed over my weak and exhausted face.

Her mother rose from the bed and her father turned towards me. They were a beautiful family. Each more beautiful than the next. Antonio favored his father but got his eyes and hair from his mother.

"You must be Seren," said his mother. She took a few steps towards me, but I held out my hands stopping her from coming closer. She smiled. "You're exactly as he described you. Absolutely lovely."

His father went to his wife's side. "I'm Anthony Simonelli and this is my wife, Rosemary. It's nice to finally meet you."

I stood silent, unsure of what to say. "How's Giana?" I asked, turning my attention towards her.

"Feeling much better," she replied. "Though, I would love to go home."

"That's not going to happen," I replied. "You are our guests here in the castle, but you are not permitted to leave until the situation with Obsidian has concluded."

"We understand," said Rosemary, moving slowly towards me.

She hesitantly reached for my hand. I allowed her to take it, watching her every move. Her eyes filled with tears as she began to tremble. "Our son is a good man, Seren. He is a good boy. He was desperate to save his little sister. I truly believe that. Please, for what it's worth, he did love you."

I pulled away, not wanting to hear another word. Rosemary began to sob. Anthony came to her side, comforting her. He looked at me with an expression I recognized intimately. "I am sorry for what my son has done," he said. "Regardless of his intent, that does not excuse him from the choices he has made. I know he hurt you and I am sorry. On behalf of our family, I am sorry."

I nodded, swallowing my pain. I left the Simonelli family without another word. I rushed back to my room, touching the mirror while I imagined his face. He appeared within five minutes. He was smiling, but his face fell as he looked at mine.

"What's wrong? What is it?" he asked.

I took a deep breath, mustering the courage to speak it out loud, but I couldn't... not yet. "I met your family just now," I said, wiping away the tears. "They're lovely."

He smiled at me. "They've been eager to meet you. I wish it was under different circumstances, but I am glad you all met regardless."

I sat silently, playing with a hair tie in my hand. "Beautiful," he said softly. "What is it? Talk to me."

I took a few trembling breaths and looked up at him. "Orion

and I are completing the rite."

His face fell. He leaned forward, shaking his head. "When?"

"Tomorrow," I whispered.

The mirror shook as he grabbed the frame on his end. "No. Seren. No. Look at me," he cried. "Look at me, Seren. You can't do this. You can not marry him. You are in love with me. I love you. Please, beautiful. I love you."

I began to cry. "I'm sorry, Tony, but I have no choice. I must complete the rite."

"No, you don't. Leave, right now. I will find you," he said, still gripping the edges of the mirror. "We will go away together. No one will ever find us, I promise. Let the magic die. Let the stupid war end. I don't care what happens. As long as we're together in the end, that is what matters."

"I can't. I can't do that to my family. I'm sorry."

"Seren, baby please. You can't do this," he cried, finally pulling away, dragging his hands down his face. "Please. I know I messed up. I know I have so much to atone for but give me a chance. Just give me time. Please."

"There is no more time, Tony. What's done is done," I said, slowly raising my hand to send him away.

"Don't," he yelled. "Don't go. Please beautiful, don't leave me!" he screamed.

I waved my hand over the reflective surface, sending his beautiful face into the darkness. I crumbled to the floor. A heaping pile of emotions and confusion.

An hour later a knock came at the door. I gathered myself enough to answer it, only to see Frankie on the other side. At the very sight of her I lost control. She caught me in her arms.

In that moment, I told her everything. Everything about how I was feeling. About how I still loved Tony. About how I selfishly wanted to go to him. Everything except that I had been communicating with him through my vanity mirror.

She stayed with me that night, gently combing my hair with her fingers while I poured my heart out. At some point in the early morning, we had fallen asleep. My body was too exhausted to dream, which I was thankful for.

When I woke on my wedding day, Frankie was still in bed next to me. I got up, heading towards the bathroom. As I passed the mirror, I could have sworn I heard a faint banging sound coming from the other side. I ignored it, knowing if I spoke to him today, I wouldn't go through with the ceremony.

I managed to shower and clean myself up. When I exited the bathroom, Frankie was awake, sitting on the edge of the bed. "Hey," she said, walking over to me. "How are you feeling?"

"A lot better now that I got everything out. Thank you for last night. I'm just sorry you were the one I emotionally vomited all over," I said, embarrassed I had shared so much with her.

"Don't you dare be sorry. All your feelings are completely valid and understandable. You are going through a lot. It's more than anyone should have to handle."

I nodded, taking a deep breath. "Well, todays the day I become Mrs. Orion Camerino," I said, trying to pump myself up.

She laughed. "No sweetie. You will always be a Salvo and don't you forget it." She hugged me as a knock came at the door. "Are you expecting someone?"

"It's probably nonna," I said, opening the door to see Orion, upright and walking.

"Good morning," he said with an eager smile.

"You're walking," I said with astonishment. "You're actually walking." He stepped into the room.

Frankie smiled at him. "Orion," she said, nodding as she headed for the exit.

"Frankie," he replied.

"I'll give you two a moment," she whispered to me, "but not too long. We have a lot to do in seven hours."

I laughed. "I'll call you when we're done." She kissed me, shutting the door behind her.

I looked at Orion, and then the mirror behind him. "Do you think you can bear the winter wind?" I asked gesturing to the balcony.

"Sure. Fresh air sounds nice." He followed me outside, away from the mirror. I lit the firepit that was at the center of my terrace as we sat, side by side on the couch.

"How are you feeling about today?" he asked.

"Anxious, nervous, weary. I'm not really sure what to expect. Will I be a different person? Will I still be me?"

"I believe so. I think we'll just have the memories of the gods in our head. And, of course, their power, but I think we'll still be us."

I smiled. "I hope so."

"I have something for you," he said, pulling a black box out of his pocket. My heart fell.

"Orion, you didn't have to—"

"I wanted to. Last nights 'proposal' didn't really happen like I had imagined but I can at least still give you the ring I had made for you."

"When did you have time to commission a ring?" I asked.

He hesitated, looking down at the box. "I... I had it made after our day at the festival last summer. I had already begun to fall in love with you, but then, after you had touched me and saw the power that you possessed, I was certain. I knew who you were. Who we were."

"Orion..." I whispered, allowing the spark inside of me to gently glow.

"I know... I know we're not in the best place right now, but I want you to know... I want you to know that I feel like the luckiest man in the entire world to be marrying you today. It is an honor to stand by your side in this life and any life after."

I smiled at him, placing my hand on his arm. "You're amazing, you know that?"

"I'm glad you think so. It's a start at least."

"Oh, I've thought that from the beginning. Ever since I first saw you with all those rippling muscles freshly showered in Frankie's room." He started laughing. "What an introduction. You had your best assets on display."

His head tilted as he gave me a side smirk. "Since you'll be my wife in a few hours, I feel the need to let you in on a little secret." He leaned into my ear, brushing his lips across my lobe. "My abs aren't my best asset."

I pulled away, hitting him in the arm.

He shrugged. "I'm just being honest."

"Says every man everywhere."

He placed the box in my palm, covering my hand with his large fingers. "I hope you like it," he said, slowly standing. He kissed me on the head before leaving.

I held the box, just staring at it. Finally, my curiosity got the best of me. I cracked the box open to see the most exquisite black diamond in the shape of an oval. The diamond was in a silver setting, with a dainty band and small white opal stones on either side.

There was a small piece of paper wrapped around the band. I pulled the ring from the box and undid the paper. It read:

Little dove, place the ring on your finger and repeat these words. "Septamor avalous".

I did as he instructed, sliding the heavy diamond on my left finger. I closed my eyes and repeated the phrase. "Septamor avalous." I felt a warm and bright light engulf me. Instantaneously, I was transported into Orion's mind. His memories.

I saw the first time we had met; except I was watching through his eyes. I felt his excitement and curiosity as he looked down at me. The moment we had touched, I could feel his power awaken in response to me just like mine had to him.

Then, the ball. His breath caught in his chest as something like hope and desire filled him at the sight of me when I was announced. He stood in the back of the room, smiling as I descended the staircase. He moved to meet me but halted. I felt his hesitation and his pain that he couldn't be the one to escort me.

Memories of the festival. Of us dancing and laughing. How happy and truly alive he was. Memories of us fighting and training. I could feel his love and admiration begin to grow. I watched as he focused on the smallest details of my person. The way my nose crinkled when I laughed. The way he noted each of my laughs and what they meant.

I could feel his desire beginning to grow. He fought against his need to touch me. To hold me and to kiss me. Then, the first time we kissed. How completely in awe. How he felt and how his heart swelled.

Memory after memory of us flashed behind my eyes. It was our story. The story of when and how he fell in love with me. The last memory was of me admitting that I was the moon goddess at his bedside.

The memories slowed as they came to an end. I felt his heart swell with hope. My mind softly faded back to my own. I looked down at the new ring that adorned my left hand.

A tear fell from my face. He truly loved me. He had waited for me this entire time. He had hoped.

I returned inside and headed straight for the door. I would focus on that hope. On the goodness and the new beginning that Orion represented. He was my chance at a clean slate. I was going to give this marriage a shot. I would try.

Nonna, Aunt Thora, Frankie, and I spent the rest of the day pampering ourselves and spending time together. Finally, two hours before the ceremony, we began to get ready. I had no clue what I was going to wear, but Frankie said she had that covered. She said it was a part of her maid of honor duties.

We got ready in nonna's room, laughing and reminiscing while we had our makeup and hair done. The champagne flowed and my heart was happy. This was what family was. This right here. No matter what, I would always have them.

Frankie brought out the dress. As she unzipped the bag, the light struck the diamonds creating a starlike effect. The dress was made of the most intricate black lace. Every inch contained diamonds and pearls sewn into it. As I slid it on, it fit me like a glove. It plunged deep in the front and exposed my entire back. The sleeves started at the top of my shoulder and trailed down.

The back of the dress was a long train that caught the shimmering light of the setting sun. My hair was pinned away from my neck, allowing the dress to be the focal point. My makeup was soft and natural. I chose a deep purple lip to complete the look.

Finally, it was time. We made our way to the limos as we drove to my wedding destination. I had no idea where the venue was, but once again, Frankie had that covered. We pulled up to a beautiful field full of white roses springing from the ground in the middle of winter. The full moon was perfectly placed, as if painted at the end of the aisle.

A body of water fed by a small spring was off to the side. White chairs created rows on either side of the aisle. The ground was covered in red rose petals. Balls of soft yellow sunlight floated above the entire field. Beautiful greenery and floral arrangements filled the tables waiting for the reception off to the side with candles and more floating balls of light. It was breathtaking.

"Do you like it?" Frankie asked.

I turned to her. "It's perfect." She kissed me on the cheek and took her place.

Nonna and Aunt Thora came to my side. "We were hoping," said Aunt Thora, "that you would allow us the honor of giving you away."

Nonna nodded.

"I wouldn't have it any other way," I replied. They looped their arms on either side of me. I held a bouquet of white roses.

The symphony began to play. Frankie took the lead, descending down the aisle first. Once she got to the front of the altar where an archway covered in vibrant sage and greenery awaited, the audience stood. Somehow, more than 500 people had arrived with just 24 hours' notice.

I took my first step towards my new future, make sure to keep my eyes forward. I saw Orion, waiting for me at the end of the aisle. His dark and curly hair was pulled back away from his face. He was in black from head to toe and God did he look good in a suit. His face beamed, allowing me to see his shapely chin and brilliant smile.

I smiled back, keeping my eyes forward. I focused on each step, fighting the urge to run. *This was right*, I told myself. This was where I needed to be. But was it where I wanted to be? With whom I wanted?

Once we got to the end, nonna and Aunt Thora kissed me on the cheek. Nonna took her place as the officiant and began the ceremony.

I handed my bouquet to Frankie while we went through the

traditional vows. Orion beamed the entire time. As nonna got to the end, we exchanged the wedding bands. I had created a beautiful thick band for him. The center strip was black, representing my night, and the outer metal was gold, representing his sun. As if we had designed the bands together, he slid two bands on my finger around my engagement ring that were gold. They curved around the oval diamond and created the illusion of the sun encompassing the moon.

We both said I do. Nonna announced us as husband and wife. Orion leaned in to kiss me. As soon as our lips met, my power answered his, sending the area around us into a mixture of light and dark. Of cold and warmth. Regardless of where my heart remained, our connection, however deep and far it ran, was undeniable.

The crowd around us erupted with cheers as we made our way to the lake. The rite was next. Our guests lined the lake holding candles in their hands. I held onto Orion, not sure of what came next. With the impromptu wedding, there was very little time to go into the details about what I could expect.

He smiled down at me. "Just in case you were unaware," he whispered, "I think you are the most beautiful thing I have ever seen."

"And just in case you couldn't tell," I replied. "I like you in a suit."

He laughed. "Duly noted."

We entered the water, hand in hand. Nonna and his mother waited for us towards the center of the pool. The water was freezing. My lips begin to shiver instantaneously. I stood by nonna and Orion stood by his mother. Once the crowd had filled in around the pool, nonna and Evaline gently helped us lay back against the fridged water. I floated, still holding Orion's hand.

I closed my eyes, trying to prepare myself for what came next. Nonna and Evaline began chanting, casting the rite spell. I began shaking. I didn't know if it was from the cold or from my nerves. I'd be lying if I said I wasn't afraid. We were walking into unknown territory.

I turned my head and looked at Orion. He met my gaze and gave my hand a small squeeze for reassurance. "It's going to be okay," he whispered with a smile. I nodded, focusing my attention back on the sky.

I could hear the coven members around us begin to chant, feeding the spell with their power. The water warmed. I focused on the stars as nonna moved closer towards me, still chanting. As she appeared over me, I could see the black crystallized dagger she held in both of her hands. She brought it up above her head. I closed my eyes, trying to remain still allowing the water to rock me gently.

The chanting echoed in my ears as did my blood pumping faster and harder with each passing second. With one quick guest of wind, I felt the dagger pierce my heart. I jolted forward, attempting to gasp for air, but none came. I looked down at the hilt sticking out of my chest. My limbs began to go numb.

Warm blood mixed with the water. I turned to look at Orion. His white crystalized dagger sank deep into his broad chest. His eyes were closed as I watched his body sink to the bottom of the lake. His grip on my hand loosened until he slipped away underneath the skin of the water.

The stinging pain in my chest was unbearable. I began to feel weak from the loss of blood. I took one final breath before slipping underneath the icy sheet of water. The liquid filled my lungs while my eyes remained open, still fixated on the stars above. Within seconds, my mind faded away. All that remained was the arms of the cold ice that pulled me towards the bottom of the lake.

CHAPTER
THIRTY-FOUR

My body jolted straight up, gasping for air. My hands went straight to my chest, searching for the dagger but it was gone. I looked down, noting that I was draped in a long white silk gown, laying on some type of altar.

Purple, blue, and green clouds surrounded, tumbling and rolling through the air. A brilliant white light came from the horizon, creating the most extraordinary and tranquil setting. The air smelled crisp and clean. I took in my surroundings, searching for something...anything familiar.

I swung my legs to the side and stepped down. The clouds around me parted, the cool fog curling between my toes. Up ahead, the blue and purple swirls parted. A figure walked towards me ever so gracefully. The light followed her acting as her own personal spotlight. As she approached, the power that radiated off her was the most intense force I had ever experienced. It was hard to remain standing in her presence.

She had beautiful with white silver hair. Her purple eyes were radiant and sparkled like the night sky. She was tall and built like a warrior. Her body was draped in a thin piece of linen, allowing her flawless, tanned skin to peek through. Her jaw was strong and was complimented by her high cheek bones and thin lips.

She peered down at me from underneath her thick white lashes. "Hello, Seren De Salvo," she said in a deep yet feminine voice. "I've been waiting for you."

"Aradia," I whispered in awe.

She smiled. "Very good."

I looked around, watching the clouds tumble past us. "Am I... am I dead? Did something go wrong?" I asked.

"Nothing went wrong," she replied. "And yes and no. You are dead, but you aren't. Walk with me. I will explain."

I took a step to follow her, hesitant about falling through the clouds. "Don't worry," she said, peeking back at me with an eyebrow arched. "They will hold you."

"Can you read my mind?" I asked.

"We are connected. One in the same. My essence is what gave you life. You are a direct extension of me. Soon, you will have the memories, the knowledge, of all those who came before you."

"And... what will happen to my memories?"

She paused, placing her hands behind her back. "You will still be you, Seren. All your memories, feelings, desires, and passions will still exist. You were designed to hold my power. To be an anchor for the covens in order to restore the energy back into the earth. I won't be hijacking your life if that's what you're asking."

We continued walking forward as I processed what she had said. "And Orion?" I asked.

She smiled. "I find him to be quite pleasing, don't you?"

I laughed. "There's no denying that."

"But there's the matter of Antonio," she said, returning her eyes forward as we continued to walk.

"You know?" I asked.

"I've watched you your entire life. Of course, I know."

"Will it... will it get easier with time?" I asked.

"That, my child, is completely up to you. I do not control your fate or destiny, nor do I know it fully. You are here because of a decision you had no choice over, but the road you now take is completely and entirely up to you."

"May I ask you a personal question?"

She nodded.

"What is the story between you and the first horned god?"

I studied her face for a sign of any emotion, but she remained stoic. "His name was Cyrus. We found each other, fell in love, and from that love, magic was born. We gifted it to those less fortunate around us. Those who would honor it and do good with it. We built a community of likeminded people who cherished the earth and strived for peace.

"Like any creation, there were those who took advantage of the power, and weren't satisfied with what they had been gifted. The first of Obsidian was born out of pure greed and... pride. Tainted by a darkness... an evil I never encountered before. This... evil, sought to destroy and conquer. Cyrus and I wanted to live out the rest of our lives in peace, but we loved those who we had shared much of our existence with. We couldn't subject them to the darkness that had risen out of our blind devotion and love.

"So, Cyrus and I chose a mortal death in order to be reborn into vessels every 300 years, so our power could restore the balance for the future generations." Her eyes fell for a moment. Something in my heart fluttered but the reaction wasn't my own.

"What is that?" I asked. "I just... I just felt you."

She smirked. "Cyrus was the love of my life. We were made for one another. Wholly and completely. Every time vessels are chosen; a part of our soul is gifted to you when you are created in the womb. That is why you and the horned god's vessel always find one another. Regardless of the distance between the two of you. Fate always brings our souls back together."

"Then, why did I fall in love with Antonio?"

"As I have said, you are still free to choose your path. I have watched many of my vessels fall in love with other males through-out history. You only have a part of my soul. The rest belongs to you entirely."

"Is it true that not all vessels are mated?"

"It varies. Your lives are tied to the power Cyrus, and I first created through our bound, but that does not mean you are cut from the same cloth."

"What does that mean?"

"You and the horned god are and will always be connected. No matter if you end up together romantically or not, the two of you will always be drawn together... long for one another because you carry a part of our bond inside of you that demands to be reunited."

"So, we have no choice but to be together?"

"You always have a choice, Seren. Some have lived long lives with others who they have loved. Others have died from broken hearts. While most accept the bond and find their happiness. Each case is different. I myself don't understand it fully."

"So, what now?"

"There is one last test you must walk on your own. This test will challenge the very thing you desire. The outcome of your choice will decide what comes next. The future *you* choose will shape the rest of eternity." She stopped at a black wooden door in front of us, attached to nothing as it floated softly through the clouds.

"How will I know what the right choice will be?"

She placed her hands on my shoulders. "Follow your heart, my child. Regardless of what you choose, you will live. The life that you live, however, is completely yours. There is no right or wrong answer here. Only the answer you seek."

The door opened into a void. Aradia nodded with a small reassuring smile. I stepped across into the darkness, completely unprepared for what would happen next.

"Wake up, beautiful," I heard his silken voice say against my ear. He kissed me softly as his hand slid down my bare body until his fingers slipped between my legs, playing with the small bundle of nerves.

I felt the smile spread across my face. A soft moan parted my lips. I pushed myself back against his firm body, feeling him hard and waiting for me.

"I need you, wife," he whispered, kissing down the side of my neck. I turned over, sliding my hands through his dark black hair, taking his lips with mine. He slid on top of my, parting my legs with his knees. The desire was unquenchable. There was no foreplay, no hesitation. With one deep thrust he was inside of me. Moving at the perfect rhythm as our breathing quickened.

He kissed me deeply, cupping my breast with his hand. He tangled his fingers in my hair, pulling my head back, exposing my neck while he licked and sucked on the sensitive skin. As our bodies moved in one passionate motion, I could feel the burning inside of me quicken before we both found our pleasure.

He laid on top of me, still tracing his fingers down my warm skin. My body felt incredible. Just like it always did after being with him. I felt him laugh tenderly against my chest as he pulled his eyes up to mine.

"Find something funny?" I asked, brushing his hair from his face.

"Not at all. I just... I still can't believe I get to wake up to you every morning," Antonio said, kissing the palm of my hand.

"I'm the lucky one," I said, bending to kiss him.

Little knocks came at the door, one after the other. Antonio looked back and smiled. "Alright, alright," he said, leaving the bed. He handed me my robe and adorned his own. Once we were covered, he opened the door. A little boy around four years old came bursting through, jumping straight onto the bed and into my arms.

A woman stood at the door with a child, no more than a year old in her hands... a little girl. The baby reached for Antonio. He took her with a look on his face of sheer happiness. She wrapped her little arms around his neck as he held her close.

"Momma, momma," the boy said, handing me a picture. "Look what I made for you." I took the picture seeing a drawing of the boy and I holding hands while we stood under a rainbow.

I made a big, surprised expression and smiled. "Anthony, I love it," I said, pulling him in closely and kissing the top of his head. Antonio returned to the bed kissing the top of the little boy's head. The little girl reached for me.

She had curly black ringlets and Tony's hazel eyes. Her little face was full, with chunky little cheeks. Anthony had straight dark brown hair like mine with Giana's green eyes. They were a perfect mix of the both of us.

Tony rubbed the side of the baby girls back. "It appeared, little Lucia has another tooth as of this morning," he said, pulling Anthony into his lap.

"You do?" I said, bouncing her up and down in front of me. "My big girl. What am I going to do with you?" I hugged her tightly, looking at them both. "They're growing up too fast," I said to Tony, making a pouty face.

"Well," he said, smiling devilish at me. "We can always work on another."

I laughed. "Really? A third?"

He shrugged. "I'm ready if you are."

I smiled, feeling my heart swell. I nodded at him as a happy tear fell from my eye. "I'd like that very much." He leaned across the children and kissed me.

"Yuck, daddy," said Anthony, pushing Tony away.

"Excuse me, Mr." Tony laughed, wrestling Anthony to the bed. "Mommy was mine first." Tony began tickling Anthony as he laughed and hollered.

"She's my mommy," cried Anthony.

Lucia laughed and clapped, pulling at the pendant on my neck, trying to put it in her mouth.

"There's enough of me to go around," I said, standing from the bed, taking Lucia with me.

We got everyone dressed and then headed down the hall of Castle Salvo. We entered the dining hall with the children. Frankie sat at a table with Joseph, Aunt Thora, and nonna. Frankie's face lit up as we approached.

"How's my adorable little man," gasped Frankie as Anthony climbed onto her lap.

"Aunt Fran, look, I drew mommy a picture," said Anthony.

"Well, aren't you talented," she replied.

"Give her to me," demanded nonna, reaching for Lucia.

I started laughing. "Well, good morning to you too," I replied, handing her over. Nonna was smiling from ear to ear as she blew into Lucia's belly.

I sat down while Tony brought me a cup of coffee and a plate. Aunt Thora looked at the two of us and smiled. "You two missed the briefing this morning," she said.

My cheeks blushed. "Oh, right... Our alarm didn't go off," I replied, smiling. Tony grabbed my leg underneath the table.

"Right," said Frankie, "just like every morning."

"Working on a third, are we?" asked nonna, smiling at Lucia as she bounced her. "Because if the answer is yes, you have my blessing to miss as many meetings as needed."

I looked at Tony and smiled. My life was so full and happy. I continued to eat while our family spoke around us about nothing and everything at the same time. The children laughed and played.

As I finished, I sat back and looked around the room. My smile faded. Something felt off. Like... like something was missing.

I stood from the table, feeling a restlessness inside of me I couldn't ignore. "Everything alright, beautiful," asked Tony.

"Yes, yes, I'm fine," I replied. "I forgot something back in the room. Would you watch the kids for a bit?"

"Of course," he said, standing and kissing me deeply. I smiled at him, kissing the kids before I headed back down the hall.

My heart felt like there was something tugging it towards whatever I had lost, but I couldn't put my finger on it. I turned down each hall, searching... for what, I didn't know.

After twenty minutes of wandering, I leaned against the window seal, more frustrated than when I started. A few members of the Soleil Coven came out of a meeting room along with Evaline Camerino, nonna's arch nemesis. Her eyes locked on mine with a cold glare of discontent.

I stood tall, not willing to back down. "Mrs. Camerino," I said first, nodding to her.

"Seren," she said, walking towards me. "A beautiful morning, isn't it?"

"It is. I was not aware you were scheduled for a visit."

"Well, sometimes business calls us at the most inopportune times. Don't worry, I won't be here long, goddess willing."

"Glad to hear it."

She paused, examining me from head to toe. "How are your children? I hear little Anthony is quite the looker."

"They are wonderful. And yes, he takes after his father."

She laughed, shaking her head. "Are you happy, Seren?" she asked, sounding more sincere than she ever had before.

I looked at her with confusion. "Of course I am. I have everything I could have ever hoped for."

She nodded, looking outside of the window. "And do you feel... complete?"

"What are you getting at, Evaline?" I said flatly.

She shrugged. "It's just a simple question. No need to get bent out of shape over it. I just find your story so enlightening. The girl, parted from her family at birth, only to be reunited later in life. A fairytale, wouldn't you say?"

"I guess you could say that."

"Well, at least someone gets a happy ending," she said, patting me on the arm before looking back out at the window. "Huh," she said, furrowing her brow.

"What?" I asked.

"A little dove," she said with curiosity in her voice. "I didn't know they flew this far south. Must be a sign of hope," she said before leaving me at the window.

My head snapped to the bird as it landed on the window seal inches from me. A dove. A sign of peace... hope... purity... and a... a promise. My heart constricted. Everything around me began to spin as I stumbled back towards our room.

As soon as I got there, I shut the door and dropped to my knees. Flashes of a life I hadn't remembered living flickered behind my eyes.

"Why do you call me little dove?" I heard myself ask.

"In your Bible, what symbolism does a dove hold?" said a man with a voice I couldn't place but knew.

"Peace, hope, purity, a promise," I replied.

He nodded, smiling at me. *"From the moment I laid eyes on you, you were all those things to me. You were a peace I had searched my entire life for. You were my hope of a love and life worth living. You were the purity that lit the way in our dark and unforgiving world. And you were a promise that I would never have to walk through this life alone again. You are my destiny, Seren. With or without the prophecy, I loved you from the first moment and I will love you till the last."*

I held my head while flashes of a beautifully sculpted man threaded through my memory. His smile. His laugh. His strong body and his tender lips. His eyes that I lost myself in. The smell of summer and sunlight. The warmth of his arms. The feeling of familiarity.

"I know, he said with hesitation, *"I know we're not in the best place right now, but I want you to know... I want you to know that I feel like the luckiest man in the entire world to be marrying you today. It is an honor to stand by your side in this life and any life after."*

I began to sob uncontrollable as my body shook.

"I will always find you." I heard him whisper.

"Stop!" I yelled at the top of my lungs, digging my nails into my scalp. "Stop!" I screamed, but... it all came flooding back.

I felt two hands on either of my shoulders. Antonio appeared, kneeling in front of me. He was speaking but I couldn't hear a word he was saying. All I could hear was my blood pumping harder and fast through my veins.

"Seren," finally came Tony's voice. "Seren, baby, what's wrong? What's happening?" he asked, taking my face, and examining me. I looked behind him. Lucia was sitting on the floor, chewing on a toy and Anthony stood next to her, watching.

My eyes filled with tears as the truth ripped through me like a dagger. I began to cry, reaching for Tony, relishing in his touch for a few more moments. I shook my head, bringing my attention back to his.

"This isn't real," I whispered, hating myself as soon as the words left my lips.

"What?" he asked, looking confused.

I swallowed. "You, the children, this marriage," I said, forcing the words to be heard. "This isn't real. This is just... just a dream."

"Beautiful, what are you saying?" asked Tony.

"I'm saying... I'm saying I'm married to Orion Camerino, the horned god. I am the moon goddess and these," I paused looking at their sweet little faces. "These children aren't real." As if I had cast a spell, the children began to evaporate within a dark haze of smoke. Tony looked back in complete horror as Lucia and Anthony disappeared.

"Seren, what are you doing?" he yelled. "What have you done?"

I cried harder, pulling away from him. "We never got married, Tony. You betrayed me. You betrayed all of us."

His face went blank as he looked at me with pain. "This could have been real, beautiful," he whispered. "All you had to do was want it bad enough and this could have been our new reality."

I cried harder. He stood, pulling me up from the floor with him. He touched my face gently and then pressed a kiss against my lips. "I will always love you."

"And I will always love you," I whispered. He vanished from my arms.

I closed my eyes, feeling a soft gust of wind envelop me. When I opened them again, I was standing amongst the purple and blue clouds. Aradia stood before me, grinning softly.

"You have made your choice?" she asked.

Unable to speak, I nodded.

"As it should be. The rite is now complete. You are officially the embodiment of my power. All my strength and power will be yours to wield. My words... my blessing completes the rite."

Crack. Lightning struck above, spreading through the clouds like a parasite consuming its host. The sky darkened engulfing the light that remained. The clouds began to roll and tumble faster and faster until the serenity of this heavenly landscape was replaced with a raging, untamable storm.

Aradia looked around us, her face full of shock and terror.

"What is happening?" I asked, confused by the change of climate.

Her eyes snapped to me. Her brow furrowed while she fought to understand what was occurring. She approached me slowly. I went to take a step back, but she whipped her arm forward too fast, freezing me in place.

My paralyzed body, now suspended in the air was useless. She stood in front of me, assessing me with her gaze. "What are you?" she asked.

"What do you mean?" I replied.

From behind her, tendrils of shadows stretched towards us from the horizon, zigging and zagging across the landscape, reaching out like dark, haunting fingers. Red lightening zapped throughout the black shadowed hands while they consumed all they touched.

Aradia's eyes flashed to the dark whisps heading towards us. Her head snapped back to me. Her face, now full of rage and terror. "No," she whispered, just before she plunged her hand inside of my chest.

A pain, like I had never felt before rattled through me, lighting every nerve ending on fire. I couldn't breathe. Couldn't think. Couldn't stop the pain I was being subjected to. I could feel her hand inside of me, reaching, searching for whatever she was hoping to find.

Her fingers trailed along the deepest and most private parts of me until I felt her grip tighten around something that laid hidden, dormant within the darkest corner of my soul. She screamed in pain, pulling her hand free with such force it broke her hold on me, sending my body freely to the ground.

On all fours, I choked, fighting to fill my lungs with air. I searched my chest for a hole, but there was none. No sign that a god had just been elbow deep inside of my body. I stood to my feet, looking at Aradia.

"What is going on?" I demanded, while the tendrils finally reached our location. They wrapped and twirled around us, growing in height and mass.

"No," she said, sounding defeated. "No. This can't be happening. Not again."

"What is happening? What is wrong?"

The shadows twirled around us. Red illuminating light boomed from beneath our feet. The shadows snaked around my legs, wrapping up each thigh in a soft and caressing manner. Aradia watched, her face shifting from panic to rage.

"No," she yelled. "No! I will not let this happen. Not again." White flames erupted down each of her arms. Panic rose inside of me as I realized she intended to kill me. She pulled her arm back, eyes locked on her target. With one massive push of force, she slammed her hand forward, sending her power hurdling towards me.

Before I could process fully the events that were occurring, the black tendrils latched onto my legs, pulling me with speed and force down through the clouds, out of her reach. Falling freely into darkness, I reached out, trying to find something to grasp onto as the echoes of Aradia's cries faded into the distance.

Black shadows danced and laced through my fingers. Small red flickers of light bounced throughout the darkness as if the tendrils were alive. I felt the shadows form against my back, cradling me for a brief moment before—

My body was torn from the darkness and slammed back into the cold water of the lake. I felt the ice first and then a fire, hotter than anything I had ever experienced rip through my body like a storm. I opened my mouth to cry out, but my screams were muted by the water that seared down my throat.

I lashed and tore through the watery skin, fighting to reach the surface as the pain of the transformation began to crystalize the blood that ran through my veins. Little by little I become immobile. I heard the ice forming underneath my skin. The wrinkles and cracking noises of the water freezing around me. I stopped moving, allowing the pain to swallow me whole.

As the ice crawled up my chest, through my lungs and then my heart, I waited for the action to consume me entirely. I closed my eyes, willing the pain to end me. For a single moment, I felt like time had stopped. Everything around me was peaceful and calm.

I could hear the trickling of the water and the last of the air bubbles leaving my nose. I floated there, completely unphased by anything around me. But somewhere deep inside, an ember sparked to life. I focused on it as the light within grew and glowed stronger and brighter than any force. The warmth consumed me as it bellowed and crawled through each layer of my skin, begging to be released.

I felt my body rising towards the surface, needing to feel the warmth of the sun. My body, as if it were a bomb, exploded, breaking through the frozen water that had formed on top of the lake. Shards of ice ricocheted from the surface high into the air with a booming sound that shook the earth. I opened my eyes, seeing the coven below me take cover from the fragments as they flew in their direction.

I threw my hand out, making a fist, commanding the ice to halt in midair. The coven looked up into the sky at the crystal-like display that hovered above them. The moonlight reached through the prisms of ice, creating rainbows and beams of pure light that reflected off every surface.

I gently floated down towards the ground. My feet made contact while everyone around me stared. Silvery white hair fell loosely down my chest. I looked into one of the shards of ice suspended in the air. My reflection looked back. Eyes, glowing a radiant hue of lavender. As I let go of my power, I watched my eyes fade back to their familiar shade of brown. The transformation was complete.

The rite was successful. I was now the living embodiment of the moon goddess… But I felt different somehow. I felt… numb.

The crowd parted, creating a path. At the end of the aisle, Orion waited. His skin had a godly glow about it. His face was as handsome as ever. For the first time in months, he looked healthy. He looked whole.

His warmth called to me. I held my head high and walked towards him. The audience watched my every step as I moved closer towards my husband. My… mate. His smile grew as he looked down at me, taking in the physical changes that had occurred.

Finally, I was in front of him. His size still surprised me. How towering and muscular he was. His eyes looked down at me as I watched his chest rise and fall. I finally, hesitantly, brought my gaze up to his, feeling the immense tug; the need inside of me that called to him, yet… something new had been awakened.

Something, foreign and dark. And this… this *thing* was greater… more powerful than anything I had ever felt. It was hungry and desperate to be whole again. I feared nothing could sate its need. Was this what Aradia was referring to? Was this why she tried to kill me? What was it? What was inside of me? What was I?

"Little dove," Orion said, snapping me out of my thoughts. I could hear the need and desire laced in his voice.

I stood in front of him, studying every inch of his being. I took a deep breath, smelling sunshine and warmth. He was who I had chosen. Who I was destined to be with. He was my duty… my—

"Orion," I said plainly, before stepping around him and shifting back to the castle without another word.

I landed in my bedroom, locking and spelling the door as I fell to the ground completely shattered and broken. I cried out in pain, yelling and screaming at no one yet everyone at the same time. What was happening to me? Was I going crazy?

Memories that weren't my own, muddled with reality... no fantasy, slammed into my head. Visions of people I didn't know. Voices and laughter coming from strangers I had never met. It was all too much. The download was ripping me apart. The goddesses. Their lives. Their pain. Their memories. I couldn't take it. I couldn't do this.

The wind blew open the doors to my balcony, causing my curtains to dance in their wake. Those same, familiar dark tendrils slowly slithered through the doorway, reaching, searching, for something. As they circled me, I laid down on the cold floor, allowing my own darkness to unleash. I watched while my shadows mixed with the others. Constellations appeared above me as stars shot across the darkness, lighting the way. Streams of red electricity zapped through the air, wrapping itself around my light until the two... became one.

Acknowledgements

Wow, this book has been a journey of self-exploration and research. When I began to formulate this story, I knew I wanted to dive into the world of magic from a modern perspective, but I had no clue where it would lead me. So much of the folklore and terminology I used throughout this story stems from my cultural background, thus, the story taking place in Italy. As I began to write and create the characters, I realized I was slowly but surly infusing them with parts of the women in my life I loved the most.

First and foremost, my nonna... my grandmother. You have strengthened and supported me in ways that have truly changed the course of my life. I love you beyond belief. There are no words that can describe what you mean to me. Your dedication to your family, your children, and your faith is inspiring. I strive to be like you each and every day. The respect I have for you knows no bounds. You are truly the rock in our family. The person that I know, without a shadow of a doubt, I can rely on. You are also fierce, strong, and successful. A true force to be reckoned with.

During the creation of Lucia De Salvo (nonna), I found myself loving this character in a familiar and admirable way. I soon realized the voice, the dedication to her family, and the power I wrote this character to possess all stemmed from the woman I admire most in my life. You are who I want to be when I grow up.

To the aunts in my life that have been like second mothers to me. Aunt Thora represents each of you. Your peace. Your loving and nurturing personalities, and your dedication to the generation that comes after you. I can't tell you how blessed I feel to be born into a family with so many strong women. Being raised by all of you... being loved by all of you, gives me the security to know that I will never be alone.

To my cousins and siblings, as you have read, I use quite a few of your names in this book and there are more to come. I love each of you for your uniqueness. Your drive. And your passions. Being the eldest, I have loved watching you all grow and flourish. There is so much more to come. I hope we can continue the traditions of our mothers when it comes to understanding the importance of family. We are stronger together. I will never forget that, and I hope you won't either. Our blood connects us, but our relationships are what grows us.

To my best friend. To my soulmate. To my Frankie. Sara. You were the part of myself I didn't know I was missing. You re-entered my life in a time of darkness. Little did I know, our happenstance reconnection would result in my gaining another sister. There are no words to describe the love I have for you. I am so honored to call you my friend, but that word fails in comparison to what you mean to me. Your strength, devotion, and love has redefined my definition of friendship. Thank you for being in my life. Thank you for always knowing what to say and how to make me laugh. Thank you for the boat trips, our Eureka getaways, and all the adventures we've yet to embark on. My life is fuller knowing that I have you in it.

I was raised and am now surrounded by so many strong, inspirational women who I revere. Being born into a family primarily made up of women meant that our events were loud, our celebrations were flawless, and our closets were always full. From sharing makeup tips to spilling our hearts out to one another, my upbringing taught me that women need to support and love other women. Now, being a mother of two beautiful little girls, I recognize the responsibility I have when it comes to living what I preach. Find your tribe. Support one another. And never forget where you came from.

ABOUT THE AUTHOR

Hailing from Kansas City, Missouri, Jessica, an Italian American and dedicated teacher with a Master's in Educational Leadership, brings a diverse background, having also graduated with a Bachelors in Fine Art, English, Business, Education, and Communications from Park University in 2015.

Beyond her professional life, Jessica is a passionate creator, finding joy in art and family time. A lifelong reader, she began writing at 16, making authorship a dream now realized during the creation of her own publishing house Dark Flame Publishing . Stay tuned for the enchanting worlds she'll unfold in her upcoming literary books!